Praise for *Innocence*

"As satisfying as it is entertaining ... *Innocence* shows Penelope Fitzgerald in full command of her powers."
— JOHN GROSS, *New York Times*

"A quite extraordinarily appealing book."
— ALIDA BECKER, *Newsday*

"*Innocence* is as civilized and intoxicating as a shot of aged brandy, leaving the reader with the same unanalyzable sensation of having briefly tasted perfection."
— ELIZABETH WARD, *Washington Post*

"Its magic, and its message, are as oblique and inconclusive as the lives of its characters, but both have a lingering power, refreshingly fictive, deliciously un-English."
— JAN DALLEY, *Literary Review*

"I know of no one who expresses so deftly and entertainingly the way in which life seldom turns out as expected. A wonderful book."
— JOHN JOLLIFFE, *Spectator*

"*Innocence* is full of eccentric, sly, and generous humor. While it is a novel that believes in happiness, a stricken sense of suffering threads the surreal vignettes and the delicious surprises — keeping happiness precious, painful, and euphoric."
— NICCI GERRARD, *Women's Review*

"This is by far the fullest and richest of Penelope Fitzgerald's novels, and also the most ambitious. Her writing, as ever, has a natural authority, is very funny, warm and gently ironic, and full of tenderness for human beings and their bravery in living."
— ANNE DUCHÊNE, *Tim̶e̶s̶ ̶L̶i̶ ̶ ̶ ̶ ̶pplement*

Books by Penelope Fitzgerald

Fiction

THE GOLDEN CHILD

THE BOOKSHOP

OFFSHORE

HUMAN VOICES

AT FREDDIE'S

INNOCENCE

THE BEGINNING OF SPRING

THE GATE OF ANGELS

THE BLUE FLOWER

Nonfiction

EDWARD BURNE-JONES

THE KNOX BROTHERS

CHARLOTTE MEW
AND HER FRIENDS

Penelope Fitzgerald

Innocence

A MARINER BOOK
HOUGHTON MIFFLIN COMPANY
BOSTON • NEW YORK

First Mariner Books edition 1998

First published in Great Britain in 1986
by William Collins Sons and Co., Ltd.

Reprinted by arrangement with Flamingo,
an imprint of HarperCollins Publishers

For information about permission to reproduce
selections from this book, write to Permissions,
Houghton Mifflin Company, 215 Park
Avenue South, New York, New York 10003.

Library of Congress Cataloging-in-
Publication Data is available.

ISBN 0-395-90872-8

Printed in the United States of America

QUM 10 9 8 7 6 5 4 3 2 1

Part One

1

Anyone can tell when they are passing the Ridolfi villa, the Ricordanza, because of the stone statues of what are known as 'the Dwarfs' on the highest part of the surrounding walls. You see them best from the right hand side of the road, driving towards Val di Pesa. Strictly speaking they are not dwarfs, but midgets, that's to say they represent adults of less than 1.3 metres, pathologically small, but quite in proportion.

Because the villa's grounds slope sharply away to the south-west nothing, from the road, can be seen beyond them. You just see the coping and the gestures of the midgets, poised against the airy blue wash of the sky. Some of these gestures are welcoming, as though signalling to the passer-by to come in, some suggest quite the contrary. You can buy coloured postcards of the villa, but the statues don't look quite the same as they do in old engravings, or even in the older postcards. Perhaps some of them have been replaced.

The owner of La Ricordanza, in 1568, was a member of the Ridolfi family, certainly, but a midget, married to a midget, and with a daughter, born to them after many disappoint-ments, who was also a midget. They seem to have been by no means the only family in this predicament, or something like it, at the time. There were, for example, the Valmarana at Monte Berico, just outside Verona. Here the daughter of the house was a dwarf, and in order that she should never know that she was different from the rest of the world, only dwarfs were allowed into Villa Valmarana as her playmates and attendants. At the Ricordanza, however, Count Ridolfi con-sulted a medical man of scholarly reputation, Paolo della Torre, who practised at Torre da Santacroce. Paolo advised him in a letter that it was all very well for the Valmarana, who had an abundance of dwarfs in both the villages beneath their walls. Travellers through those parts used to make a detour to see these dwarfs, and if none appeared the carriage-driver would offer to get down from his seat and root them out of their dwellings to be looked at. It was not realised at the time that the inhabitants of Monte Berico suffered from a lung disease and the low concentration of oxygen in their blood produced a high incidence of dwarfism.

'Such people would not be suitable to serve your worship,' Paolo went on. 'I would advise you not to lament the scarcity of them at the Ricordanza. In respect to stock, or race, we must remember that, in Machiavelli's words, Nature has implanted in everything a hidden energy which gives its own resemblance to everything that springs from it, making it like itself. We can see the truth of this in the lemon tree, whose smallest twig, even if the tree is unfortunate enough to be barren, still has the fragrance which is the soul of the lemon.' This letter was relevant, and it was civilised, but it was not helpful. With great difficulty and many enquiries the Ridolfi followed up reported instances of midget families, so that by the time she was six their only child had a retinue suitable to her position, a tiny governess, a tiny doctor, a tiny notary, and so forth, all to size. The child never went out, and was confident that the world consisted of people less than 1.3 metres high. To amuse her, a dwarf (not a midget) was sent for from Valmarana, but without success. She pitied him, because she thought how much he must suffer from knowing that, as a dwarf, he was different from anyone else at Ricordanza. Then, in trying harder and harder to make her laugh, he fell and cracked his head, which made the little girl cry so bitterly that he had to be sent away.

The Ridolfi suffered from having to practise so many deceptions on their daughter. But deception, to a quite unexpected extent, grows easier with habit. The whole property had, of course, been extensively adapted, although only one of the special stairways through the gardens remains today, with its miniature steps of grass and marble. As to the statues, none of them were made by local sculptors, though so many stone-quarries were handy. The commission was given to someone completely unknown, thought by some authorities to have been a Turkish prisoner of war.

At the same time Count Ridolfi heard of a little midget girl, illegitimate but of good family, who lived as far away as Terracina, and they arranged for her to come and live with them. Fortunately she was born dumb, or, at all events, when she arrived at the Ricordanza she was dumb. It was impossible, therefore, for her to describe the human beings she had seen while she lived outside the walls of the villa.

All the care and attention of the little Ridolfi were now for Gemma da Terracina. Having failed to teach this new and beloved friend to talk, which was something even the cage birds could do, she asked to give up studying Latin and Greek herself, or, at least, never to have them read aloud. Music was an even more serious matter. The Ridolfi had a private organist, and nobody who has ever seen it will ever forget the toy-like instrument in the salotto, whose sounds are still as clear as a bird's. It must have been a sacrifice to silence this organ, and probably quite a needless one, since there was no proof that Gemma was deaf.

But less than twelve months later Gemma began to grow at a very noticeable rate, as though her body had set itself to make up for its eight stunted years. By the next spring she was a head taller than the family doctor, who lived with the chaplain and the notary in a suite of rooms built for them over the chapel. The doctor, consulted, had very little to suggest. He tried administering oil of juniper to stunt the growth, and then, when this failed, a remedy of Pliny's, who says that Greek tradesmen used to rub a hyacinth bulb over young slaves to prevent the growth of pubic hair. The Ridolfi began to fear that their doctor was a fool. In anguish, they searched on all sides for better advice. Della Torre was, once again, of little comfort. Another letter of his, now in the Biblioteca Nazionale, points out the folly, in the last resort, of attempting to reverse Nature. 'Don't be so concerned,' he adds, 'with the matter of happiness.' There is also an exchange between Ridolfi and his brother, the Cardinal Archbishop of Florence, who says nothing about Nature, but warns that human happiness must be left to Heaven. 'Certainly,' the Count replies, 'as far as I myself am concerned, but surely I am right to exert myself on other people's account, what better study could there be?' And his daughter was not in the least concerned about herself, only about her friend. She knew, after all, that if Gemma were ever to have to go back to the outside world, where no-one was more than 1.3 metres in height, she would be treated as a monster – dumb, into the bargain, and unable to explain herself. The whole situation was cruelly embarrassing already. And the little girl took to walking a few steps ahead of Gemma, so that their shadows would be seen to be the same length.

The Count reflected that neither Nature nor Heaven has allowed for anyone, certainly not for any child, with such a compassionate heart as this only daughter of his. Impossible and unthinkable to separate her now from Gemma, and he was driven to promise her that if she could think of any way to help Gemma in her desperate condition they would try it, no matter what the cost.

She was now about eight years old, the age at which the mind works logically and without hesitation on what it has learned so far, because it is not troubled by the possibility of any other system. It was for this reason (for instance) that she had never questioned the fact that she herself was confined to the Ricordanza. She knew, on the other hand, something about pain, and that it was worth suffering to a certain extent if it led to something more appropriate or more beautiful. Sometimes, for example, when it was a special occasion, she had her hair curled. That hurt a little. The lemon trees, too, on the terraces of the Ricordanza, were sometimes dipped by the gardeners in boiling water, so that they lost all their leaves, but the new leaves grew back more strongly.

Meanwhile, Gemma had taken to going up and down the wrong steps in the garden, the old flights of giant steps which had been left here and there and should have been used only for occasional games. The little Ridolfi made a special intention, and prayed to be shown the way out of her difficulties. In a few weeks an answer suggested itself. Since Gemma must never know the increasing difference between herself and the rest of the world, she would be better off if she was blind – happier, that is, if her eyes were put out. And since there seemed no other way to stop her going up and down the wrong staircases, it would be better for her, surely, in the long run, if her legs were cut off at the knee.

2

This story is not the one given out nowadays in the leaflet provided by the Azienda di Turismo or by the Committee for Visiting the Most Beautiful Villas of Florence – it starts in the same way, but ends differently. Nor, probably, is the Ricordanza, for all its high and airy position, for all its lemon terraces, really one of the most beautiful villas of Florence. Nor, in a sense, is the present Count Ridolfi really a Count, although the leaflet calls him that, because all titles were abolished in Italy after the Second World War. And, in the course of their descent, the Ridolfi family has taken so many turns and half-turns, so many doubtful passages, that the past generations can hardly be held responsible for those of the twentieth century. No more midgets among them now. Still a tendency towards rash decisions, perhaps, always intended to ensure other people's happiness, once and for all. It seems an odd characteristic to survive for so many years. Perhaps it won't do so for much longer.

3

In 1955 Giancarlo Ridolfi, at the age of sixty-five, had made a serious decision to outface the last part of his life, and indeed of his character, by not minding about anything very much.

But his resolution was shaken not only by his love for his daughter Chiara, but by concern for his elder sister, Maddalena. This was at the time when Chiara, having just turned eighteen, told them that she wanted, before going any further with her education, to marry a doctor, Doctor Salvatore Rossi. He was young, not so very young, thirtyish, a specialist at the S. Agostino Hospital, clever, very hard-working. 'Hard-working, I suppose that means he's from the South,' said Maddalena.

Giancarlo had been born in 1890, by which time the Italian nobility had been put in their place, and no longer held important public office. His father had brought him up quietly on the small family farm of Valsassina, thirty kilometres to the east of Florence. All of them lived quietly, in reduced circumstances (the Ridolfi were never, at any time, successful with money). The old Count had his clothes made by a country tailor, and went down in the evening to drink wine, the wine from his own estate, at the village cantina, where jokes improved every time they were repeated. Until the 1900s the family had never been to the seaside and had no idea that it might be a place to go to, instead of the mountains, for holidays. In 1904 they suddenly all went to Milan, about which they had known nothing either, to hear the first performance of *Madam Butterfly*. It was as if the clouds had opened, then they went back to Valsassina. When the cinema came to the village they were allowed to go to the tattered old Terza Visione movies which were projected onto the whitewashed yard wall of the cantina. If anyone got up to go to the urinal their shadows crossed the screen in giant's form. The one other concession which the old Count made was to buy his son a new kind of toy, a wristwatch: this was in 1910, not long after the first wristwatch was created for the aviator Santos-Dumont. After that he liked to ask the small boy, whenever occasion arose – Well, tell us the time! – but the occasions weren't so frequent in a place like Valsassina where the hour of the day was obvious enough from the length of the shadows. All the same the tenants in the fields and the servants who joined in the conversation as they handed round the dishes couldn't resist asking the child to take another look – Tell us the time!

When he was eleven, the father died. The younger brother stayed on at the farm. Relatives took Maddalena and Giancarlo in hand, but they were separated. Giancarlo was sent first to England, and then to Switzerland, to learn business, but could make nothing of it, and not much more of the philosophy of Benedetto Croce, which he studied at university. He fought through the First World War in the cavalry, and was employed afterwards in the Remounts department. In 1931 his old philosophy teacher became one of the handful of professors who protested against Fascism. He was dismissed, and appealed for help. Giancarlo remembered that Croce had taught that politics were a mere passion, not the right occupation for a thinking man, but did not like to let his teacher down. As a result he found himself under house-arrest at the cliff-like family palazzo in Florence. Most of the rooms were let out, but only very low rents, if any, are paid to a man in disgrace. He was obliged to tell Annunziata, the cook, that he had no ready money, by which he really meant that he seemed to have no money of any kind. Annunziata knew this, and told him that he ought to take good advice.

His younger brother was an uncommunicative man, with a wife who was not encouraged to talk either, and a silent little son. But there was a brother-in-law, a Monsignor Gondi who was at the Curia and knew everyone in Rome. Giancarlo consulted him, and Giuseppe Gondi went so far in compromising himself as to answer by post, though in general terms. 'So far you have not been well advised. Pray and meditate constantly, and follow the traditions of your country and of the ancient nobility.' Giancarlo thought over these words and their unspecified meaning for some months, and then followed the strongest tradition of the nobility he could think of by marrying a wealthy American. But he had no acquisitive sense, and when war broke out once more she left him, an ageing father with a two-year-old daughter, and in the same precarious state as before.

How unfortunate that Maddalena, violently opposed to

Mussolini and living in England, should have married a man who quite mistakenly thought she was a wealthy foreigner, and whose main interest lay in watching waterfowl and wading birds! However much thought one took, how could such a man be made happy? The turn their marriages took brought Giancarlo and his sister together again, or at least brought both of them to the apartment in the Piazza Limbo.

In appearance Maddalena had a meagreness which suggested that she might not be long for this world, although this was contradicted by her persistent good health. Her firmness Giancarlo would have appreciated if there had been any way of telling what she would be firm about next. Take the matter of the third and fourth fingers of her right hand. They were missing, having been taken off with a pair of sharp poultry-shears by a thief sitting behind her on the 33 bus coming back from Bagno a Ripoli. The diamond ring given her by her English husband in their happier days was of course the object. The incident was not at all an unusual one, and the strong-minded Maddalena refused to make any kind of official complaint. She regarded the loss, she said, as a tax which all those who have something to be stolen must expect to pay. 'Calculate in any given year to pay out one-fiftieth of your movable possessions,' she said. On that principle, Giancarlo told her, she would lose one finger every five years. 'How long do you intend to live?'

Chiara, coming and going from an English convent school, was distressed by her Aunt Mad. There was the matter of the Refuge for the Unwanted. The failure of old people to be happy tormented Auntie Mad. The rest of the population endures their company only on sufferance. No-one, even under religious obedience, enjoys being with the old for long periods – with one exception, however, babies, who are prepared to smile at anything even roughly in human shape. Why not, therefore, a Refuge where the old folk could wear out their days looking after homeless infants? The toothless would comfortably co-exist with the toothless. 'But these ancients won't be competent, they'll forget which child is which.' 'At times, possibly.' 'They'll drop them.' 'One or two, perhaps, but what a sense of usefulness!' In the confusion of the post-

14

war, during the quarrelsome rebuilding of Florence, it was easy to do unusual things, even bribery was scarcely necessary. Pretty well all that she had left Maddalena spent on her foundation. It was in via Sansepolcro, and fortunately cost very little to run. The old women were all from the country. They were used to washing clothes in cold water, and scrubbing the floor with sand.

Giancarlo couldn't remember what his sister had been like in their childhood. Remote though it was, she must, surely, have been like something, but never, he thought, like me.

Perhaps, at the moment, sitting in the second floor flat of the decrepit palazzo, in a salon full of marble statuary, as yellow as old teeth, but with a freshness in the light from the river only a street away, they were doing no more than talking things over, as others do. What distinguished them was their optimism. Even disagreements between them produced hope.

If Chiara was to marry this Doctor Rossi, where was the wedding lunch to be? They had thought, of course, of the Ricordanza. It was true that at any celebration there Annunziata would be an absolute nuisance. Insanely cautious, she insisted that any guests from Rome (with the exception of the Monsignore), or indeed from anywhere south of the Umbrian border, were likely to need watching. Before and after they left she counted the spoons in a raucous whisper. That had happened, for instance, when Giancarlo, with the idea of raising money on the property, had given a lunch party at the villa for some Roman bankers. But the scheme had been likely to fail in any case. Giancarlo was not the kind of person who ever made money. He should have applied himself harder to his business studies in Switzerland.

But then it turned out that Chiara didn't, while deeply anxious not to distress anyone, want her wedding to be at the Ricordanza. 'Where she used to play all morning!' Mad exclaimed, 'in the shadows of the lemon trees.' It seemed, however, that Dr Rossi wasn't in favour of it. But surely Chiara had a will of her own?

'Of course she has,' said Giancarlo. 'That is why she is able to change her mind.' And it became clear to them that Chiara wanted a country wedding. 'That means the farm. I shall go out to Valsassina and talk to Cesare about it myself. He won't know what's going on, it won't have occurred to him to ask. I shall go to Valsassina tomorrow.'

4

The Count, holding himself well but stiffly, walked down to the palazzo's courtyard. The ground floor was let out to shops (one of them a hairdresser's) and small offices. The cortile was thronged with parked cars and scooters. Bicycles were always carried indoors and upstairs for safety's sake by their owners. Two horses belonging to the mounted police stood patiently, for long stretches, tethered to iron stanchions let into a marble pillar. In the fourteenth century the whole area had been a graveyard for unbaptised infants, whose salvation was doubtful.

With relief the Count got into his solid old Fiat 1500 sedan. The hollowed leather of the driver's seat fitted his sharp joints. Reluctance to start, small items out of alignment, a rattle which might or might not be something to do with the ashtrays, were no trouble, rather a consolation to a driver who recognised them all.

He drove out of the city on the via Chiantigiana. In tune to the persistent rattling, he reflected that his wife, who was not dead, but preferred to live in Chicago, and Maddalena's husband, who was not dead either, though he was sometimes thought to be, but preferred to live in East Suffolk, must both receive invitations to the wedding, but would not accept them. On the other hand the Monsignore must be asked to officiate, and would officiate, though this would have to be by courtesy of the parish priest at Valsassina. The country, as the Count drove on, the gentle inclines, the olives, vines, and vegetables, suggested that the earth here was still friendly and even protective to human beings, but it had been rewarded in every vineyard with forty-five thousand white concrete posts to the hectare. This did not disturb Giancarlo, who forgave the land its changing appearance as he forgave himself his own.

Spring was very late. At Valsassina there was a bitter smell from the straw fires which had been lit at night to keep the earth warm. They were still tying up the vine shoots and taking off the bare wood. Much more noticeably, two of Cesare's little motocultivators were rolling in procession back and forth across the ridge. The Count marvelled, not for the first time, at how much of the agricultural day consists of moving things from one place to another. He passed the little stone building, once a chapel, which the farmworkers used for their mid-day break. The ragged roof steamed like a kettle, they were boiling something up in there. Higher up, a stone cross marked the place where Cesare's father had been shot during the German retreat, or possibly during the Allied advance, there was no chance now of ever knowing which, or what he had been trying to protest against.

At the top of the rising ground Giancarlo parked in the front courtyard, where it was always supposed to be warmer (but this was a fiction) and as he got out of the car the autumn wind was waiting for him. A lizard which had emerged, as wrinkled as an old man's hand, into what looked like warm sunshine had retreated instantly. The whole of the right-hand wall was covered with a climbing viburnum, spreading upwards and outwards as it always had done within living memory, as far as it could reach. This plant had had the sense to begin shedding its leaves early.

Valsassina itself was somewhere between a farmhouse and a casa signorile and was sometimes admired for its original plan, but in fact it had been put up almost at random on the site of an old watchtower. Once inside, you always had the same sensation of no-one being there, a cavernous emptiness, with a faint sound of something dripping, and darkness, not pitch darkness but a reddish dark between the brick floors and the terracotta tiles of the ceilings. Immediately to the right as you went in was the fermentation room for the house wine. The powerful odour of saturated wood travelled from one end of the house to the other. From here, also, came the sound of dripping. Straight ahead was the dining-room, with a massive fireplace of pietra serena.

'Cesare!' shouted Giancarlo. Then he remembered that his nephew kept Wednesdays for office work.

The dining-room was as dark as the hall, the shutters were up against the sudden cold. But the outlines of knives and forks could be made out, and two substantial white napkins on the old immovable dining-table. The napkins meant that he hadn't telephoned in vain, he was expected. A door at the farther end opened, letting in the clear autumn light, and an old man appeared, making some kind of complaint, interrupted by an old woman who asked the Count decisively what kind of pasta he wanted her to cook. 'I can't hear both of you at once,' said Giancarlo. The man, Bernardino Mattioli, was, he knew, subject to mild delusions of grandeur. Cesare might well be glad to be rid of him, but as Bernardino had nowhere else to go that would be impossible. How can my nephew live here like this, he thought, a young man on his own? They say that every man in his heart wants to go back to die in the place where he was born. While he was considering this – he had been born in the bedroom directly above the room where he was sitting now – Bernardino approached him.

'I have something to say which Your Excellency will find strangely interesting.' The old woman interposed again. It turned out that there were only two possibilities for mid-day lunch, green tagliatelle or plain.

'Any decision must be in the nature of a gamble,' said the Count, 'we will have green.' She retreated towards the kitchen, and her voice could be heard calling out to what had seemed to be a deserted house, 'They want the green!' Giancarlo thought, I have to be back in Florence by half-past four for a committee meeting of the Touring Club.

At the back the two wings of the house lost their pretensions, and turned into not much more than a series of sheds. Beyond the back courtyard were deep and ancient ditches, planted with fig trees and vegetables, all cut back this year by the wind. The last shed to the left looked, from the pulley above the loft, as though it had once been a small granary. This was the office. There Cesare could be seen, sitting absolutely motionless and solid in front of two piles of papers. When a shadow fell across him and he looked up and saw who was there he rose to his feet, and fetched the only other chair, stirring up a smell of poultry and old dust. The Count lowered himself onto it, exaggerating his fragility, as a kind of insurance against ill-chance. Cesare sat down again, turning away from the desk towards his uncle.

The desk, an old walnut piece, looked abandoned and pitiful, as furniture always does once it has been put out of the house. The brass keyplates were missing and the handles had been replaced by pieces of string through the screw-holes. 'That desk wasn't out here in your father's day,' said the Count, almost as though he had forgotten this until now. But since in fact he had mentioned it a number of times, Cesare made no reply. He never said anything unless the situation absolutely required it. Conversation, as one of life's arts, or amusements, was not understood by him, unless silence can be counted as part of it.

For a good many years the Valsassina estate had been engaged in a legal petition to decide the exact location of its vineyards. When Cesare or his late father mentioned the tragedy of 1932, they were not thinking of the fate of the eleven university professors who refused in that year to take the Fascist oath. They meant that in 1932 the authorities had declared Valsassina to be just outside the boundary line of the Chianti area. This meant that none of the Ridolfi wines could be labelled or sold as classic, and their market value was reduced by a quarter. The calculations, however, had been made from the position of the house itself, whereas some of the outlying vineyards fell inside the boundary. They had deteriorated, it was true, and could possibly be described as abandoned, but Cesare was doggedly negotiating for a low interest loan to buy a new digger, which would make replanting with sangiovese grapes possible in a short time. Those borderline fields might then be readmitted as classic. It was a letter from the local Consorzio on this subject, and another one from the bank, that were planted on the desk in front of him now.

'It's cold in here,' Cesare said.

Unquestionably it was. The high windows had been designed so that the sun would never strike through them, and there was no heating in the room except a small charcoal stove. The Count was glad that he was wearing his old military greatcoat, which still fitted him very well. In a few months' time, under the Baistrocchi army reforms, the Italian cavalry would be gone for ever. When he had heard this he had silently resolved to be buried in his coat. Cesare, however, spoke as though he had only noticed the cold for the first time. His uncle stretched himself out towards the stove and as he grew a little warmer his breath became visible.

'Cesare, I've come to talk to you about Chiara's wedding. You know, of course, that she's going to marry this doctor.' The 'this' wasn't quite right, he corrected himself to 'marry Dr Salvatore Rossi.'

There was a pause, which gave him the feeling of having spoken too quickly. Cesare then said, 'Chiara came out here a month or so ago. She didn't stay long.' The Count wondered if this was a complaint, although it hardly sounded like one. Chiara ought to come as often as possible, if only because a twelfth of the estate had been left to her by her uncle, Cesare's father. It wasn't that the estate business didn't interest her, it did, and she was very quick at getting the hang of the accounts.

'Life seems an eternity to a girl at school,' he said.

'How do you know what it feels like to be a girl at school?' Cesare asked, apparently with deep interest.

'Well, I can imagine that now she's finished with it she wants to stay in Florence and, I suppose, to meet different kinds of people.'

'That she evidently did,' said Cesare.

The Count tried again. 'We were a little surprised, you know, not to hear from you. We sent you the announcement of the engagement, of course, I'm sure.'

He could be quite sure, since he could see the card standing all by itself on the light powdering of dust and cornmeal which covered the desk. Cesare followed his glance and said, 'I don't let them disturb the things in here.'

He got up, and his uncle at once understood that they were going to look at something or other on the property. Either Cesare thought this a necessary formality, or he wanted to turn over in his mind what he had just heard. The Count found that he had to check himself from making the kind of gesticulations with which people insult the deaf and the dumb. Meanwhile a section of the darkness in the far corner of the office detached itself and was seen to be a gun-dog of the old-fashioned rough-haired Italian breed. She shook and stretched herself, as a preparation for going out. It was like the action of wringing a dish-mop.

The idea that his uncle had driven out from Florence to discuss something quite else seemed not to disturb Cesare. Perhaps he gave him credit for being able, if he came to the country, to behave as if he lived there. Outside, the ragged sky burned like a blue and white fire, hard on the eyes. Everything, as though at a given signal, was leaning away from the wind or struggling against it.

They walked, not to the vineyards but along a cart track to a hillside planted as far as the horizon with olives. The ground beneath the trees had been ploughed up for potatoes, and the two of them had to go along side by side, but at the distance of a furrow apart, one foot in and one foot out; really, it would have been easier for someone with one leg shorter than the other. The tail of the old dog could be seen moving along the furrow at Cesare's heels. For some reason the Count, who was reflecting that he was too old for such outings, felt more at ease when he was walking at a higher level than Cesare, who at last came to a halt.

'The Consorzio think we ought to get rid of the olives and sell them for timber. There's all kinds of cheap cooking oil now.'

'What will you do?'

'I don't know.'

The fattore, who must have been following them, now came

up in absolute silence and joined Cesare between two lean old trees. Cesare bent down and picked up a handful of stones or earth or both, sorted them out in his palm and showed them to the fattore, who nodded, apparently satisfied. Then, noticing the Count, he wished everyone in general good-morning, and retreated down the slope. At the bottom he got onto his bicycle, adjusting a sheet of corrugated iron which he had been carrying on the handlebars, and pedalled slowly away. The wind caught the flapping edge of the iron with a metallic note, repeated again and again, fainter and fainter. The dog, crouching, followed the sound with sharp attention, hoping that the sound might become a shot. And yet when I was a boy and lived here I was impatient for every morning, the Count thought. And Chiara was always clamouring to come out here, ever since she could totter about after Cesare.

When they got back to the house the shutters had been drawn back in the spacious lavatory which had offered its row of green marble basins and urinals to shooting parties in the days of Umberto I. The shutters were drawn, too, in the dining-room. From daily habit Bernardino had grouped the oil, the salt, the pepper and the bread round the master's place, so that he could help himself at top speed and get back to work, while the Count's chair was drawn up in front of a barren expanse of table. When they sat down Cesare, without embarrassment, began to redistribute everything, while Bernardino, apparently propelled out of the kitchen, brought in the dish of pasta, its sauce freckled and dappled golden from the oven. The heat and fragrance seemed out of place in the astonishing cold of the room. Cesare began to break off pieces of bread and throw them into his mouth with unerring aim, then drank a little Valsassina. The wine, in the Florentine way, was not poured out for guests, who were expected to help themselves. The Count, whose digestion was not always reliable, pecked and sipped. How large my nephew's nose is! he thought. How large his hands! From this angle he reminds me of someone quite outside the family, I think perhaps Cesare Pavese, with those brilliant eyes, not grey, not green exactly. The large nose makes him look kindly, and I know that he is kindly, but he doesn't get any easier to talk to. In the *Inferno* the only ones condemned to silence are those who have betrayed their masters, Brutus and Judas in particular. Dante must have thought of them, before their punishment, as chatterers, or even as serious conversationalists, always first with the news. But, in Cesare's case, what if he were condemned to talk!

He pulled himself up. No one knew better than himself what difficulties Cesare must have, face to face with the bank, the Consorzio, the tenants and the stony and chalky ground, whose blood was a wine which was not permitted to be labelled classico. If his nephew were to be asked, either by divine or human authority – either on Judgment Day or by the redistribution committee of the local Communist party – whether he had made good use of his time, the answer, if Cesare could bring himself to make one, must surely be yes.

The old woman appeared, and remarking that the fire should have been lit long ago put a shovelful of hot charcoal under the dry lavender and olive roots on the hearth. The warmth of the blaze spread courageously a little way into the room and the Count lost the connection of his thoughts, found himself repeating aloud, for no apparent reason, 'If we could buy children with silver and gold, without women's company! But it cannot be.' At the same time the dog, who had been huddled underneath the table, sensed that the next course was coming and sprang convulsively to its feet. This jerked him back to attention.

'The point is that Chiara wants a country wedding, here at Valsassina. I came here, I'm afraid, principally to talk about money. We could have done that on the telephone, in fact money is the only thing one can talk about successfully on the telephone, but then . . . in any case, the expenses of the whole thing would of course be mine. The details, I suppose, aren't for you and me, but there are some caterers that Maddalena favours because she says they make pastries for the Vatican, such folly, we know that the Pacelli pope is looked after by German nuns who would never allow him to eat pastry from

Florence.' To his annoyance Bernardino, platter in hand, bent over him at this point.

'Your Excellency could not find a better place to receive your guests than Valsassina. But you will explain to them when they come that I am of better family than I seem. All the land which you have been walking round this morning, if justice were done, would belong to me.'

Cesare paid no attention whatever to this interruption. He laid down his knife and fork, but this was because he wanted to know something.

'What was it you said just now about women?'

The Count repeated the line from Euripides.

'I don't read much,' said Cesare.

'I expect you don't have time.'

'I shouldn't read if I did have time.'

Cesare used very few gestures, but one, not to be forgotten by anyone who ever knew him, was to spread both hands flat in front of him, as he was doing now. You got the impression that he had never sat at a table without enough room for him to do this. The hands weighed down firmly, as a press is screwed down, wood against wood.

'Tell me, where did she meet this man?'

'Salvatore? At a concert, it seems.'

'And he's a professional man.'

'A doctor is no more professional than a farmer,' said the Count. 'One must never under-rate what a man's profession means to him.' He still counted himself as an Army man, and hoped that his nephew might remember this, but Cesare was evidently under strain, perhaps from the necessity of saying so much at one time.

'He's a neurologist, he's a consultant at the S. Agostino. He's very clever, no doubt about that.'

'All young doctors are supposed to be clever. How old is he?'

'Rather older than Chiara, I suppose in his late twenties.'

'You mean he's thirty.'

'Well.'

'Why is she marrying him?'

'She could only have one reason. You know your cousin. She is in love. Please don't think that I claim to be an authority on the subject, however.'

'If she wants the wedding here,' said Cesare, 'why didn't she ask me herself?'

'I'm sure that she will, but just at the moment you must forgive her, she hardly knows what she's doing. I would be the first to admit that it's a regrettable state of affairs.'

'There's always time to telephone. There's always time even to write a letter. My father sent my mother a letter from the defence of the Carso. If someone doesn't write it means simply this, that there's something else more important to them, even if it's only the pleasure of doing nothing.'

'You mustn't take it in that way, Cesare. It's not an important matter.'

'You're right, of course it isn't.' As they walked out to the courtyard together Cesare said: 'I take it that the marriage won't make any difference to Chiara's interest here, I mean her part-share?'

In the end, his uncle thought, he doesn't care for anything but Valsassina.

5

Giancarlo returned to Florence not quite sure whether anything had been decided or not. He had known his nephew, of course, since birth, and was fond of him, but knowledge is not the same thing as understanding. However, a few days later Bernardino brought a message to the apartment in Piazza Limbo. 'Let Chiara's wedding be at Valsassina. But no caterers, and not the Harringtons.' This last reference Giancarlo did not quite understand.

6

Chiara Ridolfi was a beauty, but not thought beautiful in Florence. Her American mother's family had once been Scottish, her looks were northern, her delicate high colouring was suited not to a fierce climate but to the mild damp and mist of the north. Only the lids of her blue eyes were Florentine, round and languid, like those of Pontormo's angels at Carmignano, the children of a long summer. Her half eager, half diffident approach to whatever came along hadn't the ruthlessness of the ancient money-making city which in its former days had questioned the bills of the world's greatest artists. For example, she was an alert and reckless driver, but suffered from attacks of conscience, of no use at all in the streets of Florence. Her reach exceeded her grasp, so often something seemed to escape her or get left behind, so that she never felt she was doing all she could. She had a good heart. But she had no idea how to make the best of herself, or indeed how to dress at all. It was thought, because she held her head so neatly and so high, that she would come into her own when dressed up for the evening, but then, the Ridolfi had no jewellery, and Chiara didn't care whether they had or not.

A year ago, when she was sixteen, without previous explanation and without at all being able to afford it, Aunt Mad had taken her to have a dress made for her at Parenti. A Parenti was still, in the 1950s, what it had been in the 1920s, a dress recognisable at once and anywhere dresses were worn, and recognising, in turn, no style but its own. But by this time Vittorio Parenti did scarcely any cutting at all, and his confezione might be described as mere sacks, long or short. The secret (as with Fortuny) lay in the material. Parenti silk (he made only in Italian silk) was woven and finished in his own backstreet factory off Via delle Caldaie. The tissue emerged in the finest possible pleats, one half of each pleat going with the grain, the other half against, so that each crease was part of the texture itself and could never become less sharp, indeed it was not a crease, but a change in the silk's direction. The output of the ramshackle factory could only be compared to legend's least probable materials, the cloak woven of the west wind, or the wedding dress that would go through a ring. It was, of course, strictly and exclusively for the use of the house, and when the lengths arrived in the sewing-room there were instructions that all the off-cuts should be destroyed. These instructions, however, were not accompanied by high pay for the employees, who were obliged to sell what they could and there must still be numberless bits and pieces of Parenti silk in Florence, doing duty as a lining or a patch on heaven knows what, but still giving themselves away by their pale glowing colours and the trace of the inimitable pleats.

Chiara dreaded 'good' clothes, and consoled herself with the thought that at least a Parenti dress (which could never be hung up, but must be kept folded and twisted on a shelf) wouldn't be, in the ordinary sense, 'good'. There were a very few 'good' clothes left among her aunt's possessions. They had concealed stiffenings, weighted hems, curious straps and supports, taped waists, which meant that even on the hanger they presented a rigid and forbidding human shape. Aunt Mad, to take her to the appointment, wore an ancient black outfit of this kind, a Viennese suit by Knüpfe. Chiara was in her English school uniform. For the moment her anxiety was swallowed up by the fear that she might, by some outside chance, meet someone else from the convent and suffer the disgrace of being seen in uniform during the holidays.

Parenti received his clients, as he had always done, in a building next to his factory. He had known difficult times, for which he was now given credit. Since the night in 1923 when the Fascist youth had shot out the street-lights in the Oltrarno he had never consented to make anything for the women of the Party officials. (On the other hand, it might well be that the new political order had not appreciated his clothes.)

The house had no name plate or bell, and nothing written

up either on the outer or the inner glass door or on the wall inside. One ought to know one's way, or not venture up these dark stairs. But the establishment had no secrets. The second floor landing led straight through the two sewing rooms and the pressing room. Every face at the ironing tables looked up at them for a moment as they passed, and then bent down again. I hope there's another way out of here, Chiara thought.

They were kept waiting in a little place which was certainly not a fitting room, since there were no mirrors. Armfuls of silk, all in different shades of tender grey, were thrown down on a row of chairs. Without moving them, there was nowhere to sit down, and even Aunt Mad couldn't bring herself to disturb them.

'He isn't expecting us, aunt, he's forgotten us, let's go home.'

'Contessa! Contessina!'

Parenti had come into the room behind their backs. He looked much older and much smaller than in his photographs and very tired, still able, but surely only just, to sustain the fatigue of being Parenti. And yet it wasn't a studied performance, since the old maestro had never had any pretence to make.

'Commendatore, I want to introduce you to my niece, Chiara Ridolfi,' said Aunt Mad. By choosing not to complain about the five minutes wait, she had gained a little advantage. By refusing even to glance at her Knüpfe suit, he had recovered it. Now he swept the piles of grey silk to the ground, where they whispered into a diminished heap.

He said: 'I took the liberty of coming in unexpectedly just now so that I could see the Contessina of the present generation exactly as she really is, I mean when, as a young woman, she is unaware of anyone else.'

'I don't question the way you conduct your business, Parenti,' said Aunt Mad sharply.

He turned full upon her his melancholy gaze, as of one survivor to another. 'Contessa, I last made for you in 1921. For the evening, in pale biscuit-coloured pongée silk, with a belt in matching silk satin, applied with motifs of the

Florentine lily. The belt interrupted the line, and one hoped that it would never be worn.'

'Good, and what do you suggest for my niece?'

For the first time Parenti turned to Chiara.

'Please do me the favour to stand up.'

So Chiara stood up, with her arms straight down by her sides, and half-listening to the whine and mutter from the sewing rooms down the corridor. Without being asked to, but feeling that perhaps it was the right thing to do in a fashion house, she began to walk up and down a little, but very gently Parenti asked her to stop. 'Just keep quite still, Contessina, then I will tell you what to do next.' A whole minute, not less than that, passed by to the relentless chattering of the Necchis.

Then Parenti, who had been looking at her with deep professional attention, raised his hands a little, let them fall, turned away from her at an angle of almost forty-five degrees, and said quietly, 'I cannot make for her. She could not wear a Parenti.'

7

In the following year, after she had left school for good, Chiara asked her father for ten thousand lira and went to a small dressmaker, recommended (as a relation by marriage) by the barber in the courtyard. Even here she met with some opposition.

'Yes, but no one else is wearing them like this, it will have no style, think how it will look from the back.'

'I shan't have to see it from the back,' said Chiara. If there's something hopelessly wrong with me, she thought, it might as well be wrong the way I want it. Really all I need is not to have to worry. For the first time in all eternity I shan't be at school in May. I shall go to the Maggio Musicale, I shall go to every concert, I shall listen to every note.

The two dresses, one black and one white, were brought round to 5, Piazza Limbo by the dressmaker in person. 'I have told the Contessina that I have done my utmost, but she must wear something round her neck.'

'Oh, no one will look at me.'

'Think a little,' said Maddalena. 'You must have noticed that during a concert people have nowhere to look and stare first of all at the ceiling, then at their hands, then at the four corners of the hall, not, for some reason, at the performers, then finally at each other's clothes. Certainly the black dress would look better with my diamonds.' Giancarlo, who had come into the room, pointed out that she no longer had any.

'I give you my word of honour,' said Chiara, 'I'll go to the Central Market tomorrow and get some beads, some black glass beads, I like them.'

'They would not be suitable,' cried the dressmaker. 'They would not be real.'

'Well, but glass beads are real.'

'So are diamonds,' said Giancarlo, 'not more or less real, but equally so.'

There was a small diamond necklace which had belonged to Cesare's mother, and which had been deposited, when she died, in a bank in the Via Strozzi. Either Chiara's father or her aunt must have given Cesare a hint on the subject, because he wrote (he was not much of a letter-writer) to her to tell her that he remembered the necklace, but had forgotten where it was; she could have it, if she wanted it. 'He means, I suppose, that he will arrange about the insurance if you want to take it out for some concert or other,' said the Count. 'Meanwhile, your aunt keeps talking about these two dresses of yours.'

'Does she think they're ugly?' Chiara cried.

'She wonders whether they will make you happy.'

The necklace arrived from the bank in a canvas package, sewn up with linen thread. It had not been opened since 1943, when poor Aunt Lisa had died from dysentery. When Chiara had undone the thread she found a sealed envelope addressed to Cesare, in Aunt Lisa's handwriting, which she put back at once.

The little diamonds, square-cut, glittered valiantly, each with its outer and hidden inner drops of pure light. Annunziata, who had seen them before, was disappointed. She remembered them as larger, and making a better effect.

8

On their first appearance Chiara's dresses were thought peculiar, but not peculiar for the Ridolfi daughter. You had to consider that childhood of hers, shut up with her aunt during the war in the three-times-requisitioned Villa Ricordanza. Now that the girl was back from the school in England everyone wished her well, so hopeful and shining, so full of projects, so ready to regard the world as a friend. But meanwhile, how could Maddalena let her go out to the May concerts in those garments which she had apparently designed for herself and which, like her convent uniforms, must have been run up on the machine at home by Annunziata? The little necklace looked well, however. Where had that come from?

On that April evening, at the Teatro della Pergola, a pianist and a violinist were confronting not so much the audience as each other. The young energetic violinist, dark, sweaty and smelly, only just confined into an evening suit and white neckcloth, was a true Central European gypsy, defying restraint and security, as his music did. The rather older man at the piano was pale and balding, with discreet spectacles and, emerging from his cuffs, long-wristed hands whose gleaming fingertips each seemed to have an independent life. Chance and the demands of a career had bound them together, but only just, for the duration of Brahms' third violin sonata, a work which, so the programme said, 'reunited Brahms and Joachim after a rift of several years.' Before the slow movement the violinist retuned with a coarse, exuberant tzigane flourish, the pianist unobtrusively winced, then, as the music resumed, leaned forward to his keyboard in deep quiet intimacy, as to an old acquaintance, while the violinist forced obedience under what seemed the threat of instant destruction from his tiny, melodiously protesting instrument. His sweat flew visibly. The pianist raised, only once, his pallid eyelids to heaven. And to think that politicians, at that time, dreamed that Europe could become a unity! Here was a representative of one of the finest-tuned of the human species, condemned in the name of music to this unlikely partnership. When all was over, the violinist, as was his right, left the platform first and returned exultant to take his bow, while the pianist, following him, was almost obscured from sight by the resplendent woman who had been turning over his pages for him.

The Count never went to concerts, for fear of being trapped into listening to something that did not please him. Chiara was there with friends. It was old, or ageing, Mimi, an acquaintance of Aunt Mad's, who introduced her during the interval to Dr Rossi.

'My dear child, I want you to meet Dr Rinaldi, no, Dr Salvatore Rossini, no, Rossi, who is doing me so much good.'

Chiara gave the doctor her hand.

'You enjoyed the Brahms?' he asked.

She looked at him politely, but in wonder.

'Of course not.'

Perhaps we might agree about everything, Salvatore thought. No one ever agrees with me, but she might. However, it was as if another voice said this while his rational mind was occupied with a feeling which he wished to think was either amusement or disgust at the sight of a young girl wearing a diamond necklace worth – here he left a blank, for he had no idea what it was worth and it might after all be an imitation, but why should I care, he thought, I'm not a shopkeeper – wearing it in any case as if she didn't know she had it on, and quite without the elegant gesture, the Grace Kelly gesture, of lightly touching the jewels with one hand. Perhaps this young woman didn't know how to be elegant, or perhaps Grace Kelly didn't. He felt deeply irritated. He had an intimation that he was lost.

Mimi, launched on the subject of suffering, was still beside them. 'You don't know yet, Chiara, I'm glad to say, how much good one has to have done to one. To the back in particular.' She hunched her shoulders, looking for a moment like a kindly old pedlar. 'You know nothing till you're thirty-five, then everything goes at once.'

'If it's your back, signora,' said Chiara politely, 'I believe they can do wonders now.'

'Oh, but my dear, I'm told that they knock you about like drunken cabmen. They throw you from hand to hand. They listen to your bones, they listen for the click. And so I've decided that it's not my back, but my nerves.'

This girl agreed with me about the sonata, Salvatore repeated to himself. She wouldn't lie to me, she is the sort who doesn't tell lies even in a concert-hall.

Mimi, a wanderer by nature, had wandered away, and Salvatore abruptly asked Chiara to come outside with him for the rest of the interval.

'Oh, but I came with some friends.'

'What friends? Who are they? If they came with you, why aren't they here?'

'Only two of them, they're fetching me some coffee.'

'Fetching coffee is for people who can't think what else to do next. Come out with me a little.' They went out together onto the entrance steps. It had been fine weather when the audience arrived, but there must have been a change since the concert began and the sky was now a darkish olive-green, only streaked with light to the south-west, over the river. The air was damp and caressing.

'Come out into the warm rain,' Salvatore said.

'Well, but how can rain be warm?'

'Well, try it, try it. Come outside, put out your tongue, taste it.'

Chiara sat through the second part of the performance in a lightly damp condition, like washing, she thought, brought in from the line sooner than it should have been. Her hair was flattened down and the rain had given her cheeks a striking pale rose colour. Her own friends said nothing, but from their seat two rows further forward, made a light-hearted pantomime of rubbing with a towel. The Alessandri had noticed also, and were not quite so much amused, nor were Mr and Mrs Swinburne-Cacciano, or the Quaratesi party, or the ancient but inflexible Marquesa Cardoni. Their silent systems of communication and warning were the same as they would have been thirty years earlier. A dictatorship, a war and an occupation had not been sufficient to change them. Yet Chiara herself was so poor a Florentine that she listened to the second part of the concert, which was much more successful, without noticing that anyone was looking at her.

9

Salvatore, who was not a temperate person, intensely regretted having gone to this particular concert. What irritated him as much as anything else was that his mother had repeatedly predicted that if he went north to practise in Milan or Florence he would be got hold of by some wealthy, fair-haired girl who would fasten on him and marry him before he knew what he was doing. Now, in point of fact this girl was badly dressed and not fair-haired, or anyway only in certain lights, for example in the artificial light of the auditorium and the rainy twilight outside would anyone have called her a blonde. His mind chased itself in a manner utterly forbidden to it, round thoughts as arid as a cinder track.

As a favourite son, he had been obliged to receive a quite unjust amount of his mother's traditional wisdom. After he had been caught, she would say, not even with any real disapproval but with an infuriating nodding and smiling certainty, he would forget his home and even his family and they would be lucky ever to see him again in Mazzata. Curious that advice is just as irritating when it's wrong as when it's right.

She had baptised him Salvatore in honour of the Saviour, whereas his father would have preferred not to have had a

34

christening at all, and wanted, quite ineffectually, to name him Nino, after Antonino Gramsci, or perhaps Liberazione or Umanità, or even 1926, since that was the year of his birth and also that of Gramsci's last imprisonment. Domenico Rossi's choice of names could be laughed at, and was laughed at, even by the Party members of Mazzata. His one ally was a part-time book-keeper, one of those not born to succeed, with the short-sighted mildness of a certain kind of violent revolutionary. This man, Sannazzaro, was not particularly welcome in the house and often sat talking to Domenico in a windowless room which was really part of the kitchen passage. The police rightly regarded him as entirely harmless. But to Salvatore, as he grew up, his father had meant much more than his mother. He couldn't ever remember agreeing whole-heartedly and without embarrassment with his mother. On the other hand he put off for as long as he could the pain of admitting to himself that his father was wrong.

In 1913 Domenico and Sannazzaro had come up together from Mazzata in search of opportunities. They had gone as far north as their permits allowed, to Turin. Domenico had worked as a bicycle mechanic, Sannazzaro as an assistant book-keeper. They shared a copy of a weekly newspaper, Gramsci's *Grido del Popolo*. In the *Grido* they read about an Italy, a possible Italy, without poverty, favours or bribery. Mass education would come about as a matter of course, but it would take the form not just of instruction but of question and answer between teacher and learner. Every sane man is an intellectual, but most are afraid to function as an intellectual should, that is, to stay in their own communities and organise them. If only a few thousand would do this, in Calabria, Campania, Sicily and Sardinia, the south could be as prosperous as the north. Only the lack of good sense or even common sense made it difficult to envisage the great human cities of the future with their intense, tumultuous and productive life. Under present conditions every Italian family struggled against every other to get advantages for itself. When the concept of property was abolished the struggle would be unnecessary. Even within the home there would be peace. Twelve

35

brothers and sisters would be able to sit round a table without dispute. And the children's education would no longer be left to women and priests. No adult would have a mortgage on a child's character or its future. In the new community it would be free, at last, to choose.

Every life has lucky moments when sympathy opens one heart to others. To respond may be a mistake, not to respond must be ingratitude. The crowded print of the *Grido* came, in this way, in the back streets of Turin, to authentic life for Rossi and Sannazzaro. In the whole city they had not succeeded in finding one bar or câfé kept by a Mazzatano. Their own friendship, the weekly Party meetings and the *Grido* became their points of reference.

Before the strike of 1919 they met their frail leader in person. That was before he went to prison for the first time. Rossi even had the opportunity to ask him whether there was anything he could do for him, anything he could get for him or have sent to him by way of the warders. Gramsci had said that he wanted nothing except a loaf of Sardinian bread and an Italian translation of Kipling's *Jungle Book*. But his smile as he said this, not a politician's smile, showed that he recognised the impossible.

After the strike and the occupation of the factories, which was a total failure, Rossi and Sannazzaro of course lost their jobs. They sold their city shoes, resoled their boots with lengths of bicycle tires, and walked the 750 kilometres back to Mazzata. By the time they arrived they were almost starving. The village received them without enthusiasm. They had left Mazzata as failures, and returned as failures. They still attended the local Party's surreptitious meetings, in the back room of the chemist's shop. When Gramsci, from his prison cell, dissociated himself from Stalin's policies, he was declared an outcast and a heretic. The two friends, loyal to him still, became less important in local politics than the flies on the ceiling.

10

When he was ten years old Papa had taken him on a journey to see Antonio Gramsci. It was a last chance, since Gramsci, having been moved from one prison to another for the last nine years, was known to be terminally ill. There had been an international petition to the Italian government for his release, which had met with the fate of most petitions.

By 1936 he had been transferred to Rome. He was no longer an official prisoner, but was under medical treatment at the Clinica Quisisana. The rules for visiting him were relaxed. On the other hand, there were not so very many people, and almost none of his old associates, who cared to visit him.

Domenico and his son got a lift in a tomato lorry as far as Benevento, and then took the slow train to the capital, which gave them a good chance to look at each other without interruptions. Salvatore saw a patient man whom he loved, and who, he knew, had had to ask Mother's permission to make this expedition, a tired man, worn and shiny like an old suit. Domenico looked back uneasily at his bright, unaccountable boy.

When Domenico had been little his grandmother, who worked in a hotel kitchen, had edged him upstairs into the reception hall in the hopes of presenting him to a bishop (who had just arrived) for a blessing. They knelt together for a moment on the marble floor, risking everything. But the bishop, who was on a private visit and wished to indicate that he was off duty, turned his ring round on his finger so that the faithful could not kiss it. The grandmother got up and twitched the boy back to the service quarters, as though he had been in some way to blame.

All Domenico wanted now was for his son to come into the

presence of a great man. At the same time he had a few questions to ask after these many years, and of course he could not come empty-handed. On his knees, with their sandwich, he had a parcel consisting of medicines, writing paper and a woollen pullover. It was fastened with insulating tape, and anyone could tell that it had not been wrapped up for him by a woman. When they got to Rome and steamed into the old peach-coloured station in Piazza Esdraia, he tried to make it look a little more presentable.

Salvatore was disappointed firstly when they crossed the city without seeing a single one of the new Alfa Romeo two-seaters whose image he had studied in a magazine, and secondly when the Clinica Quisisana had no bars.

'It's not a prison,' his father told him.

'Can he go away if he wants to?'

'No, he can't do that, he can't go into Rome without a police guard.'

Then it's a prison, the child thought.

There was a bell in the outer gate and when they rang it was answered by a young male nurse in uniform. Salvatore saw that he was not going to be petted, as he would have been in a convent, or a hospital run by Holy Sisters. This impressed him. He was impressed because he was ignored.

The male nurse asked whether they had an authorisation from Dr Marino or Professor Frugoni, and Salvatore felt an unaccustomed admiration for his father when he pulled out of his inner pocket a note from the Professor confirming their appointment. The nurse went away, and came back to say that the patient Antonio Gramsci was not well enough to receive visits. He was now carrying a blue folder under his arm.

'Who says so?' asked Domenico.

It was about three o'clock in the afternoon. He stood there in the blank early spring sunshine, holding his son's hand.

'The management are anxious that he shouldn't see members of the public without medical knowledge, who might be distressed by certain changes in him,' said the young man, reading from the folder as though repeating a lesson. 'The tuberculosis has affected the spine – do you understand me? – and the sight is poor.'

'You can spare yourself anxiety. My permissions are all in order. In reply to a letter I sent him Comrade Gramsci himself asked us to come and see him.'

11

Salvatore had seen deformed animals, and dead bodies of both people and animals, but never anything as ugly as Comrade Gramsci. Ugliness is a hard thing to forgive at the age of ten. The thick mouth of the prisoner, his father's friend, opened darkly, like a toad's, without a single tooth in sight. The tiny crippled body could no longer make any pretence of fitting into his ordinary clothes, which hung on him, as they would have done on a circus animal. He was not sitting down, but propped standing up against the wall. The smell of illness, stronger than disinfectant, filled the room, and there was no other air to breathe. While his father unwillingly took the only chair, Salvatore, after standing up for a while, perched on the corner of the clean, hostile cover of the bed.

'We have brought a few medicines, just what we could get at the chemist's.'

'Many thanks, but no, I should prefer you to save them for someone else. All I ask for here is some kind of stimulant, but Dr Marino doesn't prescribe those. You're very good, Domenico, but I have all I need as far as I'm allowed it. My sister-in-law comes quite regularly.'

The visit was not going as it should, the present was not wanted. Gramsci, in a hoarse painful voice, difficult to follow, asked about Mazzata, and for the name of the local Party secretary. When he was told it he said, 'No, I don't know that name.'

'He's of the new generation, Nino, you couldn't have heard of him.'

'My one dread is that my memory will go. If one is forty-four, with no books to speak of, and no memory, one can't expect to write anything of value. I have no record of what's happening outside here either, except the official newspapers. My mind is still clear, but I think perhaps I've lost the gift of patience. When I was in prison I knew my friends were saying, "If he can stand five years shut up in one place or another, surely he can stand six," but in fact the fifth year in prison is very different from the fourth, and one can't tell what the sixth will be like.'

'But, Nino, this is a clinic. It's the first time I've had an answer to any of my applications to visit you. That showed me how different things are for you now.'

'It means that they don't consider me important any more. But I knew about your applications. Don't think that I've forgotten what affection is.'

By now Domenico's enthusiasm had become more like pleading. He seemed to be begging the situation to right itself and to become what he had hoped and expected.

'How could one do that, Nino? You remember Turin, you remember when the tram-lines froze and none of us could get home, and you gave us your Ten Commandments?'

'In Turin,' said Gramsci, 'I made a resolution that I would cut every strand, every connection, between myself and my family. Of course I had no children of my own then. It was only little by little that I realised how dry, coarse and squalid is a life without affection through the bond of the flesh. You'll tell me that nothing could be more obvious, and yet I didn't see it at that time.'

'I don't know how to answer you,' said Domenico hesitantly. 'This is my only son, my respect for you has never changed, I've come not only to see you once again but to ask about the things that still confuse me.'

Salvatore continued to stare fixedly at the sick man, and now it seemed to him that he looked, in his crumpled suit, more like a squab or a fledgling bird, with large nocturnal

40

eyes, disturbingly blue, and a beaked nose. On top of a cupboard full of medicine bottles there were three photographs, one of a girl, one of a boy, one of a woman with both the girl and the boy. These were evidently the prisoner's children, and Salvatore, who pondered a good deal about such things, felt sick at the thought of how the hunchback could have managed to beget them. The height of his own ambition, at the moment, was to dive into the irrigation tank in Mazzata from the topmost height of the containing wall. Now he was looking at a fully-grown man whose body was of no practical use to him whatever.

A change of tone, much like a change of temperature, told him that the discussion was now about himself. It continued as though, by some curious fiction, he was not in the room at all, and in accordance with the same fiction he pretended not to listen. His school work was mentioned. This, though in a way reassuring, was bitterly disappointing, worthy of his mother and her friends, not worth travelling to Rome for. He was ready to say, or to have it said for him, that he had passed the first of his junior intermediate exams. His father made nothing of that, but, trembling with urgency, passed rapidly on. His hands, hanging down loosely between his knees, pressed themselves together to emphasise every point.

'Of all the truths I've learned from you, Comrade, whether I've heard them with my own ears or whether I've read them, I've been interested most of all in what you've had to say about education. Through the upbringing of our children we can begin, even today, to build the society of the future. My son here is intelligent, but he will stay with me in Mazzata, I shan't lose him to the cities. He will be an intellectual for the people of Mazzata. When he goes to the liceo, I shall prevent his learning Latin. Latin is still what it has always been, the means by which one class can overawe and humiliate another. I shall go to see the school authorities and insist that he is taught simply and naturally, through question and answer.'

When he paused, waiting for words of approval, Gramsci said: 'Let him learn Latin.'

He was speaking now with increasing difficulty.

'Let him learn Latin. I learnt it. Education should never be acquired easily. Skill in a trade doesn't come without work and suffering, and after all, learning is a child's trade.'

Salvatore saw that his father was disconcerted, and although this was nothing new, he was sorry.

'And science?'

'Of course, if you're certain you can distinguish it from witchcraft.'

'Nino, in Turin you advised both of us to read Rousseau.'

'Who were "both of us"?'

'Myself and Luca Sannazzaro, you remember Luca?'

'Don't try to make me infallible,' said Gramsci, 'you can see I have enough trouble without that. In 1927, when they moved me from Ustica to Milan, I was allowed to plant a few seeds of chicory, and when they came up I had to decide whether to follow Rousseau and leave them to grow by the light of nature, or whether to interfere in the name of knowledge and authority. What I wanted was a decent head of chicory. It's useless to be doctrinaire in such circumstances.'

Shuffling himself round into a new position, he looked directly at Salvatore.

'If your father won't let you learn what you want to, what will you do?'

'I don't know, sir.'

Gramsci began to tell, in his shadowy voice, stories of his own elder brother, who had been defiant as a child and as a gesture had taken the family cat to the village baker and asked him to roast it. When his shoes were locked up to prevent his running away he blacked his feet with polish and went off just the same. The story began to steal in its own right into the hidden reaches of Salvatore's mind. He forgot the hospital room for the moment and gave way to the charm of what had happened then to someone who was indisputably here now. Gramsci went on to say a little about himself, as a crippled child, whose mother had always kept a coffin and a white dress ready for him, as he wasn't expected to last long. 'However, I have lived for more than forty years.' He, too, had felt that it might be necessary to escape from home, and with this in mind he had always kept some dry corn in his pockets, and a candle and a box of matches.

'That's enough about me,' he added resolutely, with his hinged, toothless, tender smile. 'What have you got in your pockets?'

There was a silence. 'Answer, boy,' said Domenico, threatened with humiliation. He repeated the question in their own dialect. 'Answer.' Salvatore did not at all like this concentration on his own case. The smell in the room was, he thought now, of something gone bad, or at any rate of something on the turn. Even if he didn't say anything, he could go some way towards pleasing everyone simply by putting his hands in his pockets and turning them out. But with all the force of his being he didn't want to do so.

'Bene, it doesn't matter,' Gramsci said. 'How could it matter? Perhaps, anyway, you think I'm not strong enough to be a good friend for your father?'

'No, sir, I don't think that.'

Now Gramsci moved again, sidling a little towards the right and establishing himself fairly securely against the washstand with its jug and basin of enamelled tin. There he held out his hand.

'Children don't like sick people. Are you afraid to touch me?'

'I don't want to touch you if I'm going to catch anything,' Salvatore said. 'With my cousins, there are seven of us in the house at home.'

'Seven!' shouted Domenico. 'What has that to do with it, why do you mention that?'

'You won't catch anything,' said Gramsci, and the child stepped forward and felt his hand crushed as though the bones were being ground together under the thin skin. When the travelling fair came round in autumn there was a machine called 'The Initiation' which gave you, as you gripped the handle, an electric shock. But that was not for anyone under the age of twelve.

'Now it's your turn. Since you didn't answer, I'm doing you more than justice. You can ask me anything you like.'

43

Another chance not to fail his father. It was a moment when he could do him real credit, and he knew very well what kind of credit was wanted. Immediately he could picture the two of them, their visit over, back in the station refreshment room where they had gone when they arrived, the street lights on by now, his father praising him for his good question while he himself melted a lump of sugar in a long-handled spoon, slowly, feeling satisfaction and pity.

'Ask anything you want,' Gramsci repeated. In his present position he could take out a cigarette, although his disease had eaten so far into the vertebrae that he had difficulty in balancing his head well enough to smoke it. Patiently Domenico struck match after match, trying to get the tobacco alight.

Salvatore knew by now the question he ought to put. He regretted that he hadn't wanted just now to say what he had in his pockets. That had been a mistake. He was quite well used to being told to put questions, as well as answering them, in the presence of a school inspector. That was simply a matter of knowing what was wanted. The more important these men were, the easier it was to reply. One of them had told the whole class to remain standing and to answer the question in the first lines of the Fascist Chorus of Youth: 'Duce, Duce, when the time comes, who will not know how to die for you?' Impossible to go wrong there. But Salvatore had also half-absorbed from the long droning evenings in the passage room, and from what they had earnestly tried to explain to him, the concerns of his father and Sannazzaro. Supposing he tried: 'Comrade Gramsci, sir, when the time comes, who will not want liberty?'

Courage. But the words he had formed in his mind suddenly made themselves scarce, and still wanting and intending to say something quite different he asked loudly: 'Why are you bleeding?'

And in fact a trickle of blood had appeared at the corner of the mouth of his father's friend. Gazing at the hunchback in his niche, seeing the first drop ooze past the clamped cigarette to the edge of the chin, Salvatore knew that everything could be saved if only it wasn't allowed to fall. Blessed Mary, Mother of God, Shelter of the Homeless, don't let it fall. But as Gramsci opened the other side of his mouth to answer as he had promised, and possibly even to smile, something final and disastrous happened, he leaned forward and dark liquids began to make their escape from several parts of the body. Domenico Rossi put his whole fist on the bellpush and with his other hand threw open the door. 'Get help!' The boy clattered down the shining corridors, weeping. So far in the clinic he had seen no women, but a woman was needed now. Behind one of the shut doors with their squares of frosted glass he might find one.

12

Domenico was right in believing that this visit to Rome would provide a lasting memory for his son. Salvatore's resolution, as soon as he began to be able to translate his impressions into terms of will and intention, was this: I will never concern myself with politics, I will never risk imprisonment for the sake of my principles, I will never give my health, still less my life, for my beliefs. He also resolved to be a doctor. In the end we shall all of us be at the mercy of our own bodies, but at least let me understand what is happening to them.

The sight of his father's tears as they walked back to the station was also disagreeable to Salvatore. He was reluctant to admit to himself that, for the moment, he was older than his parent, and ashamed that they hadn't got a handkerchief between them. There had been a napkin, but that was left behind with the basket and the unwanted presents at the Clinica Quisisana. Eventually they stopped in front of a little shop, and Domenico, still much moved, sent his son, by himself, to ask for a handkerchief. The man behind the counter told him that he must buy three, they were only for sale in packets of three. Salvatore stood there, solidly occupying his ground. 'My father only needs one. You must sell him what he needs.' The shop-keeper put his hand to his ear, pretending not to understand. Salvatore repeated what he had said in clear Italian. 'It's the law,' he added. He paid for a single handkerchief and counted his change with insulting care. On that afternoon he decided that as soon as possible he would be emotionally dependent on no one.

13

Hard work and opportunism are the secrets of biological success. Gramsci himself was fond of the proverb 'Where one horse shits, a thousand sparrows feed.' But from the usual source of help, the family, Salvatore received very little. All that it really came down to was that during his years of medical training he was able to lodge at a reasonable rent over a greengrocer's shop belonging to his great-aunt's step-daughter's niece.

As a medical student his call-up was deferred, and just before the Allies landed in Sicily he got himself transferred to Bologna. The following spring the great neurologist, Professor Landino, returned from a long exile, and Salvatore expected to be deeply influenced by him, but was disappointed. Honourable men are rare, but not necessarily interesting. Landino was not interesting. Neurology, however, made its appeal in the simplest possible way, for its own sake. As a junior he made notes on case after case of back injuries which had been caused two or perhaps three years earlier when the patients had come to grief in a truck or some military vehicle which had run over a mine or a pot-hole. The surgeons had removed the injured disc from the spine and fused the vertebrae above and below it to make as neat a job as possible. And now there was no inflammation, nothing to be read from X-rays or tests on the cerebrospinal fluid, and yet the patients complained of agonising pain. There were women, too, admitted to the hospital who were unable to move one arm or both, who couldn't stoop down to lift their children, whose faces were distorted and fixed into a singer's open-mouthed grimace. The pain was in their imagination, but as real, of course, as if it wasn't. In fact, it was impossible in these circumstances to attach any meaning to 'real' or to 'imagination'. There was no acceptable diagnosis to make. He was in the face of pain which left no trace, and healing without explanation. The specialists, however confident, knew no more, perhaps less, than a dog who lies down in the shade until it feels better. But whatever exists, can be known. Salvatore didn't delude himself that he was capable of great discoveries. But he thought he might set himself to see why no discoveries had been made so far. 'Gentlemen,' Professor Landino began, with a smile which acknowledged the women students but implied that he was too old to learn new tricks, 'not for nothing is neuralgia associated with artists, sensitives and degenerates.' He paused on these last words, giving them equal weight. 'We define neuralgia as pain whose origin is not clearly traceable.'

14

Salvatore's natural associates in Bologna should have been the small group of students from the South, predictable in their habits, the civilian brothel on Saturday nights, on Sundays their thick black best suits which in some cases had been inherited or borrowed from their fathers. Since they could not get used to the Bolognese food in the university cafeteria, which seemed to them designed to poison the first generation of post-war doctors, they made an arrangement with a café run by a Neapolitan, where places were kept for them every day. During his first year Salvatore considered these habits and set himself up against them. 'Any behaviour that is expected of you,' he argued, 'makes you less of an individual. As a doctor I shall have to know what is normal and take any variation from it as a danger signal. As a human being, I should do the opposite.'

In 1946 the little group gave up their black suits and either sold them or sent them back to their villages. They continued to eat at Palumbo's, and now Salvatore went with them. He had realised that if he set out to be unpredictable he would end up, as before, a slave to public opinion. He must leave Bologna as a man typical of nowhere and nothing, young Dr Rossi pure and simple, self-created, self-determined, forewarned and unclassifiable. A new city was necessary, and he went to Florence.

15

It was one of his rules never to waste time. He believed, indeed, that as a rational man he had trained himself to a point where it was impossible to waste any. The amount of time, therefore, that he spent in thinking about Chiara Ridolfi since his visit to the Teatro della Pergola in the spring of 1955 must, he thought, be in some way biologically useful.

In order to sum up his position in what seemed to him a controlled, logical and dispassionate manner, he made a written note. 'The Ridolfi family. Information about them can of course be obtained without difficulty. They have two or perhaps three houses too many, the Ricordanza, the flat on via Limbo, no doubt a farm somewhere or other. These people should be avoided until they can be analysed correctly. I am thirty. By the time she is my age she will probably have deteriorated very little except for a slight shrinkage of the breast tissue. I shall then be forty and shall almost certainly have suffered hair loss, and (judging from my mother's physique, not my father's) shall have put on a certain amount of weight. When admiring a slender or meagre physique people talk about a good bone structure, by which they mean the skeleton. What is attractive about exhibiting one's skeleton?

I doubt whether she is fitted to be a doctor's wife, therefore she should be put out of mind.

Perhaps, however, not in this particular case.'

16

At this time Salvatore was working at the S. Agostino hospital, where he was a junior consultant. He might become head of the neurology department, possibly quite soon, and on merit only. Politics and business can be settled by influence, cooks and doctors can only be promoted on their skill.

His closest friend was one of his colleagues. Gentilini, an older man, grey-moustached, not promoted, not envious, close to him professionally, which must be the strongest bond of all except that of having been young together. Gentilini was from Borgoforte, where he had only to sit down for a drink in his own piazza, even now, to be surrounded with friends, calling from table to table, while others wheeled in on their Lambrettas like late returners to a hive. In Florence he was always, and expected always to remain, a little homesick, whereas Salvatore was determined that under no circumstances would he ever be dragged back to Mazzata.

In Florence they went to the Caffé Voltaire, in Via degli Alfani, and discussed the purpose of life. This, undeniably, was reproduction. All forms of life exhaust themselves in the effort to reproduce their kind, after which, if not happy, they must at least be considered satisfied. Salvatore felt, in the course of this conversation, that he was being got at. Practically any subject, since the evening on which he had met Chiara, could make him feel this. There was little point in asking Gentilini, who had four children to support, whether he considered himself 'a form of life'. 'Contentment is an unattainable ideal,' Salvatore declared, emphasising his points on the table-cloth. 'It's strange, to say the least, that the body is content when it loses itself in its own experience and forgets itself, while the mind is only satisfied while it is absolutely conscious of itself and its own workings.'

'Why is that strange?' Gentilini asked. 'Things are in a bad way if the mind and the body demand the same thing.'

'But why "demand"?' Salvatore cried. 'What a choice of words, you speak of them as though they were bank managers.' Gentilini looked with a certain amount of anxiety at his young colleague, and asked him whether at the moment he was finding existence hard. Salvatore, raising his voice to the night sky, replied that he wasn't troubled or worried by what did exist, but by what didn't. He was threatened at every turn by the cheap stereotypes of the popular imagination – let us say the ambitious young, or youngish, arrival from nowhere, hoping to make good connections, the innocent young girl of good family, and on top of that all the stale antitheses, dark, fair, excitable, cool, South, North, the whole boiling.

'You don't consider yourself excitable?' asked Gentilini.

Salvatore replied, 'I had my first lesson in total self-discipline when I was ten. You only like to think I'm excitable because I'm from the Campania.' A new profession, he went on, should be created, to work in collaboration with medicine and experimental science, a profession devoted to clearing the human mind from preconceptions.

'In the manner of the Encyclopaedists,' said Gentilini mildly.

'Not at all, they were intellectuals, and the sole task of the intellectual is to make people despise what they used to enjoy. I don't want more contempt in the world, I want none.'

The obsessed are blind to their obsessions. To them it seems no more than a coincidence that so many unrelated things seem to refer to their one and only concern. Or it may be that the senses have become preternaturally selective, and detect it everywhere. To give an example, at an international symposium on diseases of the lung, organised by the University of

Florence, the first slide of the first lecture was a close-up of the so-called dwarfs of the Ricordanza. The lecturer, an American, had wanted to provide a catchy opening to his paper on the effects of a low concentration of oxygen in the blood. Perhaps he fancied that a murmur of appreciation and recognition might go round the hall. Pale with the desire to please, he bent his head towards the audience like a tame animal let in on sufferance so long as it behaves decently. Because of a defect in the amplification system, very little of what he said could be heard. Gentilini, whose interest in the subject was marginal, saw, when the interval came for questions and discussion, that his friend was about to get up from his seat. He took a slip of paper from Salvatore's hand and saw written on it: *Will Professor Swanston kindly inform us why, out of all the available representations of deformity in the history of art, he had to select this one? Has he any special interest in the Ridolfi family? I challenge him to tell us that.* Gentilini tore the paper into a number of small pieces, and took Salvatore's arm. 'I am forty-five,' he said. 'Allow me to know what is relevant. I have torn up your question, let's go.' On the evening of the very same day, they heard one of a group of people, not at the next table, but close enough, saying: 'Poor thing, she wants to please everybody, but she doesn't know a thing, she doesn't know how to come in out of the rain.' There was no reason, absolutely none, to think they were talking about Chiara Ridolfi, but Gentilini was alarmed, with a weary feeling that this kind of thing might go on indefinitely, when his friend rose to his feet, apparently ready to do violence. The waiter, however, like a partner in a dance, came forward from behind a pillar to add up their bill, retreating only when Salvatore sat down, or rather was replaced in his chair by Gentilini, who gripped the edge of his linen jacket.

'My feelings are perfectly in control,' Salvatore shouted. 'I simply wanted to point out, speaking with respect . . .'

'I've just realised what you remind me of,' said Gentilini. 'The old Ridolini comedies. Perhaps you're too young to remember them.'

'I remember them. We got plenty of old films in Mazzata.'

For a moment both of them sat in silence, thinking of themselves at the open-air ciné on a hot summer's night.

'But surely,' said Salvatore, 'if one overhears something said in public which is manifestly and ludicrously untrue, one has a duty to put it right immediately. You must grant me that. I appeal to your sense of responsibility.'

Gentilini wondered whether to order another Campari. They never had more than one on ordinary working days, and took it in turns to pay. He decided instead to turn the subject a little and reminded Salvatore of his project to reform mankind's prejudices by scientific means.

'How would you describe your own present state of mind?' he asked.

'I'm aware that I'm displaying unusual symptoms. I could describe them, I think, as a variant of hyperaesthesia. Professor Fregone once told me about the case of a man, I think a Russian, or perhaps Armenian, who could read what was printed on the back of a page by feeling the outlines of the letters with his fingertips, I mean through the thickness of the paper. Well, I am at the point when the faintest of sounds, sounds which would have no significance for you, affects me almost unbearably, and the lightest touch can be torture. Now, we're agreed, of course, that this kind of pain is as genuine as pain with a recognisable physical origin.'

'Well, it has an origin,' said Gentilini. 'The origin is this, that you want what, it seems to me, you can't have.'

Salvatore, calm now, turned round his empty glass.

'Why shouldn't I have her? I shall have her, if I want her as much as I do. That must be taken for granted between us.'

'And so far you've met her just this one time.'

But this turned out to be barely relevant. The turbulence arose from an argument which Salvatore was conducting with an imaginary listener, or perhaps with himself, as to the terms on which he would accept the marriage. He was to be taken, in the first place, entirely at his own value, never to be expected to behave in any particular way, never to be excused or praised or accounted for as a product or an example of one district or another, or approved of as a clever fellow or a lucky one or a successful one. Above all the two of them must take each other without explanation, and stand equal and undifferentiated before each other as human beings were once thought to stand equal before God. 'But even then, in those early days, there was a difference of sex,' said Gentilini, taking advantage of a moment's silence. There was another ten minutes before they needed to start back to the hospital. But once again he had to resign himself to listen. His friend had now taken an entirely different tack, although with the obstinacy of the lost he was bound to let it lead him back to the same starting-point, and was asking, with a show of cold rationality, why there should be even the slightest probability that he should ever meet this young woman again.

'But surely it could be arranged without much difficulty?' said Gentilini. 'You might –'

'I don't choose that it should be a matter of arrangement!'

Then Salvatore broke off, and abruptly held out his hand. 'Think of me as a cripple, if you like, don't turn away from me, take my hand.'

17

'There is no relationship more durable than friendship,' Gentilini told his wife that evening, 'perhaps because it is tried so hard.' He paused, fearing that he had been tactless, however Signora Gentilini showed no offence, but on the contrary seized the opportunity to ask him why he didn't bring his friend, Dr Rossi, round more often. Even when he did, it was just for a talk between one man and another, whereas it would be a pleasure to prepare a meal for a thinking man, and anyone could see at a glance that he was lonely.

'How can you see that?' asked Gentilini.

'He's so silent, so unsure of himself, the poor man.'

18

Gentilini's place was not where he would have liked it to be, in the university quarter and near S. Agostino, but in a back street where he was more or less resigned to living. A powerful smell of cauliflower met him as he turned the corner, still talking to Salvatore. Possibly something had gone quite seriously wrong in the kitchen, because the cage birds had been hung outside the window to get a breather although it was a cloudy day. 'So you persist in despising intellectuals as a class?' he asked, hesitating on the pavement, postponing the moment of entry into the house, where the discussion of general subjects was difficult.

'Certainly, cleverness is the curse of human history,' Salvatore said. 'Again and again the simple assert themselves, the soldierly Romans, the early Christians, no matter who, but while they're doing the necessary work of every day the intellectuals step in, and after them the vulgarisers . . . But honestly, all that matters very little. What I want to know is whether you've seen her.'

'Seen, seen . . .'

'You know who I'm talking about. I'm not asking what you think of her, that doesn't interest me in the least, I simply want you to tell me, have you seen her lately?'

'Of course not, I don't know these people.'

'I've been told she has an aunt, an eccentric, possibly of unsound mind. Don't you think that Chiara should be forcibly separated from her?'

'You can't expect me to give an opinion. But if she has an aunt, I suppose it's natural that this young woman should be fond of her.'

'Natural! It's not natural, Nature is something quite else. Do you think that a horse, or a pigeon, is fond of its aunt? Could it recognise its aunt as such?'

'Perhaps not, but in ordinary human society . . .'

'So you're trying once again to distinguish us from the rest of animal creation,' cried Salvatore in tones of angry satisfaction. 'You renounce behaviourism. Is that what I'm to understand?'

The Gentilini's maid opened the front door. So regular was Gentilini in his habits that lunch, at thirty-five minutes past twelve, was timed absolutely by his return. The smell of cauliflower gained strength. The girl looked in dismay at the two men. Salvatore had seized Gentilini by the forearms and was shaking them up and down as though he had lost his temper with an empty ticket machine. The neighbours began to come to the windows, and even out onto the balconies.

'Mere superstition . . . peasant magic . . .'

Gentilini reminded himself of his friend's deserved reputation at the hospital, and indeed in the profession, as a reliable, knowledgeable and brilliant consultant. He persuaded him cautiously into the house.

The dining-room was uncomfortably crowded. The family were all there, two of the little girls, with their clean napkins, sitting on the huge radio which stood diagonally across one corner. Everyone had to move with care to avoid dislodging the pieces of ornamental pottery and the small brass jugs which were fastened at intervals to the walls. The signora tried at first to fetch the dishes herself from the kitchen, but the servant, who had a sense of occasion and hoped that the good-looking doctor would start to shout again, insisted on managing everything herself, although she could only just push her way between the backs of the chairs and the wall. She wore a sleeveless black dress, the heavy fleece of her armpits was visible every time she lifted the casserole above the bowed heads of the family. The girls, too timid to make themselves heard directly, were interpreted at table by their brother Luca. 'Papa, Vittoria and Bice say they can feel something strange running through them from the inside of the radio, it might be a short circuit.'

'A little wine, doctor,' pleaded the Signora, kind and motherly, 'we know how hard you work in the hospital.'

'Papa, it's a scientific fact that if the girls were to spill their water on the radio the current would double in strength.' Gentilini made no intervention, except to ask his wife whether there had been any telephone calls.

'Tomato sauce is also an efficient conductor of electricity!' shouted Luca. Without warning Salvatore got up from his place, colliding sharply with the wall behind him, and throwing down his napkin, was gone. The children spread out immediately to fill the vacant space.

'Everyone in the street must have seen him leave before the main course!' exclaimed the Signora.

'He's not himself,' her husband told her.

Salvatore told Gentilini that he was afraid he must have taken leave of his senses. 'Not at all,' Gentilini replied. 'I could see that it suddenly struck you, "this won't do, this is marriage, I can't bring her to a state of life like this, I can't offer her marriage if it's going to be like this." You apparently forgot that when you start out you will be better placed in your career than I am and you won't have six children. It was an emotional reaction, you were not behaving rationally, as I imagine you intended to do.' Asked if the Signora could possibly be induced to forgive, Gentilini replied that she had always felt a great interest in his friend Dr Rossi, simply from description, and believed that he was destined to great things. This did not cause either of them the least jealousy, they were too fond of him for that. 'Of course,' added Gentilini, 'I have to admit that she is often wrong about these matters.'

Subsequently he brought a message from his wife, asking whether it would not be possible for Dr Rossi to come to them on some other day, preferably a Wednesday, when the children came home earlier and could be got rid of sooner, or perhaps he would like to accompany them one Sunday when they went up to Monte Morello or out to the country. The truth was that she had been impressed by his abrupt behaviour, which was exactly what she would have expected from a man of genius.

19

It was impossible for Salvatore to see Chiara again, no matter how many concerts he went to, or to avoid seeing her, no matter how many he failed to go to, because she had left Florence. She had to go back to England for the summer for her last term at Holy Innocents, at Champerdown in Berkshire. She had never been particularly happy there, or at any school except her primary, to which she had walked down and up the hill in her black smock in charge of Annunziata, until the villa's roof had been blown in and the water cut off. At the convent she was undistinguished, having little aptitude to offer beyond music and roller skating, which she had practised for hours round the ruined corridors of the Ricordanza. At Holy Innocents, roller-skating was forbidden.

In Florence, Gentilini feared that his friend might be developing a disordered personality. There was not much more sympathy for Chiara in Berkshire.

'You're just playing into the hands of the nuns. They want us all to get married early. It's a compensation fantasy. Never mind.'

Barney was Chiara's greatest friend at the convent. Chiara loved her because of her capacity to dispel opposition, like a tractor going stolidly through the heavy ploughland of Champerdown. Decisiveness has a nobility of its own. For her part, Barney felt a generous sympathy towards the delicate-looking Chiara, who was unlucky enough to be a foreigner.

'First things first. Now, have you written to this man?'

'I don't know his address.'

'But you could find out.'

'I could find out.'

'But you don't know what to write to him.'

'I don't know how to begin.'

'Well, at all events he was at this concert and you met him and you know his name and you know he's a doctor.'

'Yes, who's done Mimi Limentani a great deal of good.'

'Who's Mimi Limentani?'

'I don't know, I don't remember her ever not being in Florence.'

Barney looked at her forcefully.

'Tell me, what would your father and your aunt think of this man, and all their friends and so on, would they approve of him?'

'Oh, but it's not like that in Italy.'

'It's like that everywhere,' said Barney.

Chiara was silent.

'However, you met this doctor, and you were mowed down. I can see the effect it's had on you, but we must assume it won't last. And if it does, he won't like it when he hears you've done all that domestic science. He'll think you're after him.'

Chiara felt it was better to let this pass also.

'Or perhaps he's after you,' Barney continued. 'He may be an adventurer. Only you haven't any money, have you? How do they manage to pay for you here, by the way?'

'I don't know. I wish they didn't. I should have preferred the liceo. Perhaps they're selling bits of the furniture.'

'Well, you wouldn't have had my advice if you'd stayed in a foreign school,' said Barney. 'On the other hand, I suppose you mightn't have needed it, and now you do. Let me summarise it all for you. You're coming up North with us in August, aren't you? Then, when you get back to Florence, if you haven't heard from him and nothing's happened, you may have to reconsider.'

'Oh, but it will be all right, it can't be anything else, I know it, once I get home again.'

'But you're coming to us first. If it had been my grandmother's house in London I wouldn't have asked you, because it's a sink, but you get fresh air in Scotland, and you need plenty of fresh air. Besides, if you don't want to come, my parents will be insulted.'

'I do want to come, I do want the fresh air, but it's such a long time to wait.'

Barney looked at her more attentively.

'Chiara, you're getting weedy.'

At this damning word, of which she didn't know the Italian equivalent, Chiara hung her head. She accepted it absolutely. To be weedy, as she understood it, is to be alien, not to grow in the right place, but at the same time to lack stoutness and self-reliance. She knew her tendency to fragment, often against her will, into other existences. The convent was intended to provide for life a fixed basis of judgment, but it had not done this for Chiara, who could not escape from the unsettling vision of other points of view, the point of view of every living creature, all defensible. At Parenti's she had felt for the old couturier's pride (her back had stiffened in sympathy with his), but also for her aunt's disappointment, and as they walked back through the workrooms she had known that the pressers and hand-seamers had a perfect right to laugh as soon as the door shut behind her. Why shouldn't they? Why not? But the too readily-obliging 'why not?' must be a serious failing, even a disaster, unless one could remain unperturbed and stable among countless sympathies clamouring for attention, not turn and turn about, but, as it seemed, at the same time. When Salvatore had spoken to her all these distractions had settled, for the first time she could remember since early childhood, into tranquillity. The relief was indescribable. No more wear and tear of the heart.

'It's weediness,' Barney said.

20

At the S. Agostino the restless currents of energy in Dr Rossi broke out in sometimes inconvenient directions. Florence, in summer, is supposed to be empty, but in the years of the

Italian economic miracle it was as full as every other city of country people crowding in for high wages. At the same time these people had decided, by a common impulse, to discard the habits of centuries. One of these habits was the dread of hospitals. Contadini now occupied all the benches, more benches were requested on loan from other hospitals but refused because all were in use, and the new patients, well accustomed to waiting, became connoisseurs, in a few weeks, of hospital treatment. 'Treatment is only a small part of the story,' Salvatore urged the deputy administrator, who had closely studied the art of leaving well alone, 'here you've got people who've never before eaten bread with salt in it, the effect on them of permanent city life is unpredictable, we shall need both primary and secondary preventive methods.' The administrator, who had managed to resist the introduction even of microscopes for years on the grounds of economy, was dismissive. 'And yet the new clinic,' shouted Salvatore, 'dispenses antibiotics by the litre, just as the Grand Dukes once caused the fountains to run with wine.' But these, of course, were paid for by the Americans.

Without abandoning this matter for a moment, Salvatore threw himself furiously into the scandal of flood prevention. Throughout recorded time the Arno had flooded every thirty years or so, why, now that there was money to spend, was there no decent warning system so that the information from the hydrometers could be centralised and the information passed on to the emergency services in concise form. This time his indignation carried him as far as the Civil Engineering Department of the Prefettura, where he was told that such a scheme would cost forty million lire. 'The price of a footballer, and second group at that,' Salvatore said.

He glared at the umber-coloured river, sunk to its lowest point. 'Note that it's not much more than a gutter, this Arno of yours, a gutter between the hills.' Gentilini, to whom this was addressed, replied that it wasn't his Arno, and that in the Po valley they found it much cheaper and more practical to put up with the floods and give up prevention altogether. He himself would never have been able to start out on a medical

60

career if it hadn't been for the flood compensation his family received in 1924. Much more alarming, in Gentilini's view (if such things can be classified, and he was watching his friend carefully), was the affair of L'Inconsolabile.

This was a gravestone which had been executed from the sculptor's designs by a respectable monumental mason in the suburb of Rifredi. The sculptor, an elderly man named Josz, claimed to have carried out his instructions from the client exactly. But the finished work had been rejected by the directors of the Cimeterio Rifredi, who had declared it non-admissible.

The grave was that of a respectable small dealer in sports goods. It was the widow who was inconsolable, and she had ordered as a memorial a marble statue of herself, L'Inconsolabile, lying full length on the grave, beating in protest on the grating with her fists, dishevelled and in tears. The creased skirt was shown from behind in folds of greenish marble, also the slight gap, at one point, between the skirt and the top of the stocking. The widow had found the public, in general, against her. The neighbours thought it a vulgar display of new money, no art critic and not even a single artist could be found to defend it, and the Cardinal Archbishop's office ruled that on no account could it be allowed admittance to the Campo Santo. The Church's spokesman on the radio and on page 3 of the national newspapers was Monsignor Giuseppe Gondi who, indispensable as ever, was now adviser to the Sacred Congregation for Popular Religious Art. He was able to speak, too, as a Florentine. 'The duty of monumental sculpture is to illustrate a spirit, not of rebellion, but of peace, resignation and acceptance.' The widow declared, this time in an interview on Radiouno, that on the night of her husband's death she had been seized with a frightful bilious spasm and had said to him: 'If you go out of this world and leave me alone I shall knock and hammer on your grave.' – 'And so, signora,' the interviewer suggested, 'you are expressing the desire to beat, so to speak, the earth as if the departed could still hear.' – 'Not at all, I'm beating precisely because he can't.'

Salvatore's indignation was not in the cause of art. He had never given it much thought, but now that he did he saw that if art is of any use at all it must be to get rid of surplus emotion. In that way it functioned much like a dream. He had known hospital patients so heavily medicated that they were unable to dream, and compensated with hideous delusions by day. The Church, in this particular case, had suppressed the transference of human grief in the way best adapted to human beings. 'You know of course that this Monsignore is Chiara Ridolfi's uncle by marriage?' said Gentilini. Salvatore ignored him, and joined battle with an article in the *Nazione*: 'In the city of Michelangelo, Art is Forbidden.' This had good results, at least for the old sculptor, Adelaido Josz. By chance the casual attention of Federico Fellini was drawn to the just-decipherable photograph of the statue printed at the top of the article. He ordered a replica, which soon joined the heaps of magic-realist junk in Rome's Cinecittà. The original remained in a kind of half-way house, a shed at the cemetery gates full of marble limbs and crosses, some awaiting admission, some ejected. But Fellini's purchase meant that old Josz, who was not much good at pressing his claims, was paid something at last. With senile persistence he tracked down the author of his good fortune, and waited outside the hospital until he saw a man, identified for him as Dr Rossi, leaving by a private door in via del Castelaccio. Then he came forward, and introducing himself in quiet tones, told the doctor that he had put aside a small block of top-grade marble—impossible to get anything like it nowadays – as a gift, to serve when the time came for Rossi himself to die.

'As soon as I feel really ill and know that I'm done for, I'll send you word, doctor. Then you must come at once. I live up in Firenze Nova, near the Jewish cemetery. You must come before the women in my house get hold of everything, and you must take away the block which I have reserved for you.'

Salvatore managed to pronounce the correct words of thanks, but he was nearly stifled with irritation.

On all these subjects of concern, as the summer's heat mounted, he was rational, but threatened to become less so. That was because it was obvious that even chance acquaintances were in a conspiracy to drive him crazy. Take, for example, Andrea Nieve, the lawyer, a man he scarcely knew

– this Nieve had, without warning, congratulated him on his interest in the flood warning system and had asked him whether he did not feel like devoting some of his abundant energy to politics. He seemed taken aback by the violence with which Salvatore replied that the subject nauseated him. They had met entirely by chance and stood there in the Piazza della Repubblica, raising their voices to be heard against the traffic.

'Then, doctor, you agree with the philosophy of Gentile, you believe in the ethical state? You consider that politics is nothing more than a mania?'

'Much better if it were,' shouted Salvatore. 'If it was a mania, there would be an appropriate treatment.'

Nieve had another go. 'A supposition. If the Italian Communist Party had been able to keep going in the spirit of Antonio Gramsci, if Togliatti had taken more of Gramsci's advice than he did, I imagine that the Party might have appealed to you.'

'What you're saying doesn't interest me in the least. Either you think I'm someone else, or more probably you haven't been listening to me.'

'But tell me, what other solution is there? Politics may be deplorable, but short of violence, we have no other remedy.'

'Not a remedy, a drug,' said Salvatore, three inches away from his ear. 'By "physical dependence" we describe a condition where the body feels unable to tolerate existence without the drug. In my opinion, Nieve, you must be at that point. Worse still, you're a pusher in the middle of a public street, you're trying to involve me in your monstrous addiction.'

Nieve told him that he was putting things too strongly. He also reminded him that if the background noise level is high, it's more practical to lower the voice than to raise it.

Evidently Nieve saw him as a lapsed Communist, possibly one who had resigned after the XXth Congress, but in any case engaged in a warm-hearted dialogue with the have-nots. In the same way, presumably, his colleagues were beginning to see him as a sentimental hothead, a relief to them, no doubt, they could dismiss him so much more easily. Everything that he had done since he had met Chiara had run counter to his own resolutions for the conduct of his life, which, in turn, had been specially designed to run counter to what was expected of him. The least important incidents troubled him most. What did he care about the widow and her defunct husband and her bizarre bit of statuary designed to immortalise her, at least from behind? Why should he give a fuck for old Josz, or squander his time in writing to the *Nazione*? Why, going back a little, should he bother about his poor behaviour at the Gentilini home, when he had never in the least wanted to go there in the first place? These, however, were answers rather than questions, or at any rate not questions of the order of, When are the Ridolfi likely to come back to Florence?

Their goings and comings made no contribution to society as a whole and were therefore of no significance. They might be on the coast, they might be abroad. People of that sort were herded about, like cattle, according to the season by forces outside their control. He himself had volunteered to take on extra duties all through the summer and had no intention of going away at all.

21

On the 24th of June, the feast of St John, Gentilini, in an advanced state of exhaustion, was driving his battered Fiat, containing the entire family, back from Impruneta to the Fortezza del Belvedere, where they would get the best view of the fireworks in Piazzale Michelangelo. A point came, as it usually did, when all the children pleaded to get out and relieve themselves at the same moment, and he drew up where there was a bit of fallen stone wall to give them shadow. 'No delay!' called the Signora, as the boys began to compete with each other to see what patterns they could make by peeing into the dust. On the other side of the road, on higher ground, there was a house, set well back, and Gentilini recognised it as the Ridolfi place, the Ricordanza. He got out of the car, restraining his wife from following him, and looked through the locked iron gates. Above them he could read at least part of the inscription

Maggior dolore è ben la Ricordanza –
senti' dir lor con sì alti sospiri –
o nell' amaro inferno amena stanza?

The villa was one of those with a double staircase, probably added in the eighteenth century, mounting to the first floor where the main entrance now was. The ground floor was used for storage and was lit only by two round windows. This raising up of the front door made the whole house look unwelcoming and inaccessible. The lemon trees in their terracotta jars, each balanced on an empty one turned upside down, dispensed their bitter green smell: their dark green leaves were startlingly fresh against the blank, bleached, cracked and faded house. Luca, from across the road, was already pointing at the statues of the dwarfs and saying that at night they got down off the walls and came down into the city to hide in little girls' bedrooms and stick their stone fingers up their bottoms. From the passenger seat the Signora tried to control him with threats. At the far corner of the surrounding wall there was a movement. A man, not a gardener, coming slowly towards the main gates as though he had been making a circuit of the whole building. Gentilini abruptly called the children back to the car. He would rather they didn't see their father's respected friend, Dr Rossi, hanging about in this senseless fashion.

22

By September Salvatore was able to tell himself that he was over and done with his obsession, quite free from it. Impossible to overestimate the therapeutic value of daily work, although an obsession is also hard work of a kind.

The wash of tourists and visitors was beginning to recede, leaving behind it the rich fertilising silt of currency. The shops and small businesses which had faintheartedly shut in the August heat now reopened, those which had stayed open closed and the owners left for the country. Dense piles of hazel-nuts, with their leaves, appeared in the Central Market, and large mushrooms covering the counter with their wrinkled yellow dewlaps, just as earlier that morning they had covered the tree-trunks. Festoons of satchels and fountain pens hung in UPIM's windows. At the last possible moment, the names of the books to be studied in the coming academic year were given out, and the parents went humbly to queue in the scholastic bookshops. These could be considered as beginnings of a kind. Indeed, the Amici della Musica had even announced the programme for the forthcoming autumn concerts. But autumn is, all the same, the appropriate season for storing what is harvested and putting away and forgetting what will never be of use.

Salvatore's clinic – he preferred to call it an office, because it was really no more than that – was not so bad, after all, being on the third floor of the building and overlooking a plane tree growing in what was hardly a piazza, more like a widening in the Vicolo dei Semplici. On warm evenings, and they were still warm, he opened the windows and admitted the breeze which ruffled the plane's topmost boughs while the rest of its fading greenery was trapped motionless in the street below.

Between 17.00 and 18.00 he saw private patients who could afford the going rate. After 18.00 came those whose fees were paid through industrial insurance, the Previdenza, the Ministry of Health, and so on. The 18.00 to 19.00s were mostly from workshops and factories, obliged to make appointments after their working hours.

In the consulting-room all the patients had a good deal in common. All of them had a certain pride in their suffering, and were inclined to resent whatever authority had diagnosed it as 'of nervous origin' and sent them on to Dr Rossi. The word 'nervous' seemed to belittle them, and yet if they could be convinced that it was correct they showed a perceptible relief since nerves, like shadows, aren't real. All of them, no matter where they came from or why they came, were quite certain, at least before diagnosis and sometimes after it, that they knew better than any so-called professional how to cure themselves. Salvatore couldn't recall this phenomenon, or not anyway to such an extent, during either his childhood or his years of training. Nerves (the 17.00 to 18.00s knew) needed nothing more than total rest and relaxation and unfailing sympathy. Some of them had been reliably informed that part of the nerve, or one that joined up to it, could be surgically removed without pain and the operation would work wonders. The craftsmen and small shopkeepers, if they were elderly, told him that there would be no harm, now that the season was over, in their being sent to take the waters in some spa or other. If they were young, they wanted antibiotics. The country people also demanded antibiotics, but with a good dose of aconite to mix them with, no rubbish. Sometimes they asked to be blistered.

Only after he had listened to the self-healers, with a careful eye on the time, did Salvatore assert the serene will-power, of which he was incapable in his personal affairs, but which he knew was his greatest professional gift. But as soon as he began to do this and its effect was noticeable he was conscious of being the bland prototype of the 'beloved doctor', the trusted giver of advice and doer of good, so that he had to struggle, as though with a demon, with the impulse to self-contradiction. Fortunately the patients very often played into his hands with the strangely comforting words, 'doctors don't know everything'. But they would not have said this, at the very moment when Dr Rossi was making his examination, if they had believed it was true.

At just past seven o'clock on the 20th of September a patient was exhibiting, for the second time, his large coarse-skinned middle-aged durable hand. The ball of his left thumb was a little wasted away, as though it had shrunk a size or two. Salvatore asked him if he felt any pain.

'No, it doesn't hurt, and I can tell you what it's due to, it's because I've changed my work, I don't use my hands in the same way that I used to.'

'You came from the country?'

'Yes, from Mercatale.'

'Where do you work now?'

'At Mobili Spic.'

'What's your job?'

'I am in the warehouse. We pack the bits of the furniture into cardboard boxes, then with each box there's an instruction card that tells you how to put it all together again. You have to be sure to put in the right card.'

'Do you use your right hand more than your left?'

'Of course.'

The receptionist looked in from her cupboard-like outer room to ask if she could go home. Salvatore nodded. He told the patient that without fail he must come back in a month's time.

'But it's nothing much?'

Salvatore was silent for a moment, writing out the appointment card.

'I can't say yet whether it's nothing much.'

'They gave me some liniment to rub in.'

'Who did?'

'The doctor at Spic. I don't know why he sent me here.'

Salvatore looked again at the case notes. 'Yes, well.'

'Why has it got to be a month before you can tell me anything?'

'You probably think that I'm a slow worker. I expect I am. But I have to see how things go. You have my word that I will tell you as soon as I can.'

The doctor's honesty made its effect. The atmosphere in the consulting room was as tranquil as it might be in a field, under the open sky.

'Well, doctor, my thumb may get that much weaker, but at a pinch I can manage without using it . . . after all, if it's the nerves, it can't be anything much.'

'I can't say as yet whether it isn't anything much,' Salvatore repeated. 'But I can tell you that it won't help to worry about it.'

'And I'm to tell my wife to rub in the liniment?'

'Yes, let her do that.'

Salvatore showed the patient out himself, and watched him walk with a heavy, even tread up the Vicolo dei Semplice. It was dusk, raining a little, a string of lights shone hazily from the branches of the plane tree. During the day someone had pasted a fly-poster to its trunk, advertising a racing pool. *Occhi alla pista, millione in vista*. The poster gleamed red and white against the patched shadows of the gently moving tree.

He went back upstairs, made up the day's notes and then shook himself like an animal freed from its cage, putting out of his mind the probable future of the patient from Mobili Spic. While he was looking round the receptionist's room to see that the files weren't left out as a hint that she had been kept till the last minute, the bell rang once again. A boy of fifteen in the street below had got off his bicycle and pounded up the stairs in one continuous movement, probably to conform with his own idea of himself as an athlete.

'Signor dottore!'

'I'm just leaving.'

'The account for your last quarter's electricity.'

He produced a bill written in violet ink, with its duplicate, for 20,721 lira. Salvatore felt obliged to say something, if only to calm him down.

'You're not from Florence, are you? Where does your family come from?'

'Borgoforte, dottore.'

'I have a friend who comes from there, a colleague, Dr Gentilini. Do you know that name?'

The boy looked as though he was about to burst into tears. 'Dottore, there are so many names.' It was important for him to please, his livelihood depended on his commission for collecting payment on the spot. Salvatore went back into his own office and took a handful of notes out of the petty cash. At the sight of ready money the boy, trembling with excitement, took out a pen and struck the last three figures off the bill. 'Your concession, dottore.' Perhaps, Salvatore thought, I'm witnessing the first stage of a promising business career.

It was the end of his day, although he sometimes went back to the hospital to check that everything had been done according to instructions. As he stood outside his office door, trying to decide whether to go to the hospital or not, dangling his keys, ready to lock up and be done with it, Chiara came up the stairs. She was pale and shining, untidy in a frightful tweed coat, eager, unexpected, totally inappropriate to his state of mind, to the time of the evening, to everything imaginable.

'The clinic is shut,' he said coldly.

'I know it is. It's written up outside – 17.00 to 19.00. I've been waiting until it was seven.'

'You've been hanging about outside, then.'

'No, I went to Benediction in that church across the way and afterwards I sat there until it was seven by my watch.'

'But in that case you're late,' Salvatore said furiously. 'It's ten minutes past. You could have come ten minutes earlier. You have wasted ten minutes.'

'That was what I was thinking,' said Chiara, but he was not appeased.

'Why did you come here anyway? These are my consulting rooms. You have no right here, you're not one of my patients.'

'But this is the only address you've got in the book.'

'Of course it is. I live in a furnished room and eat in a câfé or at the hospital. How many addresses do you expect me to have? Listen, I am Dr Rossi, a neurologist, quite successful, thought to be getting on quite well, but of course it's not at all difficult to destroy my self-possession and upset my balance and disconcert me by turning up suddenly without warning. If that was what you intended, I congratulate you.'

Chiara refused to lose confidence. 'You remember me, don't you?'

'Yes, we met for a few moments at the Teatro della Pergola. It was raining then, and now it looks a fine evening. How the seasons pass. You could have paid this visit at any time during the past five months.'

They were still confronting each other on the stairway. The floor below was silent, but in the basement a hand printing-press was cranking away as it did every evening after working hours.

'Oh, but I couldn't,' Chiara said. 'I've been in England, then I had to go to Scotland, I've only just got back, and so I thought I ought to come and see you at once.'

'Whatever for? Whatever made you think that you ought to come and see me at once?'

Whatever happened he was going to hold out against asking her back into the building. He wouldn't open up for her and allow her to invade his particular space, quietly ordered and settled down for the next day's work.

'Did you tell your family that you were coming to see me here?'

'I can do what I like. I've left school now.'

They went down to the street, Chiara rather cautiously because she had put on a pair of new shoes which did not go very well with her coat. Once in the street she was graceful. At the plane-tree, as though it had been prearranged, she stopped, and so did he, an arm's length away. Here, in the open air, he might have come to his senses, but didn't.

'What do you mean by coming here like this?' he repeated, in pain and fury.

Now at last she believed it, and made off, quick as a shadow, down the Vicolo dei Semplice. 'It's only the second time we've met,' he said out loud, and then shouted: 'Come back! I'm saying what I don't mean!' Nobody bothered to look at him. It wasn't unusual, in that quarter, for someone to shout in the street. He felt like beating his head against a lamp post. Then he had to go back. He had forgotten, after all that, to lock up.

23

At via Limbo the telephone, enshrined in a kind of marble grotto in the vestibule, could be overheard by almost everybody in the apartment. Privacy had not been thought of when it was installed, admiration, rather, for a modern improvement. Chiara had something to hide from her father, the fact that she was unhappy.

She took her aunt's Topolino, which had been left in the courtyard, and drove up to the Ricordanza. The sensation of being high up, above the city, in the dark night air, was exhilarating. She went round to the side gate and saw that the lights were on in the gardener's house while the radio murmured a long list of winning lottery numbers. She rang the outer bell, which was inside the open stone mouth of the statue of a garden god. One year a bird had nested in it and she remembered being lifted up to feel the waiting warm young birds.

The gardener's wife had been her friend ever since she could tell one human face from another.

'Giannina, let me in.'

Giannina was moving on the other side of the wall.

'Contessina.'

'Giannina, let me into the house, I want to telephone.'

'The electricity's off in the house.'

'I know. Give me some matches. I want to telephone where no-one can hear me.'

Giannina opened up. 'Well, you're seventeen.'

Chiara kissed her. 'Nearly eighteen.'

'Where are your own keys?'

'I forgot them, I'll remember them next time.'

They went together up the rising path to the back of the house. The slope of the ground was so acute that although the front door stood at the top of a gracious double flight of steps, at the back you went straight into the old kitchens. Inside the air, and the smell of the air, was not so much stagnant as disused and resentful of disturbance.

Chiara went straight into the salone, not caring whether Giannina was following her or not, and put a call through to London.

'Where are you speaking from?' asked Barney, as clear and as like herself as if she had been in the next room.

'Oh, from home, from Florence.'

72

'You'd better make the call as short as possible, as your father's practically penniless.'

'Barney, please come.'

'What's wrong? Is it this man? Doesn't he want to see you?'

'He doesn't know that he does.'

Barney paused, saying, 'Don't rush me, I'm just turning it over in my mind.'

Chiara waited in the half-dark. The immense shutters, half folded back, laid a ladder-like pattern of cloudy moonlight across the floor.

'Barney, please come. I don't know what to do.'

'Listen, it's this way. I've absolutely got to go to Painstake, that's a house, it's the name of a house in Norfolk, it's near Flitcham, no really it's nearer to Castle Rising, that won't mean very much to you, because there's somebody I've met who's been asked there for the shooting. You know the shooting's quite different here from the way you do it in Italy.'

'I suppose it's much the same from the bird's point of view.'

'Is anyone listening to you?'

'I don't know, it doesn't matter.'

'Well, get this into your head, this man I'm talking about who's been asked to Painstake, I've decided he's the one, he's definitely my He. Now, over here you can go out with the guns all day and keep walking with the one you've decided on, even if you're half drowned in mud, and by the end of the day he has to notice you, he just has to get the message.'

'But Barney, everybody notices you, they can't help it.'

'All I want to know is whether you've understood me so far.'

'I have understood you.'

'Then you can see that I've got to go to Norfolk.'

'Please come, Barney. Think.'

'I have been thinking. I've been thinking while we've been talking, so as not to let the charges mount up. Until you get a bit less helpless I've got a duty towards you. I'll let you know my flight and you can collect me from Pisa on Monday. Then I'll be able to get back to England the week after to deal with this He.'

24

Giancarlo was a little disconcerted. Probably (forgetting how often he was away himself), he imagined that now Chiara was home at last she would not feel the need of an English visitor quite so soon.

'You're taking the Fiat to Pisa? You want to get there by nine in the evening? It seems a very ill-thought-out scheme. Where will you dine?'

'I suppose Barney will have something on the plane. You know I don't mind whether I have anything or not.'

'Shall I like this friend of yours?'

'I hope you will, I'm sure you will.'

'Does she speak clearly?'

'She has a strong character.'

'Oh, if that's all! It's to be regretted, however, that your aunt isn't here.'

'Barney knows Aunt Mad, she came and took us out from the convent on one of the feast days. And she knows some people called Harrington who did over one of the farm houses near Valsassina. She says the Harringtons would never forgive her if she set foot in Italy without going to see them.'

'In that case it's strange, perhaps, that she isn't staying with them on this occasion.'

'She's always so busy. She's only coming to us now because I particularly wanted someone strong-minded.'

'Well, you can take her out to visit them, and of course if you're going in that direction you must both go and see Cesare. You know that I didn't mean and couldn't mean that Miss Barnes wouldn't be extremely welcome. When I said that it was a pity that your aunt wasn't here, I only meant that unfortunately I shall have to spend a few days in Rome, next week, so that you will be entirely in the hands of Annunziata. Absurd that I've only just remembered it.'

He had always treated memory as a matter of convenience. So, too, it seemed, was old age. Chiara, out of love and exasperation, had tried as a child, and sometimes even now, to discount the evidence, telling him, for example, that his sight was as good as ever. 'You forget what you want to and you see what you want to.' Giancarlo took a different viewpoint. The great advantage, he claimed, which made him inclined to welcome decay, was that the substitutes were such an improvement on the originals. Glasses were stronger than eyes, and replaceable. 'Frescobaldi told me that he experienced the greatest happiness of his life when he got his first false teeth. They eat so rapidly nowadays at the Frescobaldi that one is often home by ten o'clock.'

Giancarlo could see that his daughter was in a perilously nervous state, but he was too humble, where she was concerned, to imagine that he could be of any use. That was why he emphasised the symptoms of his own decay.

25

Barney came into the apartment in via Limbo like a train drawing up at a platform, but ready, after refuelling, to take off again immediately. Her flight had been delayed and it was nearly midnight. She wanted a bath, and the sonorous iron pipes of the piano nobile groaned and reverberated in the hard duty of hauling the hot water from the trembling boiler.

'She's used to having one, she thinks showers are weedy.'

'Of course, my dear. I only want you to reassure me that Miss Barnes' visit will make you happier.'

Chiara went into the bathroom. In the sarcophagus-like expanse of marble, facing the great brass taps inscribed Installazione Niagara, Barney lay unperturbed. Her ample body had turned rose pink.

'I say, Cha, I hope you're not short of water. You run out of it here sometimes, don't you?'

'It's sometimes cut off in the afternoon in summer.'

'Why don't you have smaller baths, then?'

'I don't know.'

'For that matter, why doesn't Florence have a proper air-port?'

'I don't know, Barney. I don't care.'

'You ought to take an interest in these things.'

'Listen. Last Tuesday I went round to his consulting-room.'

'Did he ask you to?'

'How could he? I've only just come back. As soon as I could I went there. I waited till it was seven, when he stops work, then I went up the stairs to the office and he drove me away as if I was a criminal.'

'What did you do then?'

'I went home, I came back here. What else was there for me to do?'

'Did he call anything after you?'

'I didn't hear anything.'

Barney hauled out the strange old bath-plug, which was shaped like a narrow iron bottle ready for the last messages of the drowning. Then with a great broadbreasted heave she stood up. The waters surged together and she stepped out.

'He must have been deeply disturbed,' she said. 'You've disturbed him deeply, dear girl.'

'But what am I to do, Barney? Here I am, I'm eighteen, nearly eighteen, and every minute of my life is being wasted, there's not a single second ticking away now that isn't being wasted. It's all wasted unless we can be together and unless he's happy.'

'The Happiness of Dr Rossi,' interrupted Barney. 'Film neorealistico, con Marcello Mastroianni e Maria Schell.'

'Why did I ask you here? I hate you.'

Both girls had to shout above the heartbreaking sobs and bass growls of the ebbing bathwater.

76

'In ten years he'll be an Older Man. Of course, that suits some people. But you don't know him. He may have leches on everyone he meets.'

'That doesn't worry me,' Chiara said. 'All I want to know is this: is it possible for anyone to want something and then refuse to take it, not for a good reason, but for no reason at all?'

Barney was putting on a striped man's nightshirt which came halfway down her glowing, faintly hairy calves. On the face of it she looked an unlikely adviser in matters of the heart.

'I shall have to meet him, of course, first of all so as to sum the situation up.'

'But that's exactly what you can't do, I can't ask him here, not after he turned me out like that, and I can't ask him to meet me anywhere else.'

'Well, your aunt, the one who isn't here now but presumably will be some time or other, or your father, for that matter — what about them, don't they know this Rossi man?'

'I don't think so.'

Barney turned in all her striped majesty on her much slighter friend.

'Chiara, you'll have to be completely frank with me. This man won't do.'

'What do you mean?'

'He's common, isn't he?' said Barney.

Like a trace of flame, Chiara sprang to life. 'I told you that in Italy nobody thinks like that.'

'Well, I'm in Italy now, and after I've seen him I shall give you my considered opinion.'

'I don't need your opinion, Barney! I'm not buying him from a shop!'

'The signorine are disputing with each other,' said Annunziata, marching into the salotto. 'Their voices are raised.'

'What's the time?' asked the Count.

'Nearly one o'clock.'

'She is my daughter's guest.'

'Let's pray they don't do each other an injury.'

*

77

The next morning Barney, trained for field sports, got up early and went immediately to the kitchen. There Annunziata, as she had done for the whole of her working life, was heating up the remains of yesterday's tea in a saucepan. Barney pointed out to her, in the convent's serviceable Italian, that she must never on any account do such a thing again. Annunziata asked whether the signorina intended to take the work of the kitchen upon herself. 'Watch me carefully,' said Barney, pouring the reddish-green liquid into the sink. 'That might have poisoned us all. Probably though they wouldn't have arrested you, because you didn't know any better.' 'I say, your house-keeper person ought to be grateful to me,' she told Chiara, who had spent a white night, half way over the threshold of sleep.

'Honestly, I think you've been rather thoughtless, Barney. Annunziata can't change now, she's like the nuns, and then she's done so much for us, she hid things for us during the war up at the Ricordanza, and let people take the pictures, mostly the Piero da Cortonas, which no-one ever looked at anyway.'

'What people?'

'Well, everybody who came took something.'

'She did that for the personal advantage of your family, which shouldn't have been considered in wartime. Did she shelter British prisoners of war when they were on the run?'

'I think she sheltered anyone who needed it.'

'Good show,' said Barney. 'Lucky, though, she didn't poison them with the tea. That would have gone against her.'

Difficult though it was to worst her in a direct encounter, Barney, at going on nineteen years of age, could be taken in quite easily. She was taken in by the Count, who chose for those particular few days one of his easiest impersonations of himself. He became a bewildered survivor of a world grown hard to understand, with little Edwardian mannerisms learned from an English nanny and governess, when in point of fact he had had neither. Chiara, who did not quite understand that the old, as well as the young, have to defend themselves, regretted the apparent necessity of all this. She still assumed, as a child does, that those whom she loved must love each other.

The Count took the first opportunity to ask Barney whether her parents, Colonel and Mrs Gore-Barnes (about whom he was mildly curious), would like their daughter to visit the galleries, and perhaps some private collections. Barney was up to this, because she had been made to spend four, no, five terms at Holy Innocents studying art history. They had had Miss Peach, a lay teacher, for Italian and art studies, and Miss Peach had given them a list of all the artists worth remembering, with the good things to look out for in one column, and then another column for their faults, so that a balance could easily be struck.

'What were the faults of Leonardo?' the Count asked.

'Occasionally morbid and unwholesome subject-matter,' said Barney.

'Shadows too dark.'

'Botticelli, insufficiently plastic,' said Chiara.

'Michelangelo, insufficiently interested in colour.'

'Raphael, no faults.'

'The Peach was always on at Chiara to address the class, because she was Italian, and the Peach wasn't sure of her pronunciation, and thought Chiara might catch her out somewhere. It was a bit like being in a lion's cage, if one of the lions looks tricky you must never turn your back on it.'

'I know so little of lion-taming,' said the Count.

'Oh, horses are much the same, if you've had anything to do with them.'

'The horse, if I may say so, has the habit of obedience.'

'My father was in the Italian cavalry,' said Chiara.

'Then you're redundant, Count, rotten for you.'

Chiara looked restlessly out of the windows at the pure white autumn sky.

'Miss Peach might have trusted me,' she said.

They returned to the question of the study of the history of art. In truth the Ridolfi had nothing much to say about it, having absorbed it without the necessity of learning anything, rather as Barney had absorbed her ideas of weediness or of tea-making. Paintings, in one house or another, in one church or the next, had been favourites or unfavourites with Chiara all her life (just as domestic animals had been with Barney), known as only children can know their familiars, seen year by year, as she grew taller, from a different level of vision. But the Count, hoping to have struck lucky with his subject, went on: 'It has always seemed to me that one of the mistakes made in these courses of study lies in giving so much attention to the great men. There are many delightful things by quite unknown artists, little country things. I hope, Miss Barnes, that while you're here my daughter will take you over to her cousin's farm. There's a wedding-chest there painted with a design of Love Tamed by Time – it's only a pity that the companion piece, Time Tamed by Love, seems to be missing – and then there are the so-called dwarfs at the Ricordanza. I don't mean that these things are great treasures, quite the contrary, that is just my point, they are small things, local things, which would be given no doubt a considerable list of faults.'

'I'd like to see the farm,' said Barney. 'How many acres?'

26

Maddalena was in Vienna, visiting some relatives even older than herself. She received a letter from a friend in Florence. 'This English friend of our little Chiara – people who have seen her have telephoned and told me that she is a giantess, one metre eighty at least from her heels to the crown of her head, on a level with men, plum-coloured, with great bright eyes and strong white teeth. You won't think me interfering if I say that she sounds more likely to lead than to follow.' Mad tore up the letter, reflecting that Giancarlo, after all, was at home.

Chiara, however, was at that very moment driving her father to the Central Station. The car breathed faintly of the eau-de-cologne which he sometimes used, and there was the unsettling smell of leather luggage.

'Quite a tedious visit, my dear, to the Monsignore and one or two others.'

'You shouldn't go to Rome if it's tedious.'

'It's been arranged for some time.'

'I don't believe it's been arranged for some time at all,' said Chiara. 'Let's go back.'

'Oh, but I shall leave you in the company of Miss Barnes.'

Chiara was seized with distress. 'Papa, you do like Barney, don't you?'

'I've forgotten, I'm afraid, for the moment just why you asked her here.'

'But she's my friend!'

'Of course. It's just that I'm not used to quite so much straightforwardness, it's a little confusing at first. Do, please, both of you enjoy yourselves.'

It was not late when Chiara got back from the station, but she found Barney slumped like a potato sack on one of the hard divans, totally in repose.

'I love him!' she shouted as she came in. 'What's wrong with my saying that, it's true.'

'It's embarrassing.'

'But surely something can be true and embarrassing at the same time.'

'No, it can't. If it's embarrassing it shouldn't be said at all, and if it's not said no-one's going to be able to tell whether it's true or not.'

'Well then, what are you going to say to this man at Painstake?'

Barney did not reply. She was considering her tactics and the disposition of her forces. Pressed again and again as to where Dr Rossi could be found for inspection, and with whom, outside his hospital and consulting-room, Chiara could still think of nobody except Mimi Limentani, who was away, since she invariably spent the summer and early autumn at various health resorts, where she sampled the waters. Barney, for her part, knew nobody else in or near Florence, except her father's friends, the Harringtons. This friendship seemed to be based on Colonel Barnes not having seen old Toby Harrington since God knew when, and on some link of gratitude or indebtedness in the past which wasn't and perhaps now couldn't be specified. It was also the Colonel's belief that anyone who retired and went abroad to live in sunnier climes was soon reduced to asking everyone they knew to come and stay, and sit on their terraces with them, so that they could say you wouldn't be able to sit outdoors in England like this, would you?, and that it was really a kindness to give them something by way of occupation. They couldn't get down to any serious gardening in those countries because it meant taking jobs away from the peasantry, who had no idea how to make a decent lawn. Barney therefore felt no awkwardness in taking her next step.

'I can't waste any more time, Cha, I'm going to ring up these Harringtons. I'm going to ask them if they know anyone called Rossi. Do you think there'll be a lot of Rossis in Florence?'

'It's the commonest name in Italy.'

'Screw it,' said Barney. 'I shall have to get at it another way.'

She took out her address book, a trusty leather-bound friend. It did duty, too, as an autograph book, and was full of the lavish scrawls of the convent girls, ending with Annette Zamoyska who by hook or by crook would be last in this book, to which Bice Zardanelli had added, No you bloody won't, I will. Loose photographs and a newspaper cutting about worming powders fell from the album, and a list of things to be seen in Florence, divided by Barney's grandmother into 'advisable' and 'essential'.

'But what are you going to say if you get on to them?'

Barney, dialling, raised her free hand in a superb gesture. 'That depends on how they behave themselves.'

Mrs Harrington answered herself with cries of delight and astonishment, rather more than the occasion called for, but it seemed that from the moment she had woken up that morning she had known that something nice was going to happen. How was Lavinia's mother?

'And your father?' interrupted Toby Harrington. Evidently he was joining in on the extension. Certainly it didn't look as though he could have much to do.

'But your mother's up and about again? I heard about it from so many people. I mean her poor legs.'

'They're better,' said Barney. 'She doesn't like talking about them.'

'Both of them touching the ground, eh?' Toby persisted loudly.

'I'm afraid I can't think of any kind of disability as a joking matter,' said Mrs Harrington.

'Oh, young Lavinia knows I don't mean that. God, no.'

'But the point is, my dear, where are you? Are you speaking from a hotel? We'd hoped that if you ever came to Tuscany you'd make our place a kind of centre –'

'I'm only here for a week. I'm staying with Chiara Ridolfi, who I was at the convent with.'

'Then you're at La Ricordanza?' This word was very carefully pronounced.

'No, I'm at this flat in Florence. They seem to have two places, even though they're so badly off. And then there's a farm, somewhere out your way. There's some relation farming there, I think.'

'Valsassina,' said Chiara quietly at her side.

'It begins with a V. Anyway he must be a neighbour of yours, do you know him?'

Mrs Harrington hesitated.

'Cesare Ridolfi?'

'I expect so.'

'We have met him, but he seems perhaps not very sociable.'

'Repressed, if you ask me,' Toby broke in. 'But never mind all that, Madge, ask the girl when she's coming to see us.'

'I'd like to come out to your place for lunch, if that's convenient,' said Barney.

'Of course, and bring young Chiara Ridolfi with you, and her father too if you like.'

Barney took a deep courageous breath.

'Look here, Mrs H., do you know a doctor, I mean an Italian

doctor living in Florence, called Salvatore, that means Our Blessed Saviour, surname Rossi? He's a nerve doctor, that is, he doesn't deal with mad people exactly, just people who find things getting a bit too much for them. He's a proper qualified doctor, not the other sort.'

'But, my dear child, what do you want a doctor for? Aren't you well?'

'I don't want any old doctor,' said Barney. 'Only this one.'

As it happened, the Harringtons did know Dr Rossi, at least professionally. It was Madge who had consulted him. After they had settled in to their farmhouse – not straight away, but after the decoration had all been seen to, and the drains – she had been troubled with sleeplessness and had thought it might have a physical cause, anaemia, perhaps, because moving takes it out of you, even to such a heavenly place as Tuscany. She had been recommended to Dr Rossi by her own doctor, as being the best man. But in the end he had almost laughed at her, Madge went on, though in a perfectly gentle way, if Barney knew what she meant. He'd said that anaemia of the brain was an affliction of the elderly, and as she certainly couldn't call herself *that*, she had probably better consult someone concerned with the treatment of illnesses where the psychological factors were more important than the physical ones.

Barney recognised the cue for sympathy, but hadn't time for it just at the moment. 'Did he say all that in Italian? I'd have been lost.'

Yes, so would Mrs H, but she had taken Mr H along with her as interpreter.

'But Dr Rossi doesn't know any English at all?'

'Not really, but you sense his personality.'

'You'd call him the dominating type, then?'

'I'd say, compelling.'

'Did you feel overwhelmed while you were talking to him, rather as if you were losing your senses?'

Madge Harrington appeared to be taken aback.

'You see, Mummy isn't quite herself.' It's speaking evil that good may come, Barney thought. 'She asked me to find out about this man while I was over here. You see, he's very well known, only she wanted me to find out a bit more because actually nobody seems to know anything much about him. Mummy's changed a good deal lately, you know, she's quite desperate at times. She's ready to try anything.'

'But I thought her trouble was some form of arthritis?'

'That's what everyone thought, but they've changed their minds.'

'I could ring up your mother this evening,' said Mrs Harrington doubtfully. 'Or I could ring her now, if you feel it's really urgent.'

Barney felt driven to the limits of her imagination.

'No, I don't want you to do that, it might upset her nerves, she mightn't even know what you were talking about, and when she's like that a word will set her off screaming. No, the best thing by far would be if you could get hold of this Dr Rossi and ask him to lunch as well. I don't suppose he'd need a lot to eat on a working day. Tomorrow if you can, or the next day, because I'm due back in England quite soon. Then I can get an idea, you see, of what he's like. There's nothing like personal contact. I'm sure I should know at once whether he'd be the right person or not.'

'You must remember that we only know him very slightly, Lavinia. Everything in this country seems quite relaxed, but when it comes to invitations you soon find there are all sorts of little rights and wrongs.'

'Oh, but Chiara was born here, and she thinks it's a very good idea.'

27

'But is he going to come?'

It hardly seemed possible that the Harringtons had believed this story of Barney's. But Chiara was conscious, in any case, of a disturbing, though not distressing, withdrawal of reality, as though she was driven forward by some quite other motive than the old ones, and divided beyond recall from the rest of the world, who could hardly fail to realise the strangeness of her condition.

Barney, also, was somewhat surprised, but this was qualified by frank self-congratulation. She understood pretty well, however, why the Harringtons had let themselves be taken in.

Toby Harrington – 'old Toby' even then, and indeed he'd been called this since he was fifteen – had been a liaison officer with the South African Armoured Division at the recapture of Impruneta. About two years ago his wife had indulged him by letting him drive her round the old battlegrounds, and when the recession in Italy had reached its lowest point they had bought one of the fifty thousand-odd empty farmhouses in Tuscany. They had had in mind something rather different from the other villa-purchasers whom they knew, who seemed to have entered a second childhood, sitting in the sunshine, playing with adult toys. Lo Scampolo – they didn't mind their London friends referring to it as The Scampi – was only a modest place, but it was worth running it properly, and living there all the year round. It was a totally different matter from settling down, say, up at Bellosguardo where they would have had a thronged gossiping life, taking or giving refreshment with this or that informed chatterer. It was perhaps unfortunate that their little property was bounded on one side by the Ridolfi vineyards, with their almost speechless proprietor. It had only been by chance (when he had called round and offered to help them in any way, they only had to let him know) that they had realised that he spoke perfectly good English. But there had never been an opportunity to go any further, and it had been Cesare who had freed Madge Harrington at last from her illusion that Italians, as a race, were vivacious.

'The H.'s seem pretty decent people,' said Barney. 'But they've got a serious weakness, which is that they want to get to know people.'

'Why is that a weakness?' Chiara asked.

Later in the afternoon Toby rang back. 'Don't fall to bits,' Barney told Chiara. 'They've asked him and he's coming. Perhaps he isn't asked out often. Doctors and bank managers very often aren't, you know. They know too much about other people.' Chiara, who had been obliged to drive Annunziata to the Ricordanza that afternoon for some kind of conference, or possibly a dispute, with the gardener, stood poised in the doorway as though ready either to escape or advance, with the car keys dangling in her hand.

'Barney,' she said, 'I don't think we ought to do this. I can't stand the idea of Salvatore being inspected, so to speak, for two hours like that.'

'It was quite awkward for me to arrange to come here.'

'I know, I know, and I shan't forget it as long as I live.'

'You'll have to let me do things my own way. Remember that you're intending to spend the rest of your life with him, no divorce over here. You'll get a straight opinion from me without fear or favour.'

'But how can you possibly tell what he's like in that time?'

'Don't worry about that. I can sum a person up pretty well with a firm hand-grip and straight look in the eyes.'

'He won't grip your hand, Barney, he'll only just touch it, as my father did.'

'Leave the gripping to me,' said Barney. 'You can tell a lot from the conditioned reflex.'

28

Toby Harrington drove into Florence to pick up the daughter of his good friend, Colonel Barnes. He had thought it would not be uninteresting to see the Ridolfi flat, but Lavinia was waiting for him at the outer gate. There she was, solidly planted on good leather shoes from Russell and Bromley, solidly constructed herself, towering and glowing with well-earned health. Toby got out and civilly opened the door for her.

'Where's your friend?' he asked.

'Oh, she's not coming.'

'And her father?'

'He's gone to Rome.'

Toby put the car in gear.

'He's left us more or less on our own,' Barney added. 'So there's not much chance of your seeing him either. Don't think I'm knocking the Count, though, he's quite something to talk to, when you think about what he's said after he's said it you can see that he's quite witty. It doesn't really take much time to get to know him or Chiara either, they have natural good manners.'

'Were good manners taught in your convent?' Toby asked.

Barney laughed heartily, showing teeth that would not have disgraced a fine young ogress.

'You're getting at me,' she said.

As they left the city she relaxed. She felt much safer in a car with Toby than with Chiara. When Chiara was driving she no longer recognised Barney's authority, but sprang forward into or against the stream of traffic, heedless of the fines for not giving way, like a wild animal in its own habitat, whereas Toby kept peering cautiously round his substantial passenger to check on the lighthearted drivers coming in from the right. One after another the white-painted trunks of the plane-trees and the mighty billboards advertising aperitifs and building sites advanced towards them and fell behind. When they passed the Ricordanza Toby glanced up at it, but said nothing. At the turn-off to Lo Scampolo there was a small group of buildings, a shed, an unenterprising cantina and grocer's shop, and a chapel with locked doors. Then the Harrington's Hillman seemed to brace itself for the dried-out dirt road.

'I say, who's responsible for keeping this up?'

Toby said that the road was classed as local, not provincial, and that it was a matter for negotiation. Well, he was thinking, so there'll just be the four of us, if this medico bothers to turn up. Meanwhile the large bright blundering presence of

88

this robust girl intimidated him. As the tiled roof of the Scampi came in sight he was unable not to hope for her approval. There was the faint suggestion of a regimental inspection.

From a side window as they drew up came a movement between a wave and a flicker, which Toby recognised as a distress signal.

'Madge is a bit of a perfectionist, you know. I expect something isn't quite ready.'

'I'll go and help, if you like,' said Barney. 'It would be awkward for her, with me and Dr Rossi coming, if she's made a hopeless mess of everything.'

Toby thought it better to start with a tour of inspection, beginning with the outbuildings and the cellars. Here Barney emphatically condemned the ancient olive-press which Toby had put into working order with the greatest difficulty, making replicas for the wooden screws on a lathe which they'd brought with them from England. 'You could try selling it to one of those antique people on Piazza San Spirito,' she suggested. 'You never know what things will fetch.'

Toby spoke of making his own oil.

'Don't tell me that's what this cousin of Chiara uses.'

'That's a different matter, it's quite a large working estate, a fattoria, it's run as a business.'

Barney thought that in the country everything should be run as a business. But she was generous in her praise of the kitchen, where Madge, still toiling, had grown or pickled or dried everything herself, had done, it seemed, everything herself short of laying the eggs, and of the new bathroom, although there the bright ceramic tiles were sinking and rising a little as though still accommodating themselves to a new life. 'It'll help if I put all my weight on them,' Barney called out, stamping. 'They just need walking about on for an hour or two every day. They're fine.' The Harringtons felt consoled, all the more so because of her rejection of the olive-press. Total approval is never convincing.

The dining-room, too, laid out with pottery and violet-coloured glass from Empoli, looked well. The windows stood open to the languid autumn air. 'You couldn't leave them open like this in England at this time of year,' said Barney kindly.

Toby was still fussing a little over the wine, whether to serve Valsassina, which would be neighbourly, even if the neighbour seemed rather a difficult fellow, or a Chianti classico. Barney was of the opinion that doctors didn't drink wine at lunch for fear of cutting off the wrong patient's leg afterwards. Madge, too, seemed mildly anxious.

'I must admit, Lavinia, I don't quite see how your mother expects you to form an opinion of Dr Rossi, and particularly as to whether he'd be a suitable consultant for her, in such a very short time.'

'Oh, all our family are good at snap judgments, I expect it's an inherited characteristic. You know, we had to take on a new gardener and his wife this summer, and when the first couple who came, you know, for an interview, a friend of Mummy's rang up and said, "I saw your applicants at the station waiting for the bus and I don't think they'll turn out to be what you want, the husband hasn't got the hands of a working man." But when they arrived Mummy made up her mind at once. It's a gift of hers.'

'You mean she offered them the job?'

'No, she didn't, but it wasn't because of his hands, it was on account of his wife.'

'I shouldn't have thought that a gift like that could be inherited,' said Toby seriously.

Madge, after some indecision, brought the tray of glasses and olives and little bits and pieces outside into what had become the front garden. A special feature of the Scampi was the box hedge along the terrace, hopelessly out of hand when they'd taken over, but Toby had put so much work into it. Now it was stout and close-twigged enough to bear the weight of a tray, if you put it down carefully. It made something to talk about when a newcomer arrived.

Beyond the outbuildings, the road to Lo Scampolo ran into fields. No-one came that way unless they had business with the Harringtons. There were no other sounds, of cars or scooters or even of mules or donkeys, to raise expectations, or even to disappoint them.

Toby went back into the house. After all, it was only half past one. Barney sat back, resting her feet on the box hedge.

'I don't think he could have made a mistake about the day,' said Madge. 'He was quite definite about it.' She sat watching the pale, baked road.

29

Salvatore had accepted the Harringtons' invitation, which meant an inconvenient rearrangement of his day, for one reason, or rather one false deduction, only. Toby had mentioned when he telephoned that a young English girl would be coming, a friend of Chiara Ridolfi. Simply at the sound of the name Salvatore had assumed that it was a summons, practically an assignation, and the whole thing had been contrived so that Chiara and he could meet again. He asked Gentilini whether this was not probably the case. Gentilini replied that he had very little to go on, but that as far as he could see the Contessina Chiara was extremely direct and frank in her actions and not at all likely to go in for anything so complicated. She had, if he remembered rightly, walked out of a concert with him although she had come with another party, and had subsequently come straight to Salvatore's office, although for some reason that Gentilini couldn't follow she had been asked to leave. 'Try to behave with less calculation, ask yourself if you are doing what you really want to, for instance, whether you really want to accept this invitation from the Villa Harrington.' Salvatore said that it was the last thing on earth that he wanted to do. Forty kilometres each way, the language difficulty, Signora Harrington whom he remembered only dimly, his paper work left undone, probable indigestion. He had consented to go only in order to show

Chiara that he could not be treated casually. 'I can't see how it will show anything of the sort,' said Gentilini. 'However, I'm doing my best to follow you.'

'What I mean is that I think it right to treat her with ordinary politeness. Incidentally, it's struck me recently that in a non-medical sense you understand almost nothing about women.'

'I understood enough to marry and produce four children, and I can't remember noticing any particular difficulties.'

'That's precisely what I mean,' said Salvatore, with forced calm.

30

At two minutes past the half hour a Vespa approached over the rise and the dip and the rise to Lo Scampolo, and stopped in front of the house. Barney saw a thin, dark, dark-suited male creature coming to rest, switching off, and sitting still for a moment as though getting the better of a vast impatience.

'God, he's Italian-looking!' she said.

Mrs Harrington understood her perfectly. The two of them stood up, ready to support each other if necessary. At the same time Toby came out with a bottle under each arm.

'Good show, doctor, nice that you could come. I'm going to ask you to help me settle a little problem about the wine.'

'Doctor Rossi,' Madge Harrington interposed, 'this is the young friend from England who's come to see us, Lavinia Barnes.'

Salvatore bowed.

'Lavinia's just on a visit from Florence, to the Ridolfis.'

He was still standing there.

'By the way,' said Barney, 'if you're expecting to see Chiara, you're in for a shock. She won't be here today. Non c'è,' she added loudly and clearly. 'Chiara no.'

31

It had been calculated that Barney would be back at via Limbo
by about four o'clock at the latest. Chiara could hardly be
expected to wait patiently with nothing to do. There was
no-one in Florence who knew about her predicament, nobody,
therefore, that she wanted to talk to. She was supposed to
be passing the time by going to a lecture at the German
Kunst-historisches Institut on the foreground details in three
paintings formerly attributed to Belbello da Pavia. This had
been selected by Barney from some list or other as being
soothing, or at least not over-stimulating.

Two minutes after Barney left in the Harringtons' Hillman,
Chiara went, as she scarcely ever did, to look at herself in the
large mirror which hung in the salone. The mirror was an old
deceiver, the fine old glass had flattered countless arriving
and departing guests. She looked intently at her face,
slapped herself on each cheek in turn, pulled her hair behind
her ears and let it go again. Then she went down to the courtyard and unlocked, not her own little Fiat, but her father's
Lancia.

Barney had never been in this car and if she saw it following,
she would not recognise it. As a passenger, in any case, she
wasn't much of a looker-out or looker-round, more of a majestic
recliner. Chiara caught up with the Hillman, without difficulty,
in Viale Giannotti and followed it out to Ponte a Ema. Past
the Ricordanza she slowed down, ready to wave or even to
stop if Giannina or her husband happened to be at the front
gate. No-one there, it looked deserted, and she picked up
speed. At the turn-off to Lo Scampolo, the closed chapel of
Sangallo and the little shop, she hesitated, then drove straight
on to Valsassina.

On the north wall of the front yard the climbing viburnum

93

reached serenely outwards to the farthest corners, unperturbed by shadow or sun, and covered with many thousands of flowers, a population of white flowers which looked as though they could never grow less. This wasn't the time of day for their scent, and in any case the air was tainted with the smell of burning sulphur which meant that someone was disinfecting the old wine casks. To catch the viburnum's scent you had to wait until dusk, until the moment when the greenish-white flowers of the garden release their fragrance and only the shapes of white things are visible. The years when the viburnum flowered repeatedly like this were supposed to be lucky. Chiara could remember waiting as a child and then in September it had not flowered again and she had been bitterly disappointed. This year then, nineteen hundred and fifty-five, must be her lucky year. It was lucky, for instance, to find Cesare at home in the middle of the day.

He was standing in the yard. She had never seen him hurry, and he didn't now, but walked slowly over to the car.

'I'm sorry, Cesare, I ought to have let you know I was coming.'

'No, that wasn't necessary.'

'I interrupted you.' Since he had been a small boy he had had a habit of standing quite still whenever a problem struck him until he was satisfied that he had solved it or, for the time being, couldn't.

She got out of the car into the autumn sunlight.

'You're looking older,' he said.

'Well, I am older. When was I last here?'

'Last summer.'

'What were you thinking about just now?'

'The wholesale price for the 1955.'

'Are you going to put it lower?'

'The Association will.'

'And do you agree with them?'

'I don't know, because I'm not thinking about it now.'

The cousins walked into the house together.

'Bernardino will want you to go and see the rabbits and doves.'

'No he won't,' said Chiara. 'He'll see at once how much older I am.'

The rabbits and doves were kept in a stone building about half the size of the one in which the farmworkers had their lunch, though as a building it was probably much older. You could see the tiled roof and the columbarium from the house. It was closed by a solid wooden door which opened in two separate halves. Inside there was a semi-darkness, peacefully reeking of birds and animals. The squabs muttered from their loft overhead, feathers strayed down through patches of light and back into the dark, the broadly palpitating rabbits drowsed in their pens below. Both the doves and the rabbits were white. There was no feeling whatever of their fate in store, only a companionable peace, as though the whole crowded enclosure was breathing in unison, every creature deeply satisfied with its frowsty living-space. To children the place was instantly attractive.

All this livestock really did belong to Bernardino, who had sole charge of buying, selling, breeding, slaughtering and collecting the combings of the angoras. This, probably, was the origin of his delusion that the whole of Valsassina should by rights be his.

'Will he be disappointed if I don't go?'

'I don't know,' said Cesare.

Chiara cried: 'Cesare, I can't stay. I have to know what's happening at the Harringtons.'

'You mean at Lo Scampolo?'

'Yes, at Lo Scampolo, the Harringtons, you know them.'

'I've spoken to them,' said Cesare. 'You should have taken the right-hand road at the Sangallo chapel.'

'Yes, but that wouldn't have done. I wanted to be as near as I could without actually going there. And besides that I thought it would be peaceful here, and we could go out to the fields and talk about next year's prices, and I could stop my mind gnawing away at me.'

'You're very fond of these English people?'

'I've never met them.'

'It seems to me that you're not going the right way about it.'

'But it isn't them I want to meet at all. I'll try to explain, because after all it's quite easy to understand. There's somebody there, a guest, at this very moment, and all I really want to know is whether he's there or not.'

'In that case I still think you should have turned right at Sangallo.'

Cesare said this without any hint of reproach. His was a judicial nature, not a critical one. 'What do you want to do now?' he asked.

'Of course you're right, it was a stupid mistake, I'll do what you suggest, I'll go there now, straight away, now.'

'No, that isn't what I suggested.'

'Can I go by the field roads?'

'They're dry, but they won't be good for my uncle's car.'

Chiara kissed him warmly and drove back out of the main gate and up the track between the vegetable trenches and the nearest olive groves. The ruts in the road, made first by ox-carts and then by small tractors, were not adapted to the car's wheelbase and it bounded from one side to the other, as though in pain.

Bernardino, coming out of the wood store, appeared delighted. This was because the Contessina had come and gone so quickly and had stayed such a short time and was driving so dangerously up the field road. Then she pulled up and stuck her head out of the front window.

'You were right, can I leave this here and take the camioncino?'

'Yes,' called out Cesare.

'You're sure you won't need it?'

'Of course I shall need it.'

'Well, if someone brings it back this evening?'

'Yes.'

Bernardino thought he'd seen something like it at the Cine Rex, where he went every other Sunday. First the Lancia, then the camioncino! Why can't she make up her mind? What did she come for if she didn't want to stay? Long after Cesare had gone back on foot to the vineyards Bernardino was still laughing.

32

Giancarlo had told his daughter the truth when he said that his visit to Rome had been arranged for some time. Unlike most of his acquaintances he had no business matters to attend to and no-one of influence at the Ministries to whom he might drop a hint. He hoped to congratulate one or two very old friends, with whom he had served in the cavalry, on their being still alive and able to attend their club, but primarily he had an engagement to see his late sister-in-law's brother, Monsignor Gondi. This had been Gondi's idea, and Giancarlo had no objection.

The Monsignore had a journalist's temperament, mastering the given subject rapidly, never knowing more than was strictly necessary and tabulating it in his mental recesses where it would be to hand always. He could hardly conceive, even after all these years, how much Giancarlo Ridolfi avoided knowing in the interest of leading a tranquil life. The daughter, Chiara, was, as he was aware without consulting any reference, nearly eighteen. Her father and her aunt, who were responsible for her at this crucial time, seemed to him like an old gossiping country couple, with the additional disadvantage that they didn't much care for the country. This was in spite of their upbringing. They seemed to lose, rather than gain, from life's successive stages. At Valsassina his nephew had to keep things going without advice (beyond what he occasionally had time to send himself). The current low wine prices for home and export were a catalogue – one might call it a litany – of young Cesare's difficulties. Now with that powerful but awkward element, a very young woman, to launch into the family's history, Ridolfi and his sister were totally left behind by Italy's forward movement into the leadership of style and European culture. What they needed, really, was dusting off and rehabilitating, a recall to the present from the fading afterglow of old Florence. He distinguished, of course, between the two of them. Maddalena had been written off by the Gondi memory as an unpredictable old woman, or perhaps something rather less sane than that, whereas Giancarlo's amiable and unperturbed conduct of life from day to day seemed beyond classification. If he heard Ridolfi mentioned, and that wasn't often, it was always as 'delightful'. 'He was delightful.' What an epitaph, in the middle of the twentieth century, for the head of an ancient house! Giancarlo had been a student, a political idealist, and an officer, but there was an almost total incompetence in making the correct moves in the world's game, which, admittedly, was harder than most work, but just as much a matter of duty. Who else, in his position, could have married an American and been left worse off than before? Who else, for the matter of that, but Maddalena could have taken her niece to Parenti's and come away without a rag to wear? There was a certain carelessness, he supposed, which would once have been considered noble, but it was carelessness still. How had Maddalena come to lose those two fingers?

Giancarlo, for his part, accepted that he hadn't much to offer, beyond the doubtful accomplishment of being a Count who looked like a Count, and an old father who behaved just like one. In place of information he could only offer instinct and experience, and he admired the infallibility of Giuseppe Gondi. At the same time he pitied him. Gondi would never be created Prefect of a Congregation, yet he was unable to understand why. Capable of grasping so much, he couldn't see, or perhaps believe, that his virtue, hard work, relentless flow of accurate reports and genius for middle management would keep him for ever a Monsignore. Irreplaceable at his own level, he could never rise. Many small honours had been conferred upon him, but he was too useful to promote. The Secretariat commended his work, slightly altered his conclusions, and left him where he was.

During his career Gondi had sometimes been housed in some building or other in Rome itself, temporarily acquired and made officially part of the Vatican City. This depended to some extent on the changing views of the Secretariat on the importance of the various Congregations. At one point he and his staff had been moved out to a block among gasworks and tramlines where the Pisa railway crosses the Via Ostiense. Now, happily, he was back at the Vatican itself.

The Ridolfi family had never had any special rights of admission to the Vatican. Giancarlo took the 77 bus to Piazza Risorgimento, and feeling somewhat tired already, passed through the Bronze Door to make his enquiry in the reception room. While they telephoned through for him he tried to collect his thoughts, but was conscious only of mild images of reproach, tempered by the well-being of sitting down, even on a hard chair. Monsignor Gondi's office was now, it seemed, on the third floor. Giuseppe himself came forward to meet him as the lift doors opened.

'You're too kind, Beppino.'

'Not at all, in the end this saves time.'

Gondi was a solid man, but compact and rapid, as though designed by a committee for all-round heavy-duty use. His eyes and his long, delicate nose were a little like Cesare's but what could one tell from that?

'Giancarlo, I've arranged for a few people to meet you, to put you a little bit more in the picture, not of course a party during the illness of His Holiness, let us call it a conversazione. Before that we shall have time for a talk together here, simply about family matters.'

'How good of you.'

'That was what I meant about saving time. It's always possible for me to find half an hour out of the day if I know it will be profitable. In this case it will be in fact twenty-eight minutes, as you were a little late at Reception.'

In the office he dismissed the two secretaries. He would be back to sign his correspondence at half past seven.

On the desk was a crucifix and a blotter, on the wall a painting in acid mauve and orange of the Seven Sorrows by a Czech refugee and a graph showing the annual attendance of

99

pilgrims at the world's Catholic shrines. The room was furnished like a respectable hotel of the second category. The blinds were half down over a view of the city where no work can be done for personal profit, and no washing can be hung out in the open.

Gondi was not, for the moment, quite able to redistribute his attention. He took some photographs out of the blotter. 'Perhaps these would interest you, Giancarlo. You see how wide we throw our net. A sub-committee on private worship. These are Mexican images of the Redeemer, each with a hinged plastic door in the breast which can be opened to show the Sacred Heart illuminated by a bicycle lamp.' He selected several, and as though dealing cards, handed them over. 'Operated from a battery, or they can be plugged in directly.'

It was amazing how the Monsignore, as he moved from one strenuous appointment to the next, expected his relations to follow the details of his work, not only with polite attention but with something like excitement. However, it was this belief that everything which interested him was interesting that had preserved him in a condition of suspended middle age. And of course the bureaucratic faith, like all faith, must be a gift from God. But Giancarlo thought he might risk the truth without impoliteness. He looked at the photographs and said: 'But Beppino, these don't interest me in the least.' This did not quite work, in the sense of recalling Gondi to the present situation. He began to talk about some memorial or other in Florence, in the Cemetery of Rifredi. There had been some kind of scandal or difficulty. In this way the Count heard for the first time the name of Dr Salvatore Rossi. He forgot it immediately.

Now, as though some internal mechanism had corrected itself, Gondi snapped the blotter shut and with a look of reproof said: 'Well, but so far you've told me nothing. What is the news of Maddalena?'

'She's in Vienna.'

'And the casa di riposo, I mean the asylum for old women and infants? I think there were some irregularities, weren't there, but I imagine they've been put right since the war.' As there was no answer he nodded and went on, 'And Cesare, it's not easy for him up there. I hope you don't allow that to escape your attention. The old part-share tenant system is gone for good, labour costs are high. But let him stick it out. In a few years replanting will begin at the expense of the Ministry, or even of the European Community. However, in my view Cesare is too solitary. His life is bizarre. Sometimes it occurs to me that he may end up by joining a contemplative Order.'

Giancarlo felt as though with these brisk words Cesare's future was actually being disposed of. 'I don't see, in that case, who would farm Valsassina.'

'It isn't a crime to sell land for a good purpose.'

'What purpose?'

'Let us say, of having a little ready money to repair the Ricordanza.'

'I've never heard Cesare say anything about the religious life.'

'The strong current runs silently. And now, what about our little Chiara?'

'She's at via Limbo at the moment, with a school friend who's been asked to stay.'

'An English girl?'

'Yes.'

'A Catholic?'

'From the convent, a girl called Lavinia Barnes.'

The Monsignore frowned a little, turning over the index cards of his mind.

'I imagine she would be related to Lord Barnes, the Markham Castle lot. Converts, I think. Did she mention them at all?'

'She's mentioned a number of things,' said Giancarlo, 'but not that, as far as I remember.'

'And what is Chiara's present course of studies? What are her principal interests?'

'Music, but she doesn't think her voice is good enough to train. The nuns thought so, but well, we must take advice.'

'Oh, this diffidence, this Ridolfi refusal or inability to trust oneself!'

'It doesn't have to be regarded as a failing. You might think of it as humility.'

'Well, humility is an attractive virtue, though unfortunately it's impossible to give it a political form.'

'But you wouldn't object to it on that account?' Giancarlo asked, bewildered.

Giancarlo knew that to be admitted to one of the individual offices of the Vatican, instead of a waiting-room, was against protocol and a favour to him as a relation by marriage. It was a relief when the favour came to an end, and reception rang through to say the Monsignore's taxi was waiting for him in viale Vaticano.

The conversazione was to be held in the studio of a Roman princess, Billie Buoncampagno, about whom Giancarlo felt he was expected to know more than he did. This sensation was familiar to him on his visits to Rome. Giuseppe was not very enlightening, saying that 'much is due to the Princess's generosity and devoutness,' but this mattered less because it seemed that she wouldn't be present, as she never came back to Rome before October. The taxi headed for the Piazza del Popolo, and he realised that the princess's studio must be in the Via Margutta, from which the artists themselves had been emigrating for several years so that now perhaps not one was left.

In the taxi Gondi had explained that the little gathering was not to be clerical, or in the first instance social, but cultural, or, to be precise, literary. He explained, as if it were an available course of medical treatment, the suppleness of the mind, the deepening of knowledge, which might result in meeting and talking to contemporary writers, 'occasionally, you understand, as with all things'. Possibly, too, Giancarlo thought, it was part of a determined attempt by Gondi (and one could only admire him for this) to extend his Congregation's sphere of influence over all the arts, writing as well as painting (perhaps later the most intractable of all, music). But for the most part it was a courageous attempt to modernise Giancarlo himself, as the father of Chiara, and perhaps as the uncle of Cesare.

He was struck, when they arrived, by the anxious care of the manservant who had been detailed, at long distance, by the Princess to look after the Monsignore's guests. Your Eminence – Gondi rejected this title with a slight downward sweep of the head – will stand at the head of the stairs? Her Highness has authorised me to get in any other help that may be necessary –

'Simply show them in. One glass of vermouth each will be quite sufficient. They will all have left by seven o'clock.'

'Do you often give parties here?' asked Giancarlo, looking round the wide pale spaces and the wall frescoes, painted and artificially faded, with delicious traces of colour, by Campigli.

'Occasionally I give a Press conference here, when an artistic ambiente is needed. We all have our own arrangements.'

On the dot, the very tick of five thirty, when the conversazione was to begin, three guests were announced, two Italian, one French. 'They are novelists,' Gondi murmured. 'More are to come.'

'All your guests are novelists?'

'Yes, I think all.'

'You know them well?'

'I don't know them at all. I entrusted one of my secretaries with the whole matter. I believe he looked up their addresses.'

Giancarlo was amazed that any relation of his, even by marriage, could have had such a disastrous idea. He was seized with embarrassment, so strong that it resembled fear. And all this, all this time put aside by Gondi out of a crowded working life, was, as he knew, intended solely for his benefit. One of the two Italians was a Southerner, stout and impressive in his black suit, his trousers supported by a broad leather belt as a reminder that he was still in touch with the people. He struck his breast, and uttered the one word: 'Gastone'. The name evoked at once his European reputation as a humanist and his years of exile. The second Italian, a Milanese, pale, sharp and watchful, mouthed silently: 'Luigi Capponi', giving the effect of an unpleasant party game. Capponi was not so well known, and Giancarlo, not much of a reader, could not pretend to remember the title of anything that he had ever written.

Searching his memory, he sipped at his wretched glass of vermouth, which had just been distributed. It tasted strongly of parsnips. 'It's not that Beppino is mean,' he thought, 'but he's indifferent to material pleasures, which has much the same effect.'

Capponi moved towards him and without any further introduction began to explain the substance of his forthcoming novel. Its purpose, he said, was to expose the absurd pretensions of his native town of Popolograsso. In it not only the author himself but the streets, the statues, the furniture and the main drains spoke freely and reproached the citizens for their bourgeois way of life. Refrigerators, when opened, vomited over their owners, and when a couple entered a bedroom the mattress split itself lewdly and lay wide open, discharging its springs. The film rights were already said to have been sold for five hundred million lira, and Giancarlo pretended to recognise the name of the director.

Gastone had shown no signs of listening, in fact he was standing in the middle of a circle of late arrivals who kept a short respectful distance away from him, as though on the edge of a bull-pen. Now, however, he said, without even a glance in Capponi's direction: 'Satire, when all is said and done, is an ignoble art. The writer's only true subject is Nature.'

'But Nature should be satirised,' cried Capponi. 'We are all against exploitation, I trust. In this country the earth itself is the principal exploiter, a bloodsucker, living off man's work, three thousand years of sweat and mule dung on the same little terrace. In the end one has to agree with poor Marinetti. Nothing is more of a bourgeois capitalist than Nature.'

'What, you defy Nature?' bellowed Gastone.

The Monsignore interposed, pointing out, with a pastor's air of having said it more than once before, that all Nature's functions must be taken into consideration. She was not only creative. It is her business to erase the signs of damage, to heal wounds and gradually to restore the status quo. 'This surely the writer can also do by thoughtful detachment and patient observation.'

'Screw patience!' Capponi hissed, seizing the Count, for some reason, by both hands. 'Patience is the same as resignation.'

'Surely not,' said Giancarlo, freeing himself. 'Patience is passive, resignation is active.'

Gastone had been deflected, but only a little, and he now

returned to the charge, declaring that no-one was fitted to write who didn't know, from personal experience, what it was to sleep like a peasant.

'Ah, one thinks of Tolstoy,' said the Monsignore. 'You remember that one of his peasants prays to lie down like a stone and rise up like new bread.'

'Then Tolstoy was an idiot. Country bread hardly rises at all. Country people sleep as I do, or as the beasts do, with one eye open, constantly on the watch.'

Giancarlo felt a light touch on his arm. 'My name is Pierre Aulard.'

It was the tiny French writer. 'You're the Monsignore's brother?'

'No.'

'Never mind. Do you often go to England?'

'Now and then. I've been quite recently.'

'Tell me, que font les jeunes?'

'I'm afraid I haven't asked them what they're doing.'

'Do they still speak of me, Pierre Aulard, as young?'

He paused expectantly.

'You must think me very ignorant,' said Giancarlo.

Aulard fixed his large, feverish eyes upon him. 'I have been told that it's possible to live decently at the moment in London for twenty-five shillings a week. Is that so?'

'No.'

'Gentlemen,' the Monsignore was saying. For a moment his voice was in competition with Gastone's, then even that rich bass wavered and fell silent. 'Gentlemen, dottori, I have to admit to you that much as I am enjoying your company I have asked you to do me the honour of coming here partly because as a Christian and a priest' – he smiled a little – 'it is my duty to spend even the happiest moments of my day profitably. You are the experts. I am doing no more than ask you, in the name of the Church, for your professional assistance. My responsibilities at the moment, as you know, extend over the whole field of popular religious art – not only in Europe – with the exception of the cinema, which has its own distinct advisory body. My question to you is simply this: at what point does the professional artist or indeed the professional writer make contact with the man or the woman of the people? What can be hoped for in this field?'

'An example.' He picked up from the wide marble sill, which ran round the whole interior of the studio, a little statuette. It was a portrait of himself, a terracotta about twenty centimetres high, almost pyramidical because of the stiff folds of the cassock. There was no glazing except on the eyes, which were touched in with white. It was a very good likeness and surely it had been a pardonable vanity to show it as an object lesson.

The terracotta looked as if it must be by the Bergamese sculptor Giacomo Manzu, and in fact it was a genuine Manzu. The Monsignore began to enlighten them. Manzu was the eleventh son of a poor sacristan in a Benedictine monastery. As a small boy he had sat quietly in the sacristy, watching the monks divest themselves after the Mass, and turn back into approachable human beings.

This won't quite do, thought Giancarlo. 'Manzu is always the same,' Gastone rumbled. Since no-one remarked on the likeness or made any other comment, except for Aulard, who asked how much the Princess had been prepared to pay for it, Giancarlo asked if he might hold the statue and stood there with the dignified little terracotta object, which rapidly became warm in the hand.

'I'm not attempting a critical commentary on the work,' the Monsignore continued. 'It's simply a convenient way of opening what I hope will be a short, but stimulating discussion.'

'Art is finished in Italy,' exclaimed Capponi furiously. 'Artists are finished, writers as well. Essentially I work only for the cinema. All that is wanted now is film and design. Fellini, Nervi, Olivetti, Pinaferrati. Everything else is shit. The people are shit, and their art consists of chromium, straw fringes and pink light bulbs. All that we are saying and have been saying and are about to say is shit.'

Gastone confronted him ominously. 'Rhetoric, filth! Olivetti could not design a cream cheese, neither could Pier Luigi Nervi. On the threshold of Nature the man of science must pause.'

'I use the word "design" only in its most important sense.'

'What are the other senses?'

'There are none,' said Aulard, drooping like a sick marmoset.

In a private moment, under cover of the din, Gondi said quietly to Giancarlo: 'They are insane.'

'Reckless, perhaps. They're without the normal safeguards of social life.' In that way, he thought, they weren't unlike Signorina Barnes.

'They're ignoring the possibilities of a serious moral discussion, which were implied by my invitation.'

'Don't let it distress you, Beppino. They're only storytellers.' He added: 'Perhaps better to ask only one of them at a time.'

But here he had gone too far. The Monsignore could not accept advice from the frail relative whose quality of life he was improving. Gallantly he turned back to the group of guests, where jagged hostilities were flying. Giancarlo was left with his empty glass and in his other hand the little terracotta.

33

'What happened?' Barney asked. 'I came here because I was your best friend. We were best friends to the extent that Reverend Mother wouldn't let us walk round the grounds without a third for fear we should get up to something. Remember that. Admit that. I came because you distinctly said it was urgent. You said you couldn't manage without me. I came because you were showing symptoms of weediness. I've got my own life to think seriously about. I told you I'd got to go to Painstake, and this whole question of my He. But first of all it seemed I had to inspect yours. Perhaps you didn't actually ask me to do it, but in my view it was absolutely necessary as a preliminary step. That was how I saw it. Now tell me what happened.'

Barney was packing, not hastily, but with august and deliberate movements. The expression on her handsome face showed that she was deeply hurt.

'Let me just tell you, Cha, that when this Rossi found you weren't there, and I told him that straight away, he just got on his scooter and made off. The Harringtons were left flat with all their bottles and little plates and bits and pieces. They'd meant it to be nice, they'd meant to sit out on the terrace. You can't do things like that. If he does things like that, he's just not possible. Then when I got back here, poor Mrs H. drove me back, agonies of indigestion after helping her finish up everything, I couldn't leave them like that facing it all, and then I found there was bloody no-one here. I couldn't even get in, and listen to this, I had to go to the dreaded Uffizi again, it was the only place open in the afternoon, what happened?'

'I did mean to go to the Harringtons by the field-path from Terrapetrosa. But when I got there I didn't stop, I went straight on. I passed Salvatore just before the main road at Sangallo. Then when I got to the Ricordanza I turned up there.'

'Jesus Christ, why didn't you go on to Florence?'

'I don't know.'

'I suppose you were running away from him,' said Barney with queenly scorn.

'I don't know, perhaps.'

'Well, what did he do?'

'He came straight after me to the Ricordanza.'

'What did he say?'

'He said: Why weren't you at the English people's house? I said: They didn't ask me. He said, I want to talk to you, why is this place always shut? I said, it's not shut, I have the key.'

'And then.'

'Barney, he was furious. He shouted, how convenient that you've got the keys! I said, I don't always have them, sometimes I forget them and I have to try and find the gardener's wife. He shouted again, not so loudly but still it was quite loud, how convenient for you that you were born to have the keys, and if you forget them to call out for the gardener's wife!'

'You shouldn't have let him shout at you. You should have asserted yourself.'

Chiara had opened the side door, which gave almost straight onto the limonaia, so that the best thing to do was to walk in at one end and out at the other. This was the place that as a small girl she had loved above all others, particularly in the winter months, when the lemon trees were waiting in their pots to be taken out in April, all those bitter green leaves passing the long season together, and giving off a cold bitter green smell, the ghost of the lemons. The gardeners kept a number of other things in there, wheeled carts, terracotta vases, and frames for training the climbing plants, twice as tall as a man, and lying in heaps like very tall sleeping men.

'He said, why are we coming in this way? Why should we mind coming in through the front gate? I said, but don't you like it, don't you like the smell of the earth in here? Even the earth itself doesn't smell of earth like the limonaia. He said, very good, we've come here to find out what the earth smells like. Where were you at lunch-time in any case? I told him I was at the farm visiting my cousin. Who is this cousin? I said he was Cesare.'

'And then he flew off the handle again,' said Barney. 'I'm beginning to feel some sympathy with this man. Well, what next? For pity's sake don't tell me you had it off among the flower-pots.'

'We went into the house,' said Chiara. 'I do wish there'd been time for you to see the Ricordanza. There's nothing locked up inside, you just go up the stairs from room to room. The shutters were fastened, of course, so it was dark, you can't think how dark, and yet it's not absolutely dark either. You can just tell the difference between dark and pale. I rang you up from there, you know, Barney, that time.'

'The hell you did,' said Barney, flinging a pair of shoes into a suitcase. 'Well, then I suppose you thought, what can I do to make him really happy?'

'No, I didn't think of anything at all.'

Chiara looked composed and peaceful. 'It was very good of you to come,' she said.

'Cha, just tell me. Just look me in the eyes and tell me this. Were the beds made up? I mean, were there proper sheets on them? After all, we've both of us got standards. I don't want to be weedy, but we were both of us at Holy Innocents.'

'Oh, Barney, of course we were. I shall never forget that.'

Barney sat down squarely by her suitcase. 'Well, I've come to the end of the road, Cha. I can't give you any more advice, I'm not competent. I've been in bed with someone after a Hunt Ball, but we never got properly round to anything.'

'Oh, Barney, I love you, you'll always be able to give advice.'

In the fifth form Barney had held them spellbound with readings from the sixteenth volume of Burton's *Arabian Nights*, which she had selected from her grandfather's library. 'The pain which not a few newly-made women describe as resembling the tearing out of a back tooth.' 'What does he mean, "not a few"?' Chiara had asked. 'Did they all have their back teeth torn out?'

'Okay, Cha, so you and this Dr Rossi are lovers.'

'Not more than we were before.'

'You'd met him twice.'

'It wouldn't make any difference how often. Do you remember "*Amor segnoreggio la anima, la quale fu si tosto a lui disponata*"?'

Barney looked at her gloomily.

'I hope to God you're not in pup.'

34

Cesare drove down to the tobacconist's in the nearest village and bought four sheets of plain writing paper and an envelope. When he got back to Valsassina he sat down in his office and began to write a letter to Chiara. This began quite formally, saying that even though she had had to leave so abruptly it had been a great pleasure to see her a few days ago. He knew the number of days, but did not mention it. He thanked her for having the truck returned. This only took up a quarter of a page.

He could have gone on to give her the news of the farm. Last year it hadn't been practicable to make any Reserve, the special wine for the use of the family only, this year he thought it would be possible. Another thing: the day before yesterday, for no particular reason, he had gone just before sunrise to have a look at the doves and rabbits and found the casetta broken into. The door was still locked, but two panels had been taken out with an electric saw. It was clear enough that a lorry had been parked just off the track to the casetta and a little downhill, on the way to the field path. Although the ground had hardened after the recent rains the tire marks, coming, turning and going, were quite plain to anyone who wanted to read them. Unlocking what was left of the door, Cesare had been half choked by the smother of torn fur and feathers that rose, in a white cloud, to meet him. Every cage was empty, the high roosts were down and stuck out like broken bones at odd angles. A few doves, with twisted necks, lay on the ground, perhaps surplus to requirements. The doves had probably been more intractable than the rabbits. Bernardino, on receiving the information, seemed to become a little unhinged. He demanded to go out immediately in the Land Rover to look for the rapinatori, or down to the Central Market in Florence where he was certain of being able to pick out, on the heaped butchers' stalls, his own birds and animals all of whom he knew by name. The notion that all this had gone on a few hundred metres away, while he slept and dreamed peacefully, tormented him.

Since Cesare had made up his mind about the Riservata, and had found it useless to argue with Bernardino, he saw no point in including these topics in his letter. However, he went on writing with increasing speed and concentration, until all the paper was used up.

So far as he could remember, he had never written to her before. Probably there had been no necessity. When he had finished he read the letter through. Then he took the four sheets of paper, tore them into a number of pieces, and threw them away.

'At least that's something I haven't done,' he said aloud.

It was irritating, though, to be left with the unused envelope.

35

Mazzata, Salvatore's native village, was not beautiful and can never have been visited by anyone in search of beauty. A large tomato sauce cannery, intended to bring prosperity to the district, had been built under Mussolini's scheme for the rehabilitation of the South, on the very slight slope to the north of the village. The factory was in the style of the temple at San Felice, and the sauce had been renamed Salsa Imperiale. Since there had never been any provision for maintaining it the cannery had gradually rusted, flaked and declined into a semi-ruin, a ruin without doors or windows, since these had been taken away over the years for other purposes. An inscription in painted lettering, MUSSOLINI IS THE MAN WHOM NEITHER GOD NOR MAN WILL BEND could still just be made out on one of the inner walls at the entrance to the workers' recreation room. The last consignment of Salsa Imperiale, a long file of tins waiting, upside down, and full of sauce, for their bottoms to be soldered on, had been halted in that position in 1942. Ancient tins, ancient sauce and conveyer belt were all rusted together. Goats picked at the coarse flowers and straw-like grass between the fallen girders, and Mazzata's children played there when they were turned off the flattened area which had once been the threshing-ground and was now the football pitch. Often their first experience of sex was a kind of dusty scuffle in the ruins of the managerial toilet block.

There are many poorer villages than Mazzata in the South of Italy, but few more uninteresting. Salvatore, arriving unostentatiously by bus, spoke aloud to himself just under his breath, advising self-control. Everyone in Mazzata was going to behave exactly as he expected. He, too, was going to behave like a son of Mazzata coming back after making good in the city, wearing a grey suit and carrying a leather despatch case from Gherardini. If a documentary team from Radiotre were to arrive in Mazzata and make a call-out for a typical returning inhabitant, they'd pick him out in the first five minutes. The idea, or rather the fantasy, of anyone wanting to make any permanent record of Mazzata, diverted him a little as they approached the outskirts. It would be broadcast as one of the Documents of Science and Education, Number God knows what, and Gentilini would make the children listen to it in the crammed sitting-room. 'With our eyes open and our hearts no less, our journey to the South will provide a good opportunity to know better the suggestive and historic settlement of Mazzata. Sheltered in the environs of an imposing ruin . . .'

Salvatore had come back here to sell his share of the family land. He had decided to build a house outside Florence, with a garden, and a clinic standing detached from it. That would be better for the children. He would start building at once, before his marriage. The housing society connected with the hospital would give him a 2½% loan. This sale in Mazzata would provide his deposit. The Ridolfi would be asked for nothing. Like the greater part of the world's population since the war he would be deeply in debt. But in expecting nothing from his wife's family he would, he believed, put himself in an exceptional minority. His prospects were not at all bad. He could do what he had so far avoided, namely sign on to act as consultant for one of the larger insurance companies. He was almost certain of the neurology department at S. Agostino. Nothing was almost certain, of course. He allowed himself to think for a few moments of Chiara. The image which his mind supplied was of Chiara naked, dragging the unmanageable white duvet to the Ricordanza's windows and almost helpless with laughter. Curiously enough it brought with it a sensation of purity and calm. This was not what he had expected, and it unsettled him.

He knew exactly how opinions would divide, in the family and outside it, and at the Câfé Centrico in Mazzata. His brothers would impress upon him their reliance on his family loyalty and affection which would lead him to part with his share for something much less soulless than the market price. His elder sister would think him and call him an idiot for not being richer than he was. Married to the shoe-repairer, the stingiest and most intellectually dishonest man in Mazzata, she had only the experience of unhappiness to recommend her advice. After two days of discussion the shoe-repairer, who had got a little capital together by serving his time in the carabiniere, would indicate that he, together with some unknown partners, would be prepared to give rather more than the brothers for Salvatore's few clods of earth. Then there was his mother. As always he had to ring through to the grocer's shop and ask if someone could fetch her. It had taken her some time to come, even though she lived next door.

'So you've made up your mind to come at last, when may we expect you?'

'Tomorrow afternoon.'

'And you'll bring this young woman with you?'

'No, not this time.'

'Is she educated?'

Then, at the idea of his selling his part-share, she began to lament because now there would be nothing to bring him back to Mazzata. He pointed out, lowering his voice in the hope that she might lower hers, that it hadn't ever brought him back anyway.

'I only came to see you, and I'm coming to see you now.'

'Promise me that she is of good family.'

Her apparent failure to understand his letter was simply a demonstration of age and pitiable infirmity, and he had to remind himself that these would be added to her long-term demonstration of being a mother. There was no reason, by the way, why she should use the grocer's telephone instead of having one herself. He had offered to pay for the installation, but in any case there had never been a time, as far as he could remember, when they wouldn't have been able to afford one.

It was the hottest part of the afternoon when the bus drew up in the main square. The bus, an air-conditioned Pullman on its way through to Benevento, looked incongruous as it came powerfully to rest alongside the downtrodden buildings.

The only other vehicle in the piazza was a tricycle, supporting a glass case which contained biscuits of great age and packets of sweets. The tricyclist was absent, waiting until the children came out of school to make a sale. He had left his goods under the thick shadow of a plane-tree, but the sun had moved and the sweets had begun to melt.

36

When, after two days' negotiations, everybody concerned had said, both in turn and together, pretty well what he had counted on, Salvatore felt better. There is a peculiar satisfaction in predicting one's own difficulties. The matter of his forthcoming marriage was hardly discussed at all, because nobody in Mazzata had believed that what he had written to his mother was true. His engagement to a young Contessina was one of those fantasies which prove ruinous in political life, but are otherwise pardonable enough. They wouldn't, to be sure, have associated fantasy with Salvatore, but if he had arranged a good marriage, why hadn't he arrived in a new car? There was, for instance, the Giuletta Sports, of which only three hundred and twenty-three had been produced that year at Portello. The sale of the land, on the other hand, absorbed everyone, and circled round one stable point of agreement: since Salvatore had gone north, he deserved to receive as little money as possible. This, Salvatore found, was having an unfortunate effect on him. He was losing his temper, but not in the right way. He had a fierce impulse to terrify them all with generosity, to stand up in the Câfé Centrico and shout, 'The land is yours! Rather than listen to one more word, I give it to you freely!'

All business in Mazzata, until the adjournment to the lawyer's office, was done at the large table at the back of the Câfé, situated in a kind of alcove of its own, under a large advertisement of the bygone Salsa Imperiale. But on the third afternoon Salvatore had hardly got further than the door when he heard his name called out gently, his childhood name, his name as a very small child indeed, Mickey. Even his mother would never think of using that name now. Perhaps, indeed, she was less likely to use it than anyone. The word, Mickey, irritated and embarrassed him and made him burn with resentment at the thirty-year-old body in which he was obliged to operate now, but at the same time he gave way to the indulgence we all feel for the child that we once were.

He had an appointment with the shoe-maker, his sister's husband, but he could see that no-one had arrived as yet at the back table, drowned in stifling darkness. Just at his elbow, at an inferior table concealed by the open door, the gentle voice continued.

'Perhaps you don't recognise me, your father's friend.'

A spectral figure, convulsed now by an irritating cough on a peculiarly high note, a tenor cough.

'You won't have forgotten my cough. It's grown worse, I don't take pride in it, but it hasn't changed.'

Salvatore had heard it as a small boy through the bedroom floorboards, punctuating the long conversations with his father which soothed him little by little towards sleep.

'Pericle Sannazzaro. How are you, dottore?'

'Not dottore.'

'Ragionere?'

'Comrade.'

Salvatore embraced his father's friend and sat down beside him. 'I didn't know you were still living here in Mazzata.'

'Speaking with respect, of course you didn't. You don't know anything about me, why should you? I'm still a book-keeper, but now I've moved to Pantano. When I heard from your mother that you were coming, I availed myself of a lift from a business acquaintance of mine who travels in saucepans. Tomorrow is market day here, as always, that was why he was making the journey.'

The precise explanation was certainly not intended as a

reproach, but it acted as one. 'That was very good of you, ragionere.'

'I had a particular object in view.'

Sannazzaro offered his cigarette papers and a nearly empty packet of Nazionale tobacco.

'Thank you, I don't smoke. But can't I order you something?'

At once Salvatore regretted his nervous eagerness. The offer shouldn't have been made quite yet. In Florence he had lost the power of developing a subject with the proper delay and breadth of respect. But how much time, in duty to a dead father, must one waste on his faithful, coughing old friends?

'So you're making your career as a doctor, Mickey?'

'Yes, as a neurologist.'

'And it's all going well?'

'Not at all badly. You know how it is at the moment, things are getting better, production is up, the standard of living is higher, people are earning more money, and even the professionals have to benefit.'

Sannazzaro said nothing, and he went on, 'But I suppose it's childish to talk of things getting better, as though we were simply carried along from one situation to another. The Italians are imposing their will on history a little, after all these centuries, that's all.'

'Not in Mazzata.'

I know that, Salvatore thought furiously. Here I am at a disadvantage already with this frail old half-wit, with whom I'm sitting as a great favour, a favour to the dead.

'A doctor,' said Sannazzaro. 'Give me your hand.'

His touch was as cold and dry as a hen's foot.

'Let me hold it a little. Yes, the hand of a healer.'

'I don't know that we do all that much healing nowadays. The emphasis is on preventive medicine.'

Sannazzaro ignored this, and replaced the hand on the table as though it was something precious. Salvatore, with intense irritation, removed it from the oil-cloth. He ordered a mezzo of wine and two bottles of mineral water. 'Has it ever struck you,' said Sannazzaro in a melancholy tone, 'that the chances in life are not gone for ever, but that on the contrary they recur, so all that is asked of us is to recognise them? Of course, on their return they may not look quite the same. If you have ever watched floodwater going under a bridge you will have noticed that the flotsam is drawn irresistibly towards the dark arches, then vanishes, but if you cross over and keep an eye on the other side, it never seems to reappear.'

He paused, to cough a little. Salvatore tried to rally him a little.

'When did you ever see a river in flood?'

'In the Po valley, with your father, when we worked in Turin.'

The late afternoon card players were beginning to arrive, bringing a faint stir of activity to the stagnant Câfé Centrico. Pasquale, the proprietor, brought the mezzo of wine. Sannazzaro, ignoring it entirely, leant quietly forward.

'Mickey, do you believe in eternal life?'

'I was baptised, as you may possibly remember,' said Salvatore. 'I'm not sure that I want to discuss my present faith, or loss of faith, in these surroundings.' He lowered his voice. 'Why do you ask me?' Sannazzaro couldn't, surely, have heard of the absurd matter of the Inconsolabile.

'It's fifteen years now since your father was put into the earth. I miss him. Ultimately, what we human beings need most of all – I'm not speaking now in a political sense – is to be understood. You agree?'

'No,' said Salvatore.

'Still, your father, who was my closest, no, let me be honest, my only friend, is dead. That means he's gone for good, rotted away. You know of course that Antonio Gramsci spent whole nights in prison at Turi talking, I think to Trombetti, about the question of the after-life. Trombetti was a Bolognese. He shared Nino's cell in Turi.'

'I didn't know.'

'But you had the opportunity to speak to Nino?'

'I was ten years old. We didn't go to a prison, we went to a clinic in Rome.'

'Nino's great fear was that he might become so weakened

by illness that the priests would get permission to visit and corrupt him by talking of the imbecile promise of immortality which the Church holds out.'

'It's imbecile, but in my experience it's harmless. It doesn't seem to do any harm to my patients.'

Sannazzaro smiled indulgently. 'Let me explain. Nino believed in immortality, but an immortality of this earth. Every man survives in his useful and necessary actions. Every useful and necessary action passes from the father to the son – if he is a good son – in an unbroken chain.'

'I can't believe that Gramsci put that forward as a substitute for religion.'

'Why should men need a substitute for religion?' said Sannazzaro, trembling violently. 'Or women either? Do they need a substitute for unemployment, or a substitute for dysentery?'

Pasquale, who was hurling glasses into a bowl of warm water beneath the counter, looked at Salvatore and tilted his head a little backwards, nodding it up and down and half closing his eyes. This didn't indicate that he considered Sannazzaro mad, only a little cracked, a 'natural', and so, like nature, to be endured patiently. Salvatore did not make the gesture of response. It enraged him to see this pure unreproachable heart, this smalltime book-keeper who had all the nobility of life's authentic losers, sitting here in the musty Câfé Centrico, too used to ridicule even to notice it. On the other hand, Pasquale was a good sort and tolerated Sannazzaro, no doubt, whenever he came in, in a way that he himself couldn't. He was found guilty again, before a court he had never been asked to recognise. He saw himself being driven into a corner, without hope of defence, as a good son, and, more culpable still, as one who had been granted the opportunity to see Nino Gramsci in the flesh. To be reproached, what else could you call it, by the unknown Bolognese Trombetti, who, it seemed, shared the martyr's cell and preserved his thoughts on eternity, to be put down by the transparent humility of Sannazzaro, to be shamed by the casual kindness of Pasquale, what could be a more monstrous injustice to a hardworking man who had only a few days to spare for a business transaction? The old conscience, the old consciousness, risen from the dead in the form of a hollow nonentity in a book-keeper's jacket, reinforced at the cuffs.

'Mickey,' said Sannazzaro. 'I am going to ask you something. Don't sell your land. You don't mind my discussing your affairs?'

'I do mind, but since you've raised the subject, let me tell you that's exactly what my mother says.'

'And I, too, am saying it.'

Salvatore controlled himself. 'There's no mystery about it. At the present time I have a use for the money.'

Sannazzaro was convulsed for a few moments, reaching out for the mineral water with closed eyes and, from long practice, pouring it accurately into the glass. Salvatore, assuming the voice of the old-time practitioner, said: 'You should take care of that cough. Just because you've had it so long doesn't mean that it can't get worse.'

'Don't part with it lightly, Mickey. Don't sell it lightly. Hear me out. Your brothers are putting a rumour about that the Cassa del Mezzogiorno will grant a loan to rebuild the tomato paste factory. They hope to sell your land for building.'

'I know they're saying that. Why shouldn't they, if it amuses them?'

'Hear me out. Don't cut yourself off from Mazzata. Once you've sold your inheritance you'll be quite adrift. I don't say this as your mother does, for a woman's reasons, always hanging back, always frightened of change. These women, these women! If the world was in their hands, we should still be living in caves.'

'But there's nothing to keep me here, ragionere. There's nothing for me to do.' Perhaps the old man wanted him to apply for the job of community doctor. He looked at the seamed face, which struck him as having changed less than his own.

'As an intellectual, Mickey, your place is here. Here, in the country, intellectualism is poisoned at its source. Our duty, as Nino constantly told us, is to create intellectuals who owe nothing to the middle class, and who will resist the temptation to desert their birthplace for the cities. In this task the Party has failed us completely. You have the temperament for it and the education. Unfortunately you were encouraged from childhood by your mother not to co-operate, but to compete, to shoulder others aside and to advance yourself. When you told me just now that I should take care of my cough, I assume that you couldn't avoid calculating that your words, as a successful consultant, were worth let us say five thousand lire. Forgive me if the amount is wrong, I have no means of knowing the present scale of medical charges in Tuscany.'

'I don't know how much my words were worth,' muttered Salvatore.

'Mickey, they were worth nothing.'

'That's quite possible, but in that case I don't know why you call me an intellectual.'

'Every man is an intellectual,' Sannazzaro cried, 'even if not in the sense you're giving it, of a man whose words can be exchanged for cash. But not one in twenty thousand, or a hundred thousand, will take the place which an intellectual owes to society, that is, to say, to stay in the corner of the earth which gave him life and make himself listened to, as you are listening to me now. The future for which Nino suffered and died is impossible without human preparation. That was what your father expected of you. He had other sons, but you are the one he chose.'

Inconveniently, Salvatore now remembered clearly, as he hadn't done before, walking between his father and Sannazzaro, half bored, half angry at what he couldn't understand, and stopping by the case of sweets and biscuits in the piazza where Sannazzaro could be relied upon to draw out his shabby purse, more like a woman's, and treat him to something. That must have been the father of the present sweet-seller, and it was probably the same tricycle. One might think that they'd been waiting for twelve years in the dust and sunshine to betray him. All this, in common justice to himself, must be put a stop to.

'Listen,' he said, 'my land amounts to twenty hectares and a half. If one could get building permission, well and good, otherwise it's only fit for growing vegetables.'

By this time his elder sister, with the shoe-repairer, the chemist, and the local auctioneer, who also owned the garage, had arrived, with one or two supporters, at the Câfé Centrico. Out of convention they had waited for what they considered a correct interval before interrupting Salvatore's conversation with the crazy book-keeper, to which everyone in the place had been openly listening. Now time was up, and the sister and her husband advanced from their table to summon him. Sannazzaro, flustered by the presence of a woman in the câfé, sprang hurriedly to his feet. The sudden movement produced an unexplained sound of ripping or tearing, like a sharp sigh. The sister ignored both this and Sannazzaro himself. Salvatore had never detested her so much as at this moment. Pushing back his chair, he threw his arm round Sannazzaro and said tenderly, but almost at random:

'I want to tell you this, ragionere. I don't want to hide anything from you. I told you that I needed to raise some money, but it's possible that you don't know why. The fact is that I'm about to be married.'

At this Sannazzaro's face broadened into an indulgent smile. My God, Salvatore thought, even he doesn't believe it.

37

Chiara had been told that Salvatore was on a necessary visit to his mother. There was, of course, some truth in this. To endure the time until he came back she went to England. Barney was the only living being who was likely to understand what she felt at the moment.

Barney had told her O.K., come if you want to, but her father and mother, who never consulted each other's convenience or anyone else's, were away, though in separate places, for the next few months. They would let her know, they said, about their plans. To her disgust, Barney had found herself obliged to stay in London with her grandmother.

The grandmother lived in South Kensington, which Chiara remembered as a hushed district with no sky, no river and no air. But no matter, the house seemed beautiful to her, as everything at that time seemed beautiful. She loved No 23, Carlisle Gardens, the drawing-room watercolours in their thin gold-washed frames, the oils on heavy canvases, battered like a ship at sea, which hung in the dining-room, the butterflies embroidered in silk in the spare-room, the tapestry cover for the *Radio Times*, the cosseting of the windows in voluminous curtains, the beds submerged beneath under-blankets, blankets and blanket-covers, the crockery, the rockery, the immovable hall table on which lay blue-skied postcards from Barney's parents, saying that they felt much rested. Happiness destroys the aesthetic sense. When she had first met Salvatore at the concert she had known that the Brahms was badly played, now in her transfiguration she might not even have realised that.

'This place is the dregs,' said Barney.

The two of them lay in a heap in Barney's bedroom at the top of the house. It was very warm, with the murmurous central heating turned up to Full, Barney claiming that if you let yourself get too cold the hair on your legs grew more thickly. 'You have to watch it. You can get shaggy even above the knees. That's the trouble about a really cold house like Painstake.'

'Painstake!'

'You forgot, I don't blame you.'

'But Barney, did you go there?'

'I went there.'

'But what happened? What did?'

On the other side of the door an elderly voice, worn but clear, said, 'Is one permitted to enter?'

Barney's grandmother never knocked on young people's doors, because it might look as though she didn't trust them. She preferred to make some little remark, quite lightly. The door-handle turned and she came in, wearing a soft knitted suit with a Jaeger scarf signed Jaeger, and a Hermès scarf tucked through the belt and signed Hermès. This gave her an air of authenticity, but her expression was uncertain and discontented.

'This is Chiara Ridolfi, Granny. You weren't here when she arrived. Cha, this is my grandmother, Lady Jones.'

Chiara sprang up to shake hands, to apologise, to thank, and to take some small presents from Chiasso Cornino out of her suitcase.

'My dear, what pretty things, what pretty, pretty things! It's astonishing what a trick the Italians have for making these pretty things. Not like those straw hats that we used to wear from the Far East that had to be made by little children, poor creatures, sitting under water. No, with these things you can tell there was joy in the making.' She held them to her breast and looked restlessly round the room in search of something that could be tidied or altered a little without giving offence.

'I hope you're looking after your guest, Lavinia. I hope you'll see that she has fun. Are you having fun, my dear?'

Lady Jones had an unwholesome craving for admissions from young girls that fun was being had. Indeed, time spent without fun she apparently thought of as squandered.

'You're both of you going out this evening, I take it?'

'No, we aren't,' said Barney.

'But wouldn't it be amusing to go out dancing? Of course, you'd have to find a partner for your friend. Italians are always so light on their feet. I might be able to help, you know, if you couldn't think of anyone. I could telephone round a little.'

Barney said nothing, and Lady Jones, with a certain amount of hesitation, as though she was practising leaving the room, went out.

'I know she's a case,' said Barney. 'She always talks like that. One of these days I'll have a man hidden in the cupboard for her to find, what delirium for her. But you shouldn't have been so polite to her, Cha. It's the same old story. It encourages her, and besides, it's foreign.'

'How long ago did she lose her husband?'

'I've no idea. I think he deputy-governed something somewhere.'

'What did he die of?'

'I don't know. Fun, perhaps.'

Barney suddenly burst into tears. It seemed not possible,
and had never been seen to happen before. Swine that I am,
Chiara thought, inhuman that I am, why didn't I ask her
about it earlier?

'All I want you to do is to look at me,' Barney sobbed.

It was like one of those portents or miracles, when to the
terror of the lookers-on a great statue weeps, the very thing it
was created not to do.

'Just look at me, Cha. Do I look any different from usual?'

'Just at the moment, yes, of course you do. Otherwise no,
you always look the same.'

'I didn't want you to say that.'

'I'm sorry.'

'I know it's true. People don't see any change. They see I
look just the same and so they think I don't feel anything.'

'I don't think you don't feel anything.'

Chiara put her arms round her heaving friend.

'What happened about your He?'

It seemed that Barney now called him the Disaster. The
change had taken place in one day, less than one day. 'It
started off quite well, Painstake was just as usual. You know
what Painstake's like.'

Chiara had been there once, and did know. Curiously
enough the house looked, at least from the front drive, rather
like the Ricordanza. It had been built about 1734 or so in the
Italian taste, a Ricordanza set down in the East wind among
many acres of Norfolk turnips and plough and the nobly
spreading leaves of great cabbages.

Across these acres Barney had tramped and turned and
tramped again. She had things all to herself, none of the other
females were going to turn up till lunch time. At every stand she
took up her position close to the He and up to mid-day she had
felt that she wanted him more than anything on earth. The last
stand was at the end of a ride which formed a sort of wind-tunnel

for an icy north-west gale. By this time, Barney said, they understood each other perfectly. Words had not been necessary, and she herself had never been a great believer in them. But as the Land Rover bringing the lunch came jolting up the cart-track he had said, 'Thank the Lord!' then, turning to watch it arrive, 'I'm afraid I'm rather a clod about my food.'

One chance remark can do it, one change of the angle of vision under the clouds and wind. Looking at him in the clear light of a Norfolk mid-day, Barney had seen a thin trickle of saliva leaving the corner of his mouth.

'It was all like a revelation. He'd described himself exactly. He was a clod.'

'But Barney, that was nothing, he just dribbled, it wasn't enough.'

'Anything's enough if you've got the wits to understand it. This Rossi man behaved like a lunatic at the Harringtons, but you couldn't care less because unfortunately you're totally blinded by love.'

To Barney it had been a release from blindness. She had gone back to the house with the Land Rover. She broke down once again while recounting the horror of sitting through dinner next to the Disaster, considerably placed beside her by the hostess, chair to chair, thigh to thigh as he edged and fingered her in the shelter of the starched table-cloth, confident of his welcome.

'He went on and on, finally I had to pretend to reach down for something and take the opportunity to run a fork into his hand.'

'Did you draw blood, Barney?'

'I think so. Oh, he's got ordinary animal courage, if that's what you want.'

She let her firm weight slide gradually down onto the carpet. To Chiara it seemed like the fall of the great Barney, whose judgments had for so long seemed beyond dispute.

'I seem to hear laughter,' said Lady Jones on the far side of the door again. 'Such a joyous sound in this house nowadays. Of course I'm not asking to be admitted to your councils. I only came in case you might have forgotten the time.'

'We're not laughing, I promise you, Lady Jones,' called out Chiara.

38

Before going away Chiara had of course told her father that she wanted to be married at some time that would be convenient for everybody, but as soon as possible. She was in love with Dr Salvatore Rossi, the neurologist. Giancarlo was very much surprised, but he had given up the habit of showing his emotions and felt this was probably not the moment to go back to it. He asked when they were to have the pleasure of seeing the doctor at via Limbo.

'As soon as he comes back,' said Chiara. 'He had to go away. He went away seven hours and forty-three minutes ago. You understand that he can't have time off just as he likes.'

Her happiness was not discussed, it wasn't necessary, it could be felt and seen and seemed to stir the air, rather uncomfortably, between them.

'But you're in touch with him, my dear, he'll telephone us?'

It turned out that there was no telephone where Dr Rossi was staying and that although he could ring from the câfé, Chiara couldn't endure the thought of waiting all day for calls without knowing when they'd come. She would like to go back to England for the unendurable week. The telephone, with its power of idiot silence, had become her enemy. Giancarlo thought that she might regret this, and also that she seemed to have been home for a very short time – he wished now that he hadn't made the expedition to Rome – but he said nothing.

Not long after Chiara had left her aunt suddenly reappeared from Vienna. It was a city for old people, she said, for the superannuated and depressives and for women wearing felt hats – but think what they have suffered, my dear, said Giancarlo – human sufferings aren't to be thought about, said

Maddalena, only the human future. One thought might lead to the other, he replied, and then broke the news of Chiara's engagement. 'A young doctor, very well thought of.' Maddalena remembered something, though not exactly, about a concert.

That evening Monsignor Gondi rang up, the family duty call which, however, he always made as useful as possible. Before the engagement could be so much as mentioned he launched, once again, with his usual insane persistence over small details, into the matter of L'Inconsolabile. He was trying to complete his case notes before presenting the entire report on the city's activities to the Cardinal Archbishop of Florence. These notes, by the way, showed that Rossi senior had been a communist activist and an associate of Antonio Gramsci.

It was Maddalena who took this call. All day she had been out at the Ricordanza. For some reason, perhaps connected with her visit to Vienna, she had arrived there in her 'English' mood, and caused consternation by saying that the place looked cheerless and that she would 'do the flowers'. To do the flowers *all 'inglese* she needed gloves, scissors, a certain kind of pinafore, a pantry with a cupboard full of vases and glass jars and a sink, none of which were to hand at the Ricordanza – and, of course, flowers, which the Ricordanza did not provide either. Behind the evergreen private garden there were quantities of rambler roses, of a variety peculiar to this one villa alone, the result of a cross made in 1913 by the Ridolfi gardener between a wichuriana and the deep purple old-fashioned Tuscany – but 'rambler' was not the appropriate word for the rose, which in defiance of the seasons, and even of gravity, extended in deeper and deeper masses over the south-western wall. The notion of pruning had been given up for many years. Roses could be seen even in the darkness at the heart of the bushes. But they were in no way suitable for decoration or arrangement, only branches several metres long could be dragged down, spattering a myriad petals and, even in a dry autumn, drops of moisture. Apart from these roses there was only what was growing in pots on the front terraces. 'You should have given detailed instructions,' Giancarlo pointed out. Maddalena felt, every year, that she must have done so.

At the Ricordanza it had not been possible to check discussion of the Contessina's arrival there, a week earlier, with a man. The gardener had been told by a friend who was delivering a roll of barbed wire at Sangallo that she had been driving a farm truck from the direction of Villa Harrington and a man had been following her on a Vespa. The gardener himself had been coming and going, because this was the day which he reserved for selling the plants he grew on his own account, and, since these were women's matters, he had to tell his story, in an indirect way, through his wife. He had heard the van going away and seen it leave for Florence, but not the Vespa, it must have gone back to Lo Scampolo. No-one could identify the man, but everyone was ready to speculate.

Maddalena couldn't see any advantage in her brother knowing what was being said either at the Villa or by the Monsignore. Her heart sank at the thought of making further enquiries. The Ridolfi were puzzlers, rather than schemers. Without enthusiasm she learned that Dr Rossi was brilliantly clever. Clever people are not happy. Another piece of information was that the doctor didn't have girl-friends, but a mistress, in the old-fashioned way. This, perhaps, might be considered reassuring.

'I shall be here rather longer than I thought,' she said. 'I shall have one or two things to arrange which I didn't expect, I mean before we announce the engagement.'

To her surprise, Giancarlo told her that he didn't like to see her looking so worried.

'You mean I'm looking ugly.'

'I do mean that, yes. Evidently Vienna wasn't a success. Perhaps there was some miscalculation. Perhaps after all the von Hötzendorfs don't much like you.'

'They do like me. You can't be mistaken about that. About being loved yes, about being liked, no.'

'In any case, I think you need a little more rest.'

'You can't have been listening to me. I told you I had a number of things, or I suppose you might call it one thing, to see to.'

'How long will you need?'

'I don't know yet, you must let me take my own time.'

'Of course, my dear, who else's? But I still believe that it would be a good idea, grateful though I am for your company, for you to take a little holiday.'

'In God's name, a holiday from what?' asked Maddalena. It struck her that he was almost anxious for her to go. In this she was quite right. Giancarlo was afraid that she might find out, if she stayed in Florence much longer, what Annunziata had repeated to him on hearsay from the gardener's wife's sister-in-law, who had called at the Ricordanza not knowing that it was still half shut-up, and hoping that extra help might be needed in the house. The Contessina had been seen walking through the limonaia and into the house with a man, who must have induced her to go upstairs, and later shutters had been thrown open and the white summer bedcovers had been flung out to air and they had been laughing, the two of them, like children at a joke.

'Not much concealment there,' said the Count. Annunziata and he had been allies for so long (drawn even closer now, if possible, by their dread of Barney) that he did not need even to hint at instructions. He did not need to say that by means of one threat or another the depositions of the gardener's wife's sister-in-law must be silenced. But poor Maddalena mustn't on any account be concerned with the matter, and above all he wanted to avoid asking Chiara about it, because she would tell him the truth.

39

Maddalena's mind moved from point to point not rationally but in a series of clear bright pictures, showing what had been and what ought to be. Her memory worked for her without the inconvenience of regret. It was in good repair. Called upon, it reminded her that at the beginning of the summer one of the Corsini, or it might have been one of the Capponi, or both described Chiara as getting wet, or soaking wet, during the interval at the Teatro della Pergola because she had been talking to a man, a doctor, introduced by Mimi Limentani. He was said to have done Mimi a great deal of good.

She called on Mimi, who was back from her first summer vacation. Mimi, out of sheer kindness of heart, treated all visits as an unexpected honour. She paced her gleaming apartment on seven-centimetre heels, nodding her head apparently as a hen does, as a necessary part of the movement, ringing for tea, and picking up this thing or that thing which might interest or please her caller. Maddalena, she knew, had imposed a kind of pact on her not to discuss either her grandchildren or her illnesses. Nothing about those, then, but there must be other subjects; there was a vast new book she had just bought in via Tornabuoni, drawings attributed to Bertoldo di Giovanni. On huge expanses of thick paper appeared reproductions of faint scribbles in red chalk, a nose, part of a ladder, a horse's rump.

'They're so interesting, one could look at them for hours.'

She lowered the weighty volume onto Mad's fragile knees.

'Are you quite well, Mimi?'

Maddalena shut the book, the great pages closing with a voluptuous slap. Mimi's short-sighted, swimming gaze brightened. She could scarcely believe her luck.

'Oh, but you haven't come here to listen to my aches and pains. In any case, I don't really want to talk about them.'

This was manifestly untrue, and Mimi began to explain how a certain pain, originating at the base of her spine – she wouldn't try to show exactly where because that would mean twisting round and might start it off again – how this pain travelled gradually upwards, always towards the right shoulder, then across to the left shoulder, then, unless she was very lucky – she called those her white days – it began to travel back again, but here was what she was always told was the unusual and interesting thing, it didn't always take the same route back again, sometimes it even seemed to waver a little, as though wondering which direction to take.

'Who told you your pain was unusual and interesting?'

Mimi seemed a little dashed.

'I mean, which doctor told you that? Weren't you consulting someone in particular?'

'Well, I'm afraid I've consulted rather a lot of people. I don't ask much of them, you know. All I'm really looking for is freedom from pain even for a few weeks so that I can sort out my life a little and have more of it to give to my friends.'

Perhaps she really does suffer, Mad thought. I must bear that in mind.

Under close interrogation, Mimi remembered seeing Chiara at the Teatro della Pergola quite well, or said she did. Dear Chiara, such a fair complexion, sometimes she had a good colour, sometimes she looked for all the world like the Bimba Ammalata. This doll, the Sick Child, was one of the latest products of the delicacy and ingenuity of Italian commercial design. Mimi, as she now admitted, had bought three of them for her descendants, and she tapped and nodded away to her bedroom to fetch them. The dolls had little girls' faces of waxen pallor, and seemed to be on the point of living and breathing.

'I can't bring myself to wrap them up. Believe me, I'm dreading the moment when my grand-daughters come to fetch them.'

'You can always get yourself a couple of dozen more at Anichini's,' said Maddalena tartly. 'Put them away, Mimi, and never mind Chiara's complexion. Don't forget, we were talking about your health.'

Mimi sat down.

'You're so good to me today, Maddalena.'

'I'm exactly the same as usual.'

'As a matter of fact there's something I wanted to ask you. You asked me just now who I'd been consulting, and that made me think of it. I've heard, only I can't remember where, that there's a very good young doctor, a nerve-doctor, at one of the hospitals, a young man called Salvatore Rossi. Do you know anything about him?'

I should never have come here, Maddalena thought. It was idiotic.

40

On the day after next, however, there appeared under *Ringraziamenti*, the Thanks section of the *Nazione*, a paragraph repeated twenty-five times, so that it filled the entire column:

Ringraziamento. I wish to thank from the bottom of my heart Doctor Salvatore Rossi of this city, who has cured me of innumerable grievous illnesses which have tormented me for many years. The burden has now been lifted from me and I wish only to express the depths of my gratitude.

Miriam Limentani, Piazetta Spini-Ferroni 2.

Maddalena had all the Ridolfi trust in the triumph of good intentions. She was not surprised, but she felt justified. Sheer gratitude at having been allowed to discuss her ailments must have induced in Mimi a sense of unworthiness, and guilt must have prompted the memory. Or more likely she had summoned another friend to help her with her recollections, more tea, more nodding and tapping, more vaguely diffused benevolence, and the waxen Sick Children no doubt brought forth again – these, for some reason, had been a particular irritation to Maddalena – still, there it was, honourable amends, twenty-five paragraphs from one who thought she had been done good to.

By way of an answer to the Monsignore's telephone call she sent him a copy of the *Nazione*, writing across one corner that Dr Rossi was known throughout the city and its environs as the Angel of Healing. Giancarlo never read the newspapers, and professed not to know what she was doing.

41

Nothing would have kept Chiara in London except the sight of Barney's collapse. She didn't dare, in the name of humanity itself, to leave Kensington until Barney, reviving, had begun to hector her again in the old way. It was heartening to be told once again what to do and what not. There was a reassurance, as though some familiar domestic force, gravity perhaps, had been temporarily overwhelmed and reasserted itself.

'Cha, you'll have to make up your mind quite seriously to do something about him. You'd better draw up a list and stick to it very carefully. I expect your father and your aunt are going round Florence at this very moment, trying to make out that he's not as frightful as he seems.'

'What's that got to do with it?' asked Chiara absently, seeing that it would be all right for her to book into the next flight for Pisa.

But she arrived a day later than Salvatore, who was furious to find out that she was still away, and immensely glad to have the extra time to dispose of. Having made a first agreement to the sale at Mazzata, he had to see his lawyer at once, and then (for he too tried to work to a list) put aside the evening for the purpose of having an explanation with Marta.

When he got the appointment in Florence Salvatore had determined, at the grave risk of seeming old-fashioned and provincial, to make a regular arrangement with a reliable young woman. In that way he would keep both freedom and control. Greatly to his irritation, Marta was a dressmaker. A dressmaker, what else, what a comedy, and on that account he would probably have broken with her long ago, except that it's difficult to put an end to something that has started for no particular reason. If a reason had to be given it might have been convenience, since she lived not so very far from the hospital.

Marta's great attraction, on the other hand, had always been considered by her family to be her hair. She kept it long. On Tuesday evenings, since there was no hot water in the flats where she lived, she had it washed next door at the hairdresser's for whom in return she did a little sewing. Her married sister, with whom she shared a flat, had told her never to cut it, as it was something a man couldn't resist.

This hair of Marta's was somewhere between blonde and brown, a colour which, Marta's sister continued, rapidly drove men mad. Franca claimed the right to say these things, presumably, by right of seniority and of possessing the experience of marriage, although it was pretty clear that Dr Rossi was not being driven mad in the least and that Franca's experiences in the Empire style matrimonial bed were not very different from Marta's in the top room. This room was next to a kind of loft open to the sky where the washing was hung up to dry; it was divided by a curtain. Behind the curtain was a divan bed, a looking glass and a row of hooks, so that the customers could hang up their things when they came for fittings. The floor was usually covered with long pieces of white tacking thread which Marta energetically pulled out and threw down as the fitting advanced. Near the window she had her Necchi on its own table, her armchair and a pile of back copies of *Vogue* and *Moda* and *Marilyn*, tattered with leafing through. Marta also liked Funny-Books. Some of these told the story of the film in pictures, others the lives of the saints. Waiting for her to come upstairs one evening Salvatore had been reduced to looking through a Funny containing the story of a charitable monk, who caused a beggar's fleas, through prayer, to be transformed into pure gold. Marta came upstairs tired, but with her hair washed and shining.

'Why do you read this rubbish?'

She looked at him with the tolerance of a household pet who has learnt to consider anger as a game. Besides, how could anyone be angry about a book?

This evening Marta was at home, still in her black dressmaker's overall. She gave him her usual smile and began to undress. A mistress in an attic, waiting from one Wednesday to another, why doesn't she break into an aria, or both of us into a duet? They would have to finish the duet in harmony, in spite of the fact that he would be singing 'we must part' while she, an octave above, was repeating 'forever'. Marta stood looking at him with her tailored blouse in her hands. She was thirty-eight. Without this blouse and her Favorita bra, the only thing she wore that she didn't make for herself, her untidy breasts fell sideways. 'Get dressed again,' said Salvatore. The next thing, from long-established habit, should have been for him to take off her glasses.

'Don't you want it?'

'I want to talk to you seriously,' he said, walking about the room. 'I want you to attend to me, but without any feeling of resentment, there mustn't be any question of that.'

Afterwards he usually took her out to dinner at Frizzi, although she scarcely ate anything, so that she could wave at her friends and show them that she was still going with that doctor of hers. No Frizzi tonight.

The speech prepared by Salvatore as he came along a little while earlier had a political and indeed a moral basis. We were now half way through the nineteen fifties, the war had been over for more than ten years. 'It's time that we began to accept, for good or ill, the changes that have been forced upon us.' Marta, he had reflected, might interrupt him at that point and say, 'Don't I know it, no-one cares for anything now except easy money,' but he would tell her he meant something of greater importance than that. 'I mean the question of using our own free will to break out of prison – we all of us live in our own self-created prisons and we may be in danger of forgetting that this is what they are. In Italy the relationships between men and women have been fixed I suppose since long before the Christian era, but it doesn't mean that because they have lasted so long that they are necessarily right, or that there is no hope of changing them. Italy has been hurried into the twentieth century, we're all aware of that, and we must face it with reason and courage. The relationship between us has been, I hope, one of affection, but also of physical need and financial convenience. Has it ever occurred to you, Marta,

136

that whereas you've accepted overnight the miracles of Olivetti and Necchi, your dependence on men as a sex and your subservience to them is quite archaic? The truth is, however, and it's your duty to recognise this clearly, that every human relationship should be an equal partnership. It's here that I think you'll have to admit that you're falling short.'

He waited before beginning these remarks for Marta's complete attention. She hadn't put on her blouse again. With her back turned to him she was pouring water into the pot to boil up for the coffee. She looked as she bent down over the gas-ring like a half-peeled pear, the upper half shadowed down the deeply grooved spine, pale, but not very succulent.

'Marta,' he said, 'I'm in love. I shall get married. I shall get married for love. I shan't be able to see you again.'

The words surprised him as much as if someone else had spoken them, never mind, they had been said and would have to do. There would be time later for the more reasonable remarks he had prepared. Marta was still watching the coffee-pot whose tin lid had begun to chink slightly as it rose with the steam.

She said, 'Well, but aren't you always telling me that you don't hold with the old conventions and the old way of doing things?'

Salvatore wondered whether it was possible that he had made part of his prepared speech to her on some former occasion. He struggled to keep his temper. It struck him that both Marta and Chiara took advantage of him by attacking him with their ignorance, or call it innocence. A serious thinking adult had no defence against innocence because he was obliged to respect it, whereas the innocent scarcely knows what respect is, or seriousness either.

Before he could go on Marta said, 'But what about the money? How will you manage?' Seeing him stupefied, she explained, 'After all, you're not so very well off.' She used the old-fashioned term, 'not in easy circumstances', and added that she'd seen him taking his own suits to the cleaners.

'Do you mean that you've been following me?' He realised now that women might be murdered for very trivial causes.

Marta had perhaps followed him by some means or other as far as the Ricordanza when he had pressed his forehead against the cold pattern of the iron gates. But it was almost equally infuriating to be spied upon at the dry cleaners. Of course, in the first instance, he had naturally followed Marta, or rather he had said, when he first spotted her, 'May I see you as far as your house?' How had she looked then? Reasonably pretty, short-sighted even with her glasses, not quite middle-aged yet, biddable, pliant, a ready listener, quite unreluctant, except that the first call on her room was for clients' fittings. And that, after all, had been three years ago.

Marta told him that she'd watched him at the dry cleaners in order to understand him better. She went on commiserating with him, in a loud, firm voice. She had seen an article in a magazine about the disgracefully low salaries of hospital doctors in Italy. They could hardly hold up their heads, this writer had said, in comparison with professional people from the rest of Europe. Italian doctors, poor wretches, she repeated more gently, shaking her head a little. 'You know how it'll be, you'll have to start married life sharing with your wife's relations, and that'll mean a lot of give and take.'

'I haven't come here to discuss my own future arrangements,' said Salvatore, 'I don't require your advice.'

'Of course, it's better if you've got two kitchens, or even a gas-ring like this one.'

Bitterness or jealousy would have been tolerable and indeed quite in place, but no-one could mistake her genuine sympathy.

'It's not as though you had any family of your own in the city, they're all somewhere down south.'

'How the hell do you know that?'

'Somebody must have told me. Yes, Signor Gentilini told me.'

'Have you been out with him?' That was beyond belief. But Marta, it seemed, had been waiting in the rain one Friday evening at a bus-stop and Gentilini had given her a lift in his car. He had recognised her from seeing her at Frizzi's. The revelation that these two could have talked about him when he wasn't there confounded Salvatore. Traitors both. Grasping at what he could remember of his speech, which seemed to be standing by him as his one reliable friend, he began at last on the topic of Italy in 1955 and the need for a new concept of woman's place in the social structure. Marta confronted him with her arms folded four-square, as though ready for a long conversation with the neighbours on the price of fish.

'It's the women who hang back, as if they were afraid to give up their subservience. Women! If the world was in their hands we should still be living in caves.' He had the impression that he was repeating something said by someone else. 'As long as you agree with an assumption, it will continue to dominate you. Refuse your consent, and you're free.'

'Like Ingrid,' said Marta.

She was looking at the wall just behind his head and he felt compelled to turn round and look at the highly-coloured tear-out of Ingrid Bergman with Roberto Rossellini and their twins.

'If they'd been married the twins couldn't have been more beautiful,' Marta said.

'Have you been listening to me at all?'

'Yes, I have,' said Marta. 'You're finishing with me, but you don't want me to take up with anyone else.'

'That wasn't my meaning. You can't have thought that was what I meant.'

Marta turned off the gas under the coffee-pot and sat down heavily in one of her armchairs, letting her head fall sideways so that her face was hidden. He could see the nape of her neck with the thick shining hair, as though she was reaching for him blindly through the back of her neck. The attitude was familiar and Salvatore felt relieved. The money was in its envelope and she had never accused him of being ungenerous, only of being badly-paid. No Frizzi tonight, no struggling in the terribly inconvenient narrow bed in the fitting-room, best to kiss her once firmly on the neck, that will leave both of us with a good opinion of ourselves, she'll think I couldn't restrain myself and I shall believe that I'm not a hard man. Marta sat up, put both hands to the back of her head to tidy her hair and asked for a cigarette.

'How old is she, the woman you're marrying?'

'Eighteen.'

'Who is she?'

Salvatore reflected that she would know soon enough, it would be a matter for the newspapers, and that nothing in heaven or earth would stop his going ahead. There was also the luxury of repeating the name.

'Chiara Ridolfi.'

'Oh, the Contessina. I know her.'

'You don't!' Salvatore shouted.

Twenty-one years earlier Marta had been taken on at Parenti's for a period of training. Later she had been given a part-time job. Two of the girls she had worked with were still there, one in charge of the staff washroom, the other, who had done much better for herself, a head machinist, and Marta still did a bit of sewing and pressing there at busy times. She had been there on the day of the Ridolfi visit and had seen aunt and niece depart together. It was one of the excitements of the workrooms that the Commendatore might, without giving warning, refuse to 'make'.

'They walked away together. We could see them in the street. The young girl was crying bitterly.'

'How could you see at that distance?'

'I could tell.'

'Have you the least idea whether she was crying or not?'

'No.'

Salvatore knew nothing about Parenti except that he now felt an impulse to visit the establishment and fling the aged Commendatore down the stairs.

'You have to take life as it comes,' she said.

He gave her the cigarette and the envelope containing the money, to which he had added enough for the last fifteen instalments on her new machine. Marta counted it through twice.

'You're sure?'

'Yes, yes.'

'You're a good man, doctor. Don't go for just a moment.

My sister will want to say goodbye to you. She must be back by now. She won't want a good man like you to leave the house without saying a word to him.' Salvatore was appalled. Why not call them all in, the sister's husband and children, the friends and acquaintances from Frizzi, the clients, the hairdresser, the tripe-seller from the corner of the street, Gentilini, let it be a farewell in style.

'God bless you and your work,' said Marta in a deep, serious tone, 'you will know what I mean by that.'

'I don't know at all.' Evidently she was not going to cry, as when she felt like doing so she always took off her glasses. 'You can cry a little, if you like.'

'That would be boring,' said Marta. 'When I first met you, you told me that to be boring was the unforgivable sin.'

Good God, thought Salvatore, does she think she's never bored me? The door trembled, and Marta's sister, broad and highly-coloured, advanced, without knocking, into the room. Salvatore had always been her hero because of his defence of the Inconsolabile. She was violently anti-clerical and thought of him as her ally against the machinations of the priests. Now she flung down a copy of the *Nazione*, folded at Mimi's advertisements, seized both Salvatore's hands, and noisily kissed them.

'Miracle worker, you honour our house.'

Salvatore told himself that he hadn't controlled the situation in the way that he had planned because his energies had become fragmented. This in turn was due partly to Marta's unaccountable reactions and partly because of the image she had left with him of Chiara walking down the via delle Caldaie in tears. Impossible, with an idea like that in one's mind, to conduct a reasonable conversation with another woman, let alone two others, one of them waving a newspaper at him like a maniac.

Later that evening Gentilini asked him: 'How did you get out of the room in the end?'

'I don't know. Backwards, perhaps.'

'Exits are the most difficult part of life. Still, Marta wasn't a bad sort. There are a good many worse women than Marta.'

He saw that Salvatore couldn't as yet have seen the announcements in the *Nazione*, but thought he would wait a little while longer before mentioning them.

42

When Aunt Mad had written her letter to the Monsignore she drove out again to the Ricordanza. Apart from any other concern, the Azienda Autonoma di Turismo had just notified the Count that they were considering the villa for next season's tour of the most beautiful houses and gardens. This, like Mad's lost fingers, seemed a tax only to be expected. It was the Count's business to confer with the gardener and the gardener's family as to what kind of a front could be put on things. Maddalena only had to prepare them a little.

She arrived, however, to find only one subject of conversation still. The entire neighbourhood had come to the conclusion that since the Vespa, on the remembered sunny afternoon, had never been seen to go on to Florence, and since it had come from Lo Scampolo, it must certainly in the end have gone back there. The man in question, then, the violator, must have been Toby Harrington. Signor Toby had a black Vespa, no question about that. As a result the Harringtons, who had hoped to live and entertain their friends in a land of smiles, found themselves looked at with resentment and could scarcely get served at the crossroad grocers.

This fortunate turn of affairs proved to Aunt Mad that she had gone the right way about things. Good intentions, she had always known, justify themselves. In due time, also, it led to the Count's visit to his nephew, and to Cesare's message: Let Chiara's wedding be at Valsassina, but no caterers, and not the Harringtons.

Part Two

1

Cesare had said that it would suit him best to have the wedding in February, before Lent, and before the ploughing and dead-wooding began. Perhaps he had not expected sunshine, but the day was so fine and windless that although there was still snow on the hills they were able, once the fires were lit, to leave the front door open so that the guests could walk in and out of the house as they chose. The almond trees were in full bloom already. Sometimes you do get weather like that in February.

The battered little church below Valsassina was too small for all the guests to be asked to the wedding and the nuptial mass. It was crowded out, then emptied, and left with a bewildered and dishevelled air, its one bell swinging against the blue sky in its open wooden belfry. From the church and from the Sangallo road the cars streamed up to the farm. Like defending troops the lines of bottles stood ready. Champagne was not served, only the last year's Reserve, probably the best ever produced at Valsassina.

So many of these people knew each other, and approached each other, dressed to the nines, at high pitch, that Cesare saw that his first duty was to look after any strangers. Inside the house, in the passageway, he found the enormously tall English girl, strong enough to shoulder a sack of grain, to whom he had been introduced outside the church. She was standing by herself, looking at the painting of a mythological subject on the cassone.

'You're interested in these paintings, signorina?'

'No, not a bit,' said Barney.

'Well, we shall soon be sitting down to lunch, then there'll be no need to look at these things.'

Barney looked at him sombrely. 'This is your place, isn't it?' Cesare nodded.

'You're the cousin?'

With an effort he replied, 'Yes, I'm the cousin. Today everyone must enjoy themselves.'

'I can't see why,' said Barney. 'I'm not at all sure that Cha ought to marry this man. What do you think?' He said nothing and she repeated, 'What do you think?'

2

Looking at the photographs of a wedding taken nearly thirty years ago one can't believe that so many, who now look as they do, once looked like *that*. This is particularly true of the pictures taken from one end of the tables, down the whole length of them, the guests leaning forwards, most of them with their best faces ready, a few unawares, thinking about something else except themselves. The unselfconscious are likely to be caught in strange attitudes which can now no longer be explained. Professor Pulci, for instance, seems in one of the pictures to be earnestly holding out some dish or other, as though taking up a collection for charity – this was the Professor Pulci who, in 1944, sat gravely checking his catalogues of missing objects, working among broken sewers and gas-mains and after midnight in the candle-lit rooms of the Palazzo Medici-Riccardi, ignoring both the American Commission for the Protection of Cultural Treasures and its British counterpart, ignoring also the German positions a few hundred yards away in Forteza da Basso. Half of everything she knew about pictures Chiara had learned from him as she grew up without quite realising it, seeing him in this house or that, frowning, pointing or explaining. He had been one of her true educators, so too had been the head teacher from her primary school, embittered now because the free school dinners were to be abolished – she was perhaps best avoided by anyone who didn't feel like discussing this matter – but in the photographs even she looks radiant and is therefore practically unrecognisable. One arm is raised and she seems to be on the point of grasping Bernardino as he waits to serve in his white cotton gloves.

At another table, the smiles are more controlled. It can be seen that Monsignor Gondi is now on good, if stiffish, terms with Salvatore. The parish priest, a little deaf, is smiling with great geniality. He refuses, however, to be impressed, and wouldn't have been if a Cardinal or an Archbishop had come to solemnise the marriage. At the opposite end, among the guests from América (though not Chiara's mother) and from England (though not Aunt Mad's husband), Mad herself looks unexpectedly cloudy, like one of those images in a 'spirit' photograph which is later explained as a fault in the negative. Giancarlo always photographed well, he would have been ashamed not to. He bends towards Signora Rossi, Salvatore's mother, agreed not (from this angle, at least) to look much like her son. And then Chiara, evidently without a care in the world, so lucky in that she always looked at her best in white, no jewellery, though, not even those small diamonds.

3

Annunziata had brought the tablecloths and the best napkins from via Limbo, causing offence to everyone at Valsassina except Cesare, but creating long and narrow spaces of pure starched whiteness, seeming to invite stains, which soon appeared. The fault lay with the generosity of the Tuscan food, with its wealth of meat and of one sauce only, the salza rossa, as though Abundance was running to meet Need, careless of appearances. Mimi Limentani was asked, 'Surely you're forbidden to eat meat?'

'They've forbidden me to eat everything, cara. By this time I don't know what's going to kill me.'

4

Lady Jones had come in default of Barney's parents. They were escaping the winter elsewhere. 'The Count is quite delightful. And his sister, too, of course.' She looked round restlessly. 'If only it was Rome, there would be somebody one knew from the Embassy.'

5

From Mazzata, only Salvatore's mother had come. The brothers, the sister, the shoemender, had declined the invitation. Salvatore had expected this, knowing that they would be mortally offended at finding that he had told them the truth. If they had known it was the truth they would have offered him even less for the part-share.

To his mother he had sent quantities of money for travelling expenses, suggesting that she should ask Sannazzaro to come with her and look after her. This was quite implausible, and as a means of paying Sannazzaro's fare without hurting his feelings it had evidently failed completely, for the old man had not even written. In church and at the lunch Signora Rossi was being looked after first by the Count, then by Gentilini, and now more successfully still by his wife. The Gentilini children had disappeared to make a nuisance of themselves on the farm. The two mothers, old and middle-aged, recited their trials and sorrows. Sons were so much more trouble to bring up than daughters, yet the reward was greater. Strange to think that there were so many human beings born into the world, millions every day, and yet no two were alike. A mother would always know her own. The more suffering he caused her, the more she would recognise and welcome him. A man has only to look honestly at his mother and he knows himself a child again.

Fortunately Salvatore was unable to hear these remarks. He was at the head of the next table but one, talking to Aunt Mad. Suddenly she turned round to Cesare, who was patrolling the tables, and said:

'When the time comes for speeches, it is you who should speak.'

'But I don't speak,' said Cesare. 'You know that, aunt.'

'You could say something pleasant about Salvatore, a kind of introduction.'

'I don't know anything about him,' said Cesare mildly.

'I certainly don't want to be described,' said Salvatore. 'That's one thing I hope to be spared, to know exactly what kind of man I am.'

'Well, I should be glad to know what kind of man you are,' said Aunt Mad.

'The kind that loves your niece Chiara, and would give his life for her.'

In the atmosphere of wine and winter sunshine this sounded not at all absurd, in fact it was not absurd and no-one thought it was. Aunt Mad seemed moved, others sitting nearby also seemed moved and began to clap their hands in frank admiration. Mad looked up again at Cesare, who said calmly, 'You see how much better he speaks than I do.'

6

'Such a quaint old man,' said Lady Jones. 'Such a character. If only one had more Italian. I thought at first he was employed here in some capacity, but as far as I can make out from what he told me . . . he was certainly waiting at table. But of course he may have made a vow of humility.'

7

'Your daughter is looking very beautiful, Giancarlo,' said an old Ricasoli who had known him for years without number. 'I don't know that I could have ever, quite honestly, have said that before, but today she is looking very beautiful.'

'Ah, that's what it is,' said Giancarlo. 'I didn't quite know what it was, I thought she was looking happy.'

'And how do you get on with your new son-in-law?'

'Very well, as well as one can get on with a doctor.'

They walked together for a little, arm in arm. They were talking about their bowel movements. Loyalty from that quarter was the one thing necessary, said Ricasoli, for absolute peace of mind.

8

Monsignor Gondi was looking for Cesare to ask him whether it might not be appropriate to address a few pastoral words to the staff. Both Annunziata and Bernardino seemed to some extent to have forgotten themselves, but a day of festivity should not mean a day of disorder. Cesare, who was the tallest person present except for Signorina Barnes, was easy enough to pick out in a crowded room, but just at the minute he was not to be seen.

9

When was it that Signora Gentilini began to feel not herself? She had left the table, and Gentilini, in his turn, was deeply and not very willingly occupied with Salvatore's mother, who was explaining to him her unaccountable gift for foretelling the future. He was wondering how it would be humanly possible to get back to the hospital by five o'clock. 'My son,' she told him, 'who is a man of science, can't account for how it was that I was able to predict his father's death, not only as to the year, but as to the day.' Collect the family, thought Gentilini, make my goodbyes, find out who's parked in front of me and ask them to move. He looked round unobtrusively but couldn't for the moment see his wife. It was Cesare who found the Signora lying shapelessly outside one of the lavatories allocated to the ladies, just as Barney came storming out of the other one.

'What's wrong with her, is she pissed?'

Cesare shook his head. That was quite out of the question. Unlikely that she had taken any wine at all.

Barney knelt down. 'Well, she's not dead. I've done my Red Cross up to Grade One. Perhaps it's her time of the month, or a bit of a collapse. I know who she is, she came with that doctor, she's his wife, I think, I'll go and get him.'

As she scrambled upright Signora Gentilini opened her eyes, with their large yellowish whites, and said:

'Non so capacitarmi . . . mi vergogno . . .'

'What's she ashamed of?' asked Barney.

'She wants to recover,' Cesare said.

'You mean that she's afraid of embarrassing her husband. You mean he hardly ever takes her out with him in public and she's afraid that if she screws it all up and calls attention to herself she'll never be allowed out again. She's downtrodden to that extent.'

Cesare did not deny this.

'He must be a brute.'

'I only met him today for the first time.'

'And he's a brute.'

'No.'

Signora Gentilini sat up, and clinging to Cesare's arm began to talk in a rapid, broken manner. Anyone would think that she was not used to going out, not used to company, but the fact was that she hadn't eaten or drunk anything although everybody had pressed her, and that had caused a little faintness, also there were so many people, so many new faces and no two of them exactly alike, the truth was that she hardly ever went out formally nowadays, a mother had so little opportunity except for a giro with the family, her husband had warned her that it might be too much for her but that was ridiculous, as a girl she had had invitations every day of the week. She then fell back against the wall and shut her eyes again.

'Give me a hand,' said Cesare.

'You don't mean you approve of all this?' said Barney, who had been able to understand in part.

'You take her feet.'

And Barney picked up Signora Gentilini's ankles, swollen in their strap shoes. Cesare, at the top-heavy other end, walked backwards. The weight of the Signora, who was quite a short woman, was unbelievable. There was a stiffness, too, in her deep sighs, as though she was wearing leaden corsets. At the corner of her bright red lips a bubble rose and fell cautiously. Her right hand still kept its grip on the long handles of the grey suede bag which matched her outfit and which was now dragging along the ground.

They had to avoid the front rooms through which the guests were milling, the kitchens and the kitchen passages. Still supporting the weight with his left arm Cesare opened, behind his back, a small door. Then they had three steps down to negotiate. They were like criminals, or pious relatives at a funeral, crossing a yard now where a curly-haired bitch came out and looked soberly at Cesare, waiting for permission before sniffing at the handbag and the shoes.

'My God, we don't need her,' said Barney.

'She's old, let her be,' said Cesare. With the dog at their heels they struggled into the farm office.

'Well done, Signorina Lavinia.'

'Not to worry,' said Barney, 'everyone tells me I'm very strong.'

Cesare gave his cautious smile.

They eased the inert Signora into the dusty chair. 'I still think she ought to brace up,' said Barney. 'I mean morally. I usually tell people what they ought to do. That's what she needs.'

'You must think of what she wants,' Cesare said. 'Wait here.'

Barney was left only for a few minutes with the heaving, tightly-clothed wife and mother, subservient to men. The scent, she thought, even in the cold of Cesare's office, which got no sun, was strong enough to make a cat sneeze. Then he was back, with a sandwich of bread and ham.

'Did you get that from the kitchen? I could have gone.'

'No, Annunziata's there.'

'Well, but I'm not afraid of Annunziata.'

'You would be if you saw her now.'

'What's she doing?'

'Counting the forks.'

He gave her the sandwich. 'I have to go back to my guests. Make her eat something as soon as you can, and then take her back to the others. Don't brace her up. Let her be.'

As he went off the Signora gave a kind of lunge and Barney held out a piece of bread on her hand, as though she was feeding a horse. 'Gently, good girl, take it easy.'

The mouthfuls of bread had a good effect. 'You're better now, signora,' said Barney. 'Much better.' It never occurred to her that her Italian might not be understood, and it always was.

She helped the poor female to her feet and vigorously dusted

153

her off. Her skirt had been made in the old-fashioned style, for walking and for being looked at, not for sitting down, and it had creased lamentably. But in the grip of a new, or renewed, worry Signora Gentilini no longer cared how she looked. She cried, 'Where are my children?'

'Come with me,' said Barney. 'We'll find them.'

'It's not the girls . . .'

'Why not, don't you want the girls?'

'Luca is so imaginative and daring. Often people misunderstand what he does.'

Before they had crossed the yard the two little girls met them, pleased to be the bringers of bad news. Luca was doing very wrong. He was in the dove-house. They pointed.

The casetta had been restocked since Bernardino's loss. It was locked, but Luca had climbed up from the outside and forced open one of the louvres. The doves were escaping. They had only one wing clipped and after soaring boldly out, one after another, against the blue winter sky they reeled sideways like broken toys and lurched towards the ground. Luca was imitating them as they fluttered grotesquely towards the open fields, stretching out his arms like an idiot, and stamping his feet.

'Luca! Your clothes!' the Signora said. 'Do your mother's wishes mean nothing to you?'

'What were you doing?' asked Barney.

Luca looked round and saw Barney. He was terrified.

'He was driving the birds mad,' declared the little girls. 'He told us that he could drive them mad in this way.'

Barney took Luca by the elbows and shook him once.

'Cretino.'

The eldest girl took her hand, the younger one clung to her mother. Both of them wept because the beautiful birds were loose. 'They'll come back at feeding time,' said Barney, who wasn't sure whether they would or not.

Luca walked after them in silent rage and dejection. The huge English signorina did not even look round to see whether he was following or not.

When Barney marshalled the four of them into the house, leaving them with Gentilini, Chiara had gone to change her dress. Cesare was surrounded with people, but when he was near enough for her to be able to hear he remarked, 'Brava Lavinia.'

10

When Barney had heard that Cha's bridesmaids were going to include one of the Capponi girls, and one of the Rucellai, and one of the Frescobaldi, and that there was no way of avoiding this as she had known them ever since she was born, Barney asked to be counted out.

'They'll all be half my size. I don't mind towering, I just don't want to dwarf people.'

In the end the two of them saw each other only for a few moments after the wedding and clung to each other in one of the great raftered bedrooms looking out over the wintry land. Chiara had taken off her plain white dress, which lay discarded on the floor, and put on another one of plain grey flannel.

'None of them thought much of my dress, Barney. I could see they hated it.'

'Well, they couldn't wear it themselves, that's why. It's all right on you, though.'

'Please don't let us drift apart,' said Chiara in tears.

'You sound like my grandmother,' said Barney. 'But keep smiling, we shan't drift apart, I've decided not to.'

'Please tell me if there's anything you want, or if there's anything in the world I could do for you.'

'Blow your nose,' said Barney. 'Since you've raised the subject of what I want, though, I was thinking that your cousin might take me out to dinner.'

Chiara looked startled. 'I don't know that he ever asks anyone out to dinner.'

'Well, never mind it,' said Barney. 'I'll manage without. God bless, Mrs Rossi.'

11

They were married, they drove away together, they were going to Misurina d'Ampezzo, in Salvatore's new second-hand car. The car was a Fiat, because the company had just started a road breakdown and rescue service for Fiats only. It had been a great surprise to Chiara to find Salvatore making such a practical decision, just as strange as if, for instance, Cesare had given way to imagination. Of course, Salvatore couldn't practise as a neurologist without being, for the most part, calm and sensible, it was just that until today she hadn't had any experience of it. Now she had a problem, as it hadn't occurred to her that she could love him any more than she did, but to take in this new aspect of him her love would have to expand, and show that it had expanded.

'None of them thought much of my dress,' she said.

'What does that matter, it suits you, it's how I like to see you.'

'You don't care about it, do you?'

'Not in the least.'

'I don't either.'

She looked sideways at the stranger. He was quiet, rational and predictable, and she saw that he wouldn't any longer be driven to a frenzy by any small thing that she happened to do or say. When they reached the bedroom of the ski-hotel, lined with wood like a cigar-box, and were sitting together half crazy with happiness, she began to take off the grey dress and to tell him at the same time that she wouldn't have known where to go for her clothes this time, she was no good at shopping, and then a woman, not a young woman, middle-aged in fact but kind-looking, had called round at via Limbo and asked if anything had been decided yet, and if not whether she could be given the job of making the wedding-dress and perhaps another dress as well. She was a good worker, she said, trained with a good house. 'We were surprised, because it was very early on and we hadn't put the announcement of the engagement in the paper.'

'How did she know about it, then?'

'Well, it turned out that her lover had told her.'

'Why did he know?'

'She said he was very well educated and knew everything that was going on.'

'He didn't suggest that she should come and see you?'

'Yes, he did, he thought it would be a good way for her to make a little more money. She said that he was always very thoughtful.'

Salvatore got to his feet.

'You won't wear that dress again.'

Chiara, who had been gently turning the sleeves the right way out, felt her heart miss a beat. He pulled the dress away from her so violently that her hand felt scorched. His intention had been to tear it up immediately, but Marta's new machine sewed strongly and it was not so easy. Salvatore had strong wrists however and there was a sharp crackling as one of the sleeves parted company with the top.

'Just tell me this,' he shouted, very dark and very pale. 'Did she bring her sister with her?'

'What sister?'

All that Chiara understood clearly was that when they had left Valsassina he had thought she looked all right, and now he didn't. She sprang to help him, not only because he had taken against the dress, but because of a certain wildness in her that wouldn't let him have all the destruction to himself. Between them they were stretching and shredding the fine grey material into jagged pieces. The pieces drifted about, cluttering up the carpet.

'What sister?'

Salvatore looked at her. 'Your hand is bleeding.'

'I know, I don't mind.'

'Why don't you mind?'

'It doesn't hurt much.'

'Why doesn't it hurt much?' he asked furiously.

And now it appeared that they couldn't go down to dinner, she had nothing else but her ski-pants and some knitted things and their attention had been drawn to a strict notice in the dining-room, No Ski-Dress. Salvatore therefore rushed out like a lost soul through the thin drifts of snow to find some sort of shop that was open and to buy her something, anything, anything at all.

12

It was not till after the wedding that the Azienda di Turismo finally gave definitive notice that the Ricordanza must be opened on certain days to group visits during the forthcoming spring. Failure to comply would mean liability for a greatly increased tax on their richezza mobile, private property and family farm, and a fine for their negligence in performing their common duties as citizens. To some extent this was an exercise of the imagination. Every year the authorities published lists of the principal families of Florence showing their declared income and, in the opposite column, the official estimate of what this really was, allowing for bank deposits, which were not declared, and the two differing sets of books kept by all private companies. Only the Ridolfi, perhaps, with their poor grasp of reality, might be written off as having scarcely more income than they admitted to. And the Turismo would perhaps not have bothered themselves with the Ricordanza if this had not been the year of the cypress disease, when it became clear that most of the old villas in the environs would be in an unpresentable condition. For miles around Florence, the great trees drooped like sink-brushes. But the Ricordanza had no cypresses, and its lemons and roses had never been known to fail.

There was no grant for repairs. Giancarlo had assumed that

there wouldn't be one, and he was right. He pointed out that the premises were shabby, and the garden steps, in particular the grassy staircase of the midgets, possibly dangerous. Robiglio, the Deputy Director of Tourism, dismissed this objection immediately. The travel companies would be liable for any accidents outside the building, the parties would be covered by the package insurance. Their tour of the house would be twenty minutes only, which hardly gave them time to hurt themselves, and they would be hurried back for tea at the Ugolino gold course. 'It will be excellent for children,' Robiglio added vaguely.

'Certainly,' said Giancarlo, 'provided you can find children that don't fall over.'

'We shall have to add an extra page to the brochure, and a photograph. An extra page, that is, summarising the legend connected with the Ricordanza. Unfortunately, though, the story as it stands won't do at all. It wouldn't be attractive to tourists in any way.'

'I should need a little time to think about that. Nobody in the family does very much writing.'

He thought of Chiara, who spelled incorrectly in four languages, and then of Cesare.

'I can supply a writer, no worry about that,' said Robiglio. 'A reasonable fee will be paid, and the Azienda can make an appointment any time convenient to you. Only your approval is wanted, this is fiction, not history.'

Giancarlo at first thought nothing much about the matter, then it began to hover on the threshold of his mind. What do I think about the story? he asked himself. I don't even know if we've got the right version. But no, that's not the point. The right version would presumably be true, and a legend doesn't have to be true, it has other things to do. On the other hand, some of it, some part of it, must have taken place, because there are the letters in the Biblioteca Nazionale. Now the whole story is being altered in the interests of tourism. Should I mind if it was being altered to please myself?

It was the moment to take advice from his family. Chiara

(how odd it was, now that she was back, to ring up and ask for her, as though she was an acquaintance, in a flat which he must bring himself to accept was where she lived, while he himself was speaking from her home, where she didn't live any longer. – The enormity of this!) – Chiara was touchingly ready to help him, but said she was afraid she would be of no use.

As a tiny child, before the war, she had spent a whole day at the Ricordanza with her father. Giancarlo was still under house arrest and they had had to bring with them two men from the questura, who went to have something to eat with the gardener and Giannina. Aunt Mad had not been there. They had simply walked about the gardens all day. What was walking to Giancarlo was running, at that age, to Chiara. She found it difficult to manage up and down the grass staircases, impossible on the giant steps. She was, for that summer only, the right size to re-enter the past. The Count had arranged all this with unusual concentration, imagining that it might be for the last time.

After the war, at the beginning of the Reconstruction, when Chiara was not quite twelve, there had been an evening party at the Ricordanza. The party had really been given by and for Annunziata, to celebrate the gradual withdrawal of evacuees, refugees and partisans from the various rooms, the removal of the corpses in the rose-hedge and the digging up of barrels of oil under the graves in the chapel where no graves were supposed to be. There was wine, no food, but lights in the garden, where the great rose-bushes rampaged. Chiara, small, thin, and still as flat as a board, wore a black dress because her uncle had been killed and her aunt was dead. She moved from one group to another and they interrupted what they were saying and gave her an affectionate word. From head to heel long shivers of excitement passed through her at the realisation of what could be made manifest, like the scent of the roses itself, from human beings known and half known to each other, dressed differently, speaking and behaving differently from their everyday or earthly selves. The women were made up; the men, who couldn't be, compensated by the additional effort they made, as though they were compelled to amuse on penalty of sinking into the earth. Only gradually it came to her – or perhaps it was more and more so as the night went on – that as she listened, anxious to learn, almost all of them turned out to be speaking unkindly about someone else who was present, but out of earshot. The unkindness produced laughter and a kind of gentle intoxication. The garden was divided not only into moonlight and shadow but into areas of risk and safety as the guests, moving up or down, in or out, or under cover of the music, might or might not happen to overhear what was being said about them.

When she had taken Salvatore through the limonaia and made love with him in the vast bedroom she believed she would feel differently in future about the Ricordanza and come to think of it tenderly and sentimentally as you were supposed, after all, to think about the place where you spent your childhood. Nothing seemed to have changed, however, and she only had to shut her eyes to see the unlucky Gemma, the cripple, floundering up the grass stairs.

'Suppose we forgot it,' she said. 'Suppose we got rid of the whole thing.'

'And your husband, what does he think?' Giancarlo asked rather stiffly.

Salvatore must have come in while she was speaking and taken the telephone from her. Everything had to be repeated once again. 'I am putting it to you simply as a member of the family,' said Giancarlo.

'The story is a superstition,' answered Salvatore. 'I have no opinion, none at all. A superstition concerns things that don't exist, and it isn't possible to have an opinion about things that don't exist. Ask me anything else, anything. Please don't get the impression that I'm holding back, you can be sure that I'll answer absolutely frankly.'

Giancarlo would very much have liked to ask him what his ideas were about marriage, but knew that the moment for this was not now, or ever.

Cesare was, as always, a satisfactory listener. He thought it would be an opportunity, even if the Turismo wouldn't help, to get a bank loan to replace the grass staircases, which in his opinion couldn't be older than the eighteenth century.

Maddalena was against any kind of change.

Largely because he had seen him again, after too long an interval, at the wedding, Giancarlo also consulted Professor Pulci. The professor replied from London: 'I can't tell from your letter how serious you are. I take it that you're appealing to me in reference to my earlier work on the myth as a justification, a theory which I now reject as totally misconceived, but perhaps I'm flattering myself in thinking, old friend, that you remember any of my books. The Ricordanza material, including the statuary, shows that at some unspecified time one branch of your family was considered kindhearted but incompetent, and ill-judged in carrying out their good intentions to a grotesque degree. This of course may well have been so then and may even be so now. The story is an illustration only. I am taking the banal point of view. However, if you are asking me whether the character of a family and perhaps their general prosperity could improve or deteriorate because someone has been allowed to fiddle about with their definition through myth, then I think my answer may surprise you. It is yes. Thirty years ago we none of us believed in either magic or miracles, but I notice that both of them have managed to survive very well without our belief. I should be inclined to leave the story alone.'

As to Beppino Gondi, Giancarlo was determined not to consult him at all. It must have been entirely a coincidence that the Monsignore opened his regular check-up call from Rome by saying: 'You remember Luigi Capponi?'

Giancarlo did not. He was reminded impatiently that Capponi was a well-known novelist and cinéaste. 'You met him last year at one of my conversazione.'

'Was he a Milanese?'

'Yes, yes. Now he has the idea, which will of course depend

on what financial backing he can obtain, of writing a screen play on the subject of the Ricordanza.'

'I'm surprised that he should find it at all interesting.'

'You've remembered who he is?'

'Yes, that's why I'm surprised.'

'Well, the mutilated girl, you understand, mutilated by your family, the mutilated child of the people. That is what interests him. Capponi of course is a communist, but I flatter myself that I have a little influence with him and I have a notion that I can induce him to give the whole tragic story a Christian colouring, in the manner of Pasolini.'

'You'd better hurry,' said Giancarlo, 'or it won't be a tragic story.' Gondi did not understand this, and was too proud to ask for an explanation.

Meanwhile the Deputy Director of Tourism was anxious to go to press. The Count assumed that Robiglio would have chosen for the job of rewriting the legend, a writer or a journalist connected with his own family or his wife's family or failing that someone who wasn't a writer at all but to whom he owed an obligation or some money. He never discovered, however, what connection there was, if any, between Robiglio and Signorina Monti. She was a journalist, on the Woman's Page of the *Nazione*, accustomed, as she pointed out herself, to solving problems very rapidly. She appeared at the flat in via Limbo at nine o'clock in the morning, wearing dark glasses, and dismissed immediately all the usual little politenesses. At the prospect of having a decision made for him by someone who was not his sister and not his late sister-in-law's brother, the Count felt a delicious relief. Is it not a natural duty, after all, for the weaker to follow the stronger?

'I have every confidence in you, dottoressa,' he said.

'You think it'll be an easy job.'

'Not at all. In fact, I have the impression that in spite of all we have been promised since the war, journalism is still not an easy profession for a woman.'

'Probably not,' said Signorina Monti. 'I myself can't afford to rely on impressions.'

Giancarlo saw that he had deserved this reply, but no longer felt so friendly towards Signorina Monti.

She began, 'I know the story in question, of course. I've been living here in Florence for nearly two years. When I arrived I made it my business to familiarise myself with all the aspects, even the most trivial. Robiglio is right, the story as it stands won't do. Are you sure there's no grave?'

'There used to be a small family chapel, in fact there still is, but it's been closed for a long time.'

'And none of the family were buried there?'

'I fear not, I'm very sorry, I'm afraid it never occurred to them.'

'A grave is a prime attraction for international tourism. It doesn't matter that Juliet's tomb in Verona is an old horse trough. If the Protestant Cemetery in Rome is shut there's a special opening made in the wall so that you can have a look at the grave of Keats. You insist that there's no tomb at your villa?'

Giancarlo told her that the little Contessina, like most of the family, was buried in the vaults of Santa Maria a Quarto. 'Not her,' said Signorina Monti impatiently. 'The other one, the legless one.'

'If she ever existed.'

'You've no idea where she was buried. She was a nobody, more or less bought over the counter, it wouldn't have been thought worth recording. I daresay the dogs' graves were marked, and the cage-birds'. Not to worry, Count. I've had to manage with much worse material than this.'

13

In the Monti version of the story, Gemma da Terracina avoided the fate in store for her by escaping from the Ricordanza. She climbed over the wall at a spot where there was now a pull-in on the opposite side of the road, so that photographs could conveniently be taken by visitors sitting in their coach. Gemma was said to have been dearly loved by all. The statues of the midgets facing outwards were looking regretfully after her. Those looking inwards were waiting to break the news to the little Contessina. 'To have a hearty laugh at her disappointment, I suppose,' said Giancarlo. Robiglio approved of the alterations, but hesitated over the location of Gemma's flight. The pull-in was for three small or two long vehicles only, and once tourists were allowed out of their coach to take photographs it was difficult to get them in again. But the story itself he liked, it had atmosphere and struck, he thought, a bright note. Before sending it to press he added: 'Thus the "good intentions" of the Ridolfi were frustrated, and it was at this time they gave the villa its name, as a memory or reminder of their own folly.'

14

Salvatore knew that he was more than ever obliged to defend himself on all sides against merciless attacks in order to retain the little ground he had gained. These attacks were largely, though not entirely, by women.

The most irritating, perhaps, was his mother, who (as he now found out) had burst into tears at the wedding and told everyone within earshot that if he had searched the whole world he could not have made a better choice. She had no reason to say this and he couldn't conceive why she had said it. Repeating again and again that her son must have thought, when he made up his mind to marry, first and foremost of his old mother, she had cut him off, by a kind of instinctive encircling movement, from his independence. Ingratitude to those who have given us life is a luxury and Salvatore now felt deprived of it. Marta, on the other hand, hadn't burst into tears, but had taken the opportunity to make another two hundred thousand lire. Then, Giulia Gentilini, who refused, in the teeth of the evidence, to admit that he was ill-mannered and unpredictable. Only Chiara was not in the grand conspiracy. However much they disagreed there would surely never be anything to forgive.

What is all this about happiness? he asked himself. – We never talked about it in Mazzata.

They had a flat a long way out from the centre, via Emilio Münz 261. There were two rooms, a cucinetta, and a shower. The agent had called it luminoso and so, being four floors up, it was, as light, in its way, as via Limbo, but while he was showing them round it was quite difficult for them not to get in each other's way. Chiara threw her clothes and possessions all over the place and felt immediately at home. She had a poor grasp of time, and was not the sort of person on whom watches keep going for very long, but fortunately she could hear the tocco from the bell of the junior school across the road. Salvatore was punctual, but impatient. The lift in their block often didn't work, and rather than wait to find out whether it did that day or not he would take to the stairs. Then, four floors down, she could hear the engine of the Vespa, for he hadn't parted with that, roaring, fading, rising again and dying away abruptly as he turned the corner southwards towards the Agostino.

Running down and even up the stairs was a simple counter-irritant against rage. The flat was what Salvatore could afford at the moment. The money from the sale of his inheritance was still in hand, but the 100% mortgage at 2½% which he had hoped for, and still did hope for, from the hospital, in fact it was his contractual right, had not come through as yet. 'I've been to them time and again,' he told Gentilini. 'What is wrong with them, what possible authority have they not to do this?' Gentilini reminded Salvatore that he was popular with his patients but not with the S. Agostino's finance committee, and in particular not with the Chief Administrator (formerly the Deputy Administrator).

'He didn't like the trouble about that woman's grave in the

Campo Santo at Rifredi. He didn't like your recommendations about the contadini and the effect of commercial bread on their diet. After all, you're not a nutritionist.'

'Nor is he. It's impossible that he can be so childish. He must know his own ignorance.'

'He isn't ignorant of how to manage a committee,' said Gentilini. 'In any case, your place is perfectly all right for a young couple with no children. Giulia, when we were first married, would have been glad of it.'

'My God, do you think I want Chiara to live a life like Giulia's?'

'Has your wife complained about the flat?' asked Gentilini stiffly.

'I don't want to ask her what she thinks.'

'That strikes me as absurd. Marriage, surely, means free discussion on every subject, and particularly, I should have thought, about where you were going to live.'

'You understand that Chiara mustn't be limited in any way, she's still very young, she may quite likely want to study, and I of course should have no objection, none whatever, she might enrol at the University this autumn.'

'As it happens, Giulia herself is a state registered nurse. It's simply that until the children are older she hasn't time for anything outside the home.'

They walked on in silence (they still went to the Caffè Voltaire) and then Salvatore said: 'Did you think, just now, that I was criticising your way of living, and possibly your wife?'

'Yes, I did,' said Gentilini.

15

Chiara and Salvatore quarrelled, but not so successfully as they made love. Chiara had no gift for quarrelling at all and could scarcely understand how it was done, nor, really, had

Salvatore, since his argument was with himself, and he was therefore bound to lose. When they had torn up the grey dress together in the hotel they had hardly known whether they were for or against each other. When Salvatore's temper rose Chiara became not frightened but reckless, as when driving through the city's traffic. They knew each other, to be honest, so little, and had so few memories in common (the concert, the limonaia, the wedding) that they had to use them both for attack and defence. They loved each other to the point of pain and could hardly bear to separate each morning. The bed was on the narrow side so that it was impossible to lie for very long either back to back or six inches of hostility apart. This led to truces or reconciliations of a kind, rather too easily made. The bed had come from Valsassina. It was made of walnut, an old country piece of furniture. Chiara had remembered that it was in one of the upstairs rooms, and, determined to be practical, had asked if she could have it sent to Florence. Cesare had said that she was welcome to it. She could take anything she liked.

Salvatore and Chiara never quarrelled twice on the same subject. Each battle, as it closed, was recorded in their memories, as in an elementary history book. In these books you usually get three or four causes of hostilities given, and afterwards three or four results, which have to be learned by heart. It must have been eight weeks or more before there was any kind of dispute between them in public.

16

That spring Professor Pulci gave a dinner party. He did this only because he happened to have alighted for a season in a villa up at Bellosguardo, belonging to the Istituto Hodgkiss. The Hodgkiss Foundation for Fine Arts had built the house two years earlier for its course directors, the Institute itself being in the city, onto which the Professor descended daily, changing buses at Porto Romano. The Hodgkiss congratulated themselves on securing Pulci, who had always been elusive, and was now old enough to be referred to as mythical.

Although the Professor, when he took the trouble to think about it, was a hospitable man, the dinner party was entirely dictated by the situation. Finding himself temporarily in a large house with someone to do the cooking, he allowed the idea of guests to enter his mind. 'You will act as my hostess,' he said to Maddalena, of whom, as her brother's sister, he was genuinely fond, and then there was nothing further for him to worry about. He told her to invite Giancarlo, Chiara and her husband, Cesare if it was possible to drag him away from Valsassina, and then a young English historian, Burton Murray, or it might be Murray Burton, who had come with a letter of introduction from the Institute.

'What's he doing here?' Maddalena asked.

'He is beginning his doctoral research, or perhaps concluding it. Possibly he won't be staying here so very long.'

'Well, that makes seven,' said Maddalena, 'and you haven't asked any of the Americans.'

'They see me every day,' said Pulci.

Maddalena pointed out that there were only two women, and that except for Burton, or Murray, all the guests would be from the family, which might make him feel awkward. Pulci said that in that case he would ask Mimi Limentani.

'What made you think of her? I shouldn't have thought you saw her from one year's end to another.'

'She has been attending my lectures, the public course, and she came up to speak to me afterwards. When she went away I asked the secretary who she was, and I was told that she was a good woman, a kind woman who did kind things.'

Maddalena couldn't deny this, although she believed that the Professor was speaking at random and that his mind was already with his students in the seminar room overlooking the green expanse of the Giardino dei Semplici. Otherwise he could scarcely have thought that kindness was a qualification for a dinner guest.

17

On the evening of the dinner party, in the middle of that very wet April, there had been no rain for twenty-four hours, and the air glittered.

The Villa Hodgkiss had been built on an acute slope on the east side of Bellosguardo, off the via S. Maria Marignolle. Although it had been commissioned to represent all that was new and uncompromising in post-war Italian reconstruction, the house still had a largish terrace tiled with glazed terracotta and looking out northwards towards Florence over one of the most stupendous and banal views on earth. 'Like a postcard!' cried Mimi Limentani, with great satisfaction. Young Burton, who had arrived punctually, nicely dressed and on the make, stood uneasily beside her. The river gleamed, the Duomo's pale stripes were clearly distinct, the cypresses marched up the Arcetri hill.

'Imagine having that outside your front window,' she said. 'Imagine having that to look at every time you want to empty the ashtrays.'

Burton looked at her with dismay.

'You must have seen it so often.'

'Every day, but it's not too much.'

'Don't go on about the view, Mimi,' Maddalena called from inside the salon into the bright evening air. 'Signor Murray is an art historian.'

They were not alone on the terrace. A small boy and an even smaller girl were playing there. They had none of the furious imagination which would have made English children, confined in the same area, a menace. The girl in her pinafore, the boy in his school overall, circulated slowly on their miniature tricycles, counting the red and black squares of the tiles.

'How many are there?' asked Burton in Italian.

'Two hundred and fifty-six.'

'How many are there usually?' He smiled, to show that a smile was expected.

The little girl looked at him patiently.

'There are always the same number.'

'Angels!' Mimi exclaimed. 'Where do these angels come from?'

Burton hoped he was not going to be put upon. He had the touchiness of those who are learning to put the great masters in their places. Once inside things went better. He was presented by Maddalena, this time under his right name, to a handsome, rather dangerous or defiant looking doctor and to the dottoressa, who seemed to be the Count's daughter although she looked too young for that, but then the Ridolfi aunt herself looked as old as the hills. Somebody, it seemed, was still to come, but as time passed the Professor showed no anxiety. Nobody looked at their watches, perhaps they had none. The cook appeared, with her husband in a white jacket, offering Camparis. It turned out that the boy and girl on the terrace were the cook's children, and she now took them away, carrying the two tricycles under her arms. 'How nice to see someone from London,' Chiara said to Burton. Her voice was so gentle, and yet so enthusiastic, that it made her remark sound sensible.

'Do you know London well, Contessina?'

'I don't know it at all. I know Carlisle Gardens,' she added.

Burton turned slightly towards Dr Rossi.

'Isn't that near Harrods?'

'How should I know?' said Salvatore. 'I've never been out of Italy.'

He spoke Italian, and so, now, did Burton. 'I'm sorry, I didn't mean –'

'Why should you think I have been to London?'

'I hadn't thought about it at all. I suppose most people have to go at one time or another.'

Burton felt the unfairness of being confronted by a man who was apparently even more ready to take offence than he was himself. But the doctor's black glance changed to a smile, as difficult to resist as all the others in the room. 'When I'm not on duty I don't always think before I speak,' said Salvatore. 'It's a fault, you must overlook it.'

There was a telephone call, which the Ridolfi aunt took; Cesare would come within half an hour. There seemed no chance of anything stronger to drink, everything must be faced on a Campari. The Count approached Burton and asked him whether he thought the English concept of fair play had been extinguished by the war. 'My point is this, that if the concept was exported, in one of its forms, to provide the basis of the American constitution, now that the Anglo-Saxon element is no longer the most important one in the United States it should be replaced by something else – let us say the Italian attitude, which I take to be unadulterated fatalism.'

'I can't quite picture it, sir,' said Burton. 'If a government was fatalistic I suppose it wouldn't make any provision for the future.'

'On the contrary,' said the Count. 'Every situation would be regarded as a probable disaster.'

Maddalena slightly separated them. 'There aren't enough women in this room,' she remarked. 'But even if there were, the men would find a way to talk to each other.'

'That is not at all true,' said Giancarlo. 'If I had the opportunity I would talk to women all day. As it happens, just a moment ago Pulci and I were discussing camomile tea and the way it should be made.'

Burton, seeing at last his chance to make some impression on the Professor, asked him who had designed the villa.

'I don't know who it was,' said Pulci, 'I must ask them at the Hodgkiss.'

'Of course he had to meet the challenge of a steep site,' Burton pursued, 'but that's true of any hill town.'

Mimi asked him whether he wouldn't like to come out on the terrace again, now that the lights were coming on. Maddalena thought that they should start dinner. Giancarlo detached the young Burton and quietly asked him for his help. 'If I might just take your arm for a moment.' This was not, though it might have been, one of his affectations of old age. The Villa Hodgkiss was an exercise in split levels, or perhaps into how many levels a villa could be split. The areas of the living-room, some of them almost isolated and too small to accommodate more than a coffee-table, were connected by flights of polished stairs, and two of these flights apparently led nowhere at all, or rather to glass doors which were never opened. The Count treated all this as though it was a preliminary course in skiing, mildly availing himself of Burton's help. Gently the guests descended, the three women on their high heels negotiating the steps like dancers. The dining area only came into view at the bottom, after a sharp turn. In its centre was placed, in fact fixed, a round table of pale green marble, with the shapes of twelve plates, twelve knives, twelve forks, let into the surface in darker green mosaic. On an evening such as this when only eight guests were dining, none of the real plates, knives, or forks quite covered their green stone images. The Institute, presumably, had not liked to argue on this point with their architect, who had reserved the right to design all the furniture, much of it immovable. And there was no place at all indicated for the spoons, which looked like intruders.

From long practice, one might say centuries of practice, these Florentines became convivial. Because Cesare was late, because the son-in-law was felt a little as a dangerous quantity, because the English visitor still looked aggrieved, they all exerted themselves to make things go, to pacify time and to flatter the long mild evening into hours without regret. English sentences turned into Italian and back again half way through, so that Salvatore could have no feeling of disadvantage. Every topic was treated affectionately, but, as it were, on sufferance, so that if anyone should find it tedious even for a moment, it could be ushered politely out to wait for its next turn. The Count said nothing further about the English sense of fair play, but told one or two personal reminiscences. He was speaking of a philosophy which had been talked about for a short while in his youth, lorianismo, the doctrine that the further people lived above sea-level the stricter their morality became. Of course, such ideas could really only have been proved by experimentation. He told them about a woman he had known in Navarre, and another in Toluca, at 3000 metres, and another, he said, in Scotland. Mimi, who seemed to go everywhere, had never been to Scotland. 'You must come with me,' said Professor Pulci, with sudden gallantry. 'It will do you good, you will never be ill again. In Scotland no-one is allowed to eat anything after six o'clock, that's why the health benefits.' Chiara asked Burton whether this was true, then saw that he was confused, not liking to contradict the Professor at this stage, and said that she herself had only been there once and felt she didn't know any country properly, not even her own. She asked Burton whether he'd ever been to Painstake, in Norfolk. 'No,' he said, 'but I don't think there's anything there, is there?' He meant that there were no pictures or collectable objects of any importance. The noble turnips, the cabbages, the thousands of acres, the woods where Barney had suffered, went for nothing, Chiara could see. But his nervousness was disappearing, and he smiled back at her without guile. Maddalena was speaking now of the old couturier Parenti, who was said to be very ill. He was being nursed at home, and had sent a message asking whether it would be possible to see her. Several years ago, he wrote, he had had a difference of opinion with the Contessa. 'He wants to die forgiving and forgiven!' cried Mimi, her eyes full of tears.

'I don't think so,' said Maddalena. 'He wants the pleasure of a last disagreement.'

By ill-chance, the ill-chance of being too much welcomed and too much reassured, Burton, hearing the conversation glide by, mentioned that by the end of the week he would be homeless. His pensione needed his room for another booking. 'They're making out that they need my room,' he repeated. His intention of being asked to stay at the Villa Hodgkiss was quite clear, and lay there as though designed to trip someone up. Professor Pulci perhaps did not notice it. Giancarlo and he, like old lovers, were smiling together over an unfinished anecdote. Certainly, he didn't take up the suggestion. Burton made things worse by adding, 'Of course, I should be out all day.' Chiara could not let this pass and said in distress, 'Well, but you mustn't worry about that. There are so many places where you could go. We could put you up' (what a strange phrase that was, she left in English because there was no Italian equivalent) 'we could put you up, you must stay with us.'

'No,' said Salvatore, 'no-one can stay with us.'

Chiara gave a troubled smile. The doctor, without explanation, shouted 'No-one.' Perhaps he was not quite sane. Burton thought now that he remembered something about one of the family being strange in some way. Providentially there were sounds outside, the sounds of arrival at a luxury villa – the electric alarm rang from the outer gate, a buzzer answered from the kitchen, the Alsatian barked, the cook's children called out in treble voices and Cesare came in. Everyone rose or half-rose from the table except for Salvatore and Chiara. Burton took the opportunity to say, 'Please don't think. I'm very sorry if. I'm sure I'll be able.' But Rossi and his wife were still talking, bent towards each other across the table, and Chiara was crying out,

'What do you mean? I'd live with you anywhere! I'd sleep with you on straw in a cowhouse!'

Cesare came down the split levels without any apology, as he had made one already on the telephone. He said good evening to everyone present and sat down. 'It's good of you to invite me, Professor,' he said. 'I've never been here before, I've often wondered what it was like inside. How can you bear this table?'

'I cannot,' said the Professor. 'I shall advise the Hodgkiss to send artisans to chip it away.'

The soup came in again for Cesare with a flourish, he had created a diversion, but not enough it seemed, and Chiara, oblivious of time and place, was crying out:

'Everyone knows how generous you are!'

'Why have you been talking about me?' asked Salvatore loudly. 'Why do you need to discuss me? Who said I was generous?'

'Everyone knows it. I'm only saying what everyone knows. At the S. Agostino if anyone gets into any kind of trouble they go to you. When the nuns come round with the collecting box they're told to try Dr Rossi.'

'They're lying about me.' Salvatore could be seen wildly searching his memory for some evidence of meanness. 'Who have I helped? When have I ever helped a living soul?'

'People want to come to us, they want to see you.'

'Tell them I'm not an exhibition. There are other things to see in Florence. Or tell them that if they want to come to us there will be a charge, a small charge to see the unpleasant Dr Rossi.'

Both of them got to their feet, acting, surprisingly, in complete harmony, and both pushing away their plates which slid hissing over the marble towards each other. Then they both walked up the steps. It was like a sudden accident, an irreversible spilling of grease, ink, or blood when the surface which only moments ago was so clear, so serviceable, now stares back, ruined. Giancarlo turned to the Professor, who, as host, had risen once again, this time dislodging his pale green dinner napkin and half disappearing under the table to retrieve it. 'My dear Pulci, it must have seemed very important to them to say these things.'

'They're so young!' Mimi cried.

'How young is Rossi?' asked Cesare, beginning on his soup.

'They'll come back,' said the professor. 'They'll finish the discussion outside the house, then they'll come back.'

This was not so, and a car was heard driving away. The Count looked round about him and saw that the young guest from England, who had looked so disheartened, wasn't so any more. Probably, and indeed understandably, he was composing the whole incident into an amusing story to be told later, so that for him the evening would not have been wasted.

The guard dog barked again, the buzzer sounded. Chiara had come back, having refused to go with her husband in the car. Now she had no money for her bus-fare down to Porto Romano. It was the bus-fare she wanted, not a lift, not a taxi. She stood at the top level, with a certain dignity, as though she had made it impossible for herself to come any further. With the exception of Cesare, who still had his soup to think about, everyone searched for small change, no-one had any. In the end a book of bus tickets had to be borrowed from the cook.

18

True to their own system of misunderstanding, Chiara and Salvatore said nothing about the dinner party. Chiara, when she arrived back, remembered that she hadn't a latchkey or the special second key, recommended by the agent, which had to be turned once to the left and twice to the right. But the door of the flat had been left so that it opened at a push. Salvatore was lying stiff as a block of wood in the wooden bed. As she took her things off she saw and tasted the noisome darkness into which they were heading of their own free will, and she also saw that quarrelling becomes much easier with practice, easier every time. Professor Pulci, who had always shown her so much patience, would scarcely have believed that she would grow up into what she was now. Salvatore turned over and put his arms round her and she felt as though her mind had been crushed and now the blood was running back into it, blood from wood. 'I don't want to talk about it,' he said. But as soon as she was alone she conducted an interrogation with herself. She couldn't believe that she was supposed to be ashamed of the two rooms, the shower and the cucinetta. She usually met her friends somewhere in the centre because the flat was far out, but it had been her intention to ask everyone in turn, everyone who didn't live in Florence, to come and visit them. She had made a list, if she could remember where she'd put it. It was more difficult to keep tidy in a small place than a large one, but Salvatore had never minded about that. Usually when he came back from the hospital he would put everything into its right place, the clothes in particular, but quietly, without comment, as though it was something he expected to do. It wasn't possible that he could lose control of himself because of a chance invitation to via Emilio Münz, 261.

Chiara, as it happened, was right. After he had said 'No' the first time, Salvatore had been redeemable, but between that and 'no-one can stay with us' he had been maddened and totally overcome by an enormity which struck him as he looked round the dinner-table, that was that the whole company, the whole boiling of them, had jumped to the conclusion that he, as a man from Mazzata, was jealous of this Murray, or Burton, apparently some student of Pulci's, because without a word to him Chiara had begged him to stay with them in their home. The Englishman himself had believed it, first stammering idiotically in his High School Italian, then smiling to himself like a sated lizard. Immediately Salvatore decided to allow them to indulge themselves. I am a guest in this house, he thought, on no account let me spoil the entertainment. 'No,' he repeated. 'No-one can stay with us.'

Chiara, even if all this had been explained to her, would have found it beyond her comprehension and even beyond her imagination. The Ridolfi family were so constituted as not to feel jealousy and as a result they never suspected it. This was a serious fault in them, as it would be in anyone.

19

'Cha, have you seen that handout they're giving out at the Turismo, well, they've got that story different.'

'Barney, where are you speaking from?'

'The way they've got it down here, the little girl gets away quite all right and it's your family that's left on the wrong foot, did you know that?'

'Barney, are you in Italy?'

'Yes, I am, I'm in Florence. I'm in a telephone box actually. I got this leaflet thing in via Tornabuoni.'

'But where are you staying? Why aren't you staying with us?'

'You haven't asked me, and I take it that means your husband doesn't like me. Probably he's not keen on any of your friends.'

'He will be, please give him time. But anyway there's via Limbo, why didn't you tell us, why didn't you go there?'

'I got on all right with your father, I think, but I had to tell that housekeeper of yours, remember, that she was poisoning us, and if I went there I might have to put her right again in some way and that might make for an unpleasant atmosphere.'

'But Barney, you never used to mind about the atmosphere.'

'Quite likely I'm changing in some ways.'

'Are you in a hotel then?' Chiara could hardly bear the thought of this.

'No,' said Barney. 'I'm staying with the Gentilinis.'

Chiara hesitated.

'But is there enough room?'

'Not really, but they've put the two little girls on a kind of sofa thing in the living-room, I mean you're supposed to be able to turn it into a proper bed, but it doesn't, quite.'

'I didn't know they'd invited you,' said Chiara forlornly.

'They didn't exactly, but the Signora kept writing, because she's taken a great liking to me.'

'Barney, why?'

'On account of something that happened at your wedding, I might tell you about that later, but the point is that these letters of hers always ended, "We think of you with affection and trust to have the pleasure to see you again one day." Well, now she has the pleasure. I shan't stay long because there's no bath, only a shower.'

'When can I see you? When?'

'You can see me now, that's actually what I've come for. You can come straight away and pick me up from this telephone box.'

'Yes, of course, but where would you like to go first?'

'I want to go out to the farm.'

'To Valsassina?'

'Yes.'

'But Barney, there won't be much to see out there, the weather's been so wet. There ought to be wild tulips out there now, and wild asparagus in the ditches but I don't believe we'll find any.'

'I don't like asparagus,' Barney said. Chiara could hear her putting another gettone in the box and giving it a good hard blow.

'Well, we'll go out if you like, but Cesare won't have time to speak to us, they're so busy.'

'He'll have to speak to us.'

If he doesn't she may stab him with a fork, thought Chiara. She said she would pick Barney up immediately.

20

'I've got my licence now,' said Barney on the way out to Valsassina, 'so I'll probably be able to make suggestions as to how you can improve your driving. But it's a bad thing to have a licence in one way, because now I have to drive my grandmother about. I have to put her off near the back entrance of Harrods and leave her there and collect her, as if she was a dust-bin. I like cars, though. I like heavy vehicles. Did you tell Salvatore you were going out for the day?'

'He's at the hospital. I don't want to interrupt him unless it's really important. I'll tell him this evening,' said Chiara. She appeared a little bewildered, and looked pale. Barney was unmoved.

'Well, come on, tell me everything, how's the marriage going?' she asked. 'Is it wonderful?'

'It's wonderful.'

Barney stared straight in front of her. As they had sat together the evening before, the guileless Signora Gentilini had discoursed upon everything, the good and the bad together, including what she had witnessed of Chiara's marriage, never unkindly, but rather as if she was repeating (as she frequently did) the plot of the last film she had seen, and always ending with a word of praise for Doctor Rossi. There were always disagreements at the beginning of matrimonial life, because you couldn't have love without quarrels, any more than a child can learn to walk without falling. And then, a man as clever as Salvatore Rossi had worries which ordinary women like herself couldn't guess at. Things might upset him which simply wouldn't be noticed at all by the rest of the world. While she talked and the radio hawked and crackled the Signora worked at some very elaborate table mats in pale green nylon which seemed unlikely ever to be used. Her hands and her voice moved together hypnotically.

Barney marvelled at her own restraint in not mentioning any of this now to Chiara. 'I was telling you I've changed,' she said. 'The nuns thought so when I last went back to the convent. They noticed that I was less noisy. Well, what do they expect? They kept asking after you, by the way. Some of them are coming to Rome to fix up something or other with the mother house, and they told me they might be passing through Florence, they're always rioting about these days, no image of tranquillity now. Anyway, they thought I was different. Perhaps it's that my sympathies are getting broader. That can happen, you know.'

'Marriage is wonderful,' Chiara repeated. 'Mine is, anyway.'

Her failure in hospitality depressed her immeasurably. There was no explanation she could give that wouldn't make Salvatore appear cruel and idiotic, and herself idiotic, possibly weedy, and incapable of standing up for herself.

'Barney, why don't we turn off and go back to Florence. You haven't even seen where we're living yet. We could go to the flat and have some coffee. It'll be dismal at Valsassina, the roof leaks and they'll be having to retie the vines and if we're not careful we'll have to help.'

'Have you ever done that before?'

'Yes, often.'

'What's it like?'

'Very dull. Not as dull as labelling by hand when the machine breaks down, but dull.'

'We'll go on.'

They found Cesare in the fields. He received them without surprise, and told them that if they wanted to stay they had better help to retie the vines. The rains seemed to be occupying his thoughts completely. His old dog stood watching him with a martyred expression. She would not consent to sit down, having tried it once or twice and found that the earth was not warm enough.

The vines were still in flower and stood bound with plastic to their wires, their subsidiary branches straggling down, some even broken. With the perseverance of all climbing plants they had begun to turn their light green flowers, as soon as they touched the crumbling earth, up again and towards the light. But the effort was too much and the vinestocks were like massed rows of stunted patients, each waiting for a few minutes' attention. Higher up, men and women were moving diagonally to and fro against the threatening sky.

Barney and Chiara, assigned to a row, began work on the plants alternately. Chiara was very much quicker than Barney, and had to stand waiting for her. Cesare came down the slope and told them it was going to rain again and asked them if they would like a couple of sacks for protection.

'My coat's quite good, I got it in London, in the sales,' said Chiara. 'And so is Barney's.'

'They don't look it,' said Cesare, who shared the delusion of all Italian farmers that sacks are waterproof.

'We don't want sacks,' Chiara told him. 'If it's going to rain, we want you to go to the house and tell them to see about some coffee.'

He walked away, neither fast nor slowly. 'Come on,' said Chiara. Barney doggedly snipped off her last length of plastic.

'I don't mind doing this now I've got the hang of it,' she said, 'but it isn't what I came here for. When we get indoors

I'm going to tell your cousin that I'm in love with him.'

Chiara looked at her distractedly.

'I don't want you to think you've got to go away, Cha. I'm perfectly willing for you to hear what I've got to say.'

'But Barney, you never said you were going to do this. You've made me bring you out here on false pretences.'

'I can't see the objection. All these friends of yours, these Florentine females you asked to be bridesmaids, they've had years and years to have a go at him and they've simply missed their chance.'

'But I didn't know you were in love with him. I never even thought about it.'

'You didn't have to think about it and you don't now. After all, I'm going to do the talking.'

'But it may be a mistake, Barney, another disaster, like at Painstake.'

'My God, if you're going to throw that in my teeth.'

'It's just that I'm not quite sure that Cesare is like the men you meet in England.'

'You don't know whether he is or not. You've never met any men in England. You don't know anything. You're just an innocent who hopped into bed with the first man you saw when you got out of the convent.'

'Well, but I've known Cesare all my life. He taught me to add up – two grapes, four grapes. He taught me to ride a bicycle. You don't know him at all.'

'I know him better than you knew this Rossi man,' said Barney. 'As a matter of fact, I got to know him at your wedding.'

'It seems to me that more went on at my wedding than I bargained for.'

They turned down towards the house, Barney walking resolutely a couple of paces ahead.

'What did he do at the wedding?' Chiara called out. 'What did he say?'

Barney answered over her shoulder. 'He said "Brava Lavinia." '

'Was that all?'

'How would you translate that into English?'

'I don't think you could.'

Cesare was not in the dining-room, and seeing that even Barney's courage was failing, Chiara summoned up her own. She found him in one of the sombre bedrooms at the top of a ladder. From the ceiling above his head, from the four corners of the room and beyond it, could be heard the relentless regular full-toned drip from roof to floor, the voice of the rainy season.

'It's a matter of finding tiles the right size. They're all graded, the smallest at the top.'

'Cesare, I want you to stop thinking about the roof, and don't worry about coffee, we can have some at the cantina at Sangallo on the way back. I want you to come and sit down.'

Cesare came back to the dining-room and sat down, as though he had heard those two words only. Chiara sat opposite him and gazed at him frankly, as though this cousin and this old table, heavily marked and scored, both of them known to her for nearly twenty years, were about to change into another table and another man.

'Thank you both for your help,' he said.

'We didn't do very much.'

'No.'

'Lavinia has something to say to you. That's why she asked me to bring her out here today.'

Cesare turned his mild glance, the courteous attention of a busy man, on Barney. He laid both his hands down flat on the table.

'I'll tell you what it is,' said Barney. 'It won't take long, because I know exactly what I want to say, I've been thinking it over for some time. As far as I can see, all Italian men get married, unless they're . . .' she hesitated and Chiara, who was still looking steadfastly at her cousin, supplied the phrase 'uno di quelli'. Barney nodded. 'Right, well, as far as you're concerned I'm prepared to marry you right away. I've got a little money, or anyway I will have when my grandmother dies, and that'll be useful, I expect, because I know the whole family's a bit short, and I'm quite sure that when I've had a really good look at this place I shall be able to help you a lot, particularly with the machinery side of it, and the staff, they need a woman's hand. Possibly you think I'm getting desperate because I'm twenty-one next year and my youth will pretty well be over. That isn't it, though. I've had people after me and I still have. Now I'm getting to the real point. I want you to listen to me carefully. I'm in love with you. I love you.'

'Yes,' said Cesare.

There he sat with his hands on the table, as though locked to the wood. He looked, not away from Barney, but straight at her, as good manners demanded. The long nose, the mild grey eyes, the usual tender but distant expression. 'Is that all you've got to say?' cried Chiara, jumping up, outraged. Cesare could be seen to be making an honest, even painful attempt to think of something more to contribute, but nothing came. 'She's my friend. She's come over from England, she's come all this way simply to tell you this.'

'Yes,' said Cesare.

'We'll go straight back to Florence.'

'Yes.'

He went out with them to the cortile and looked into the car to see that a dozen bottles of wine had been put in for Chiara, as usual. As he shut the door he said, 'But I don't want you to go.' Chiara looked at him in uncomprehending reproach and let in the clutch.

The drive back was less awkward than Chiara had feared, because Barney talked at great length, not resentfully, but out of the injury she had done herself. She acknowledged, with gloomy generosity, that she ought to have taken a warning, and Chiara felt as she had felt at 23 Carlisle Gardens, that something quite indispensable threatened to give way if Barney, accustomed to command, was forced to retract. How could Cesare simply take it for granted that she was in love with him, Barney said. He couldn't have even given it a moment's thought before.

'He might have been thinking about it in the evenings, when he's sitting alone by himself,' said Chiara, and as she said it the words acquired a certain resonance, as though reminding her of something without defining it.

'Perhaps he was taken aback,' Barney went on. 'Perhaps it wasn't a good idea to say I could help him run the place, after all it's his and although it certainly does need money putting into it he's not managing it too badly.'

'A twelfth of it is mine,' Chiara put in without knowing why she did so. She was relieved when Barney took no notice.

'He never actually said he didn't care about me. Do you think that's a hopeful point?'

'Oh, yes, it might be, yes.'

'And then he said he didn't want us to go.'

'Yes, he did say that.'

'Would you say there's a bit of hope there?'

'Oh, yes, probably.'

'There isn't though,' said Barney. She then returned to her first point, how could Cesare have accepted it so calmly when she said she loved him? The discussion was in the form of a sad arabesque, always, as the figure came back to its starting point, taking a slightly new direction. After a few times round Barney asked whether Cesare ever wrote letters. 'Does he write a lot of letters to you?' she asked. Chiara, frantic to console, searched her memory, but couldn't think of a single one. 'Do you think that's a hopeful point? I mean, if he's never written any letters before he might take to it once he got started.'

'I shall have to get some petrol, Barney, I'm sorry. Perhaps you'd better mop up a bit.'

'I haven't been crying,' Barney said.

'No, but you look as though you've been facing a firing squad.'

Outside the garage where they filled up there was a tiny câfé. The proprietor was bringing his chairs out onto the shining pavement. It must have been raining here, Chiara said to him, although where we've been, out beyond Sangallo, it's been quite dry. The man said that he hoped to get rid of his wooden chairs this season and buy plastic ones which could stay out in all weathers. Who, these days, has any use for a wooden chair? Barney, during these remarks, stood by with an expression of blank disbelief. It was as though she was unable to credit that such things could be discussed.

They sat down, and Chiara asked the proprietor to bring a

câfé corretto, which Barney swallowed, first that one, then another. Against the grinding din, a few feet away, of cars coming and going from the garage, she intoned to the traffic and the blue evening light

> 'No game was ever yet worth a rap
> For a rational man to play,
> Into which no accident, no mishap
> Could possibly find its way.'

'It's the brandy,' she added. 'That was poetry. Normally I don't think about poetry ever. It's quite interesting. It's the effect of the brandy.'

'I know, but I thought the coffee was supposed to slow it down.'

'Have you got any money?'

'Oh yes, I can pay.'

It suddenly came to Chiara that Salvatore might have come home early from the hospital – this had happened before, though only once – and found nobody there. The thought that she might have caused him bewilderment or loneliness was like the edge of a sharpened knife.

'I shall have to go home now,' she said.

'Right, what's stopping us?'

'I may have to be sick.'

'Don't give way,' said Barney, beginning to reassert herself. 'Incidentally, I can guess what you're going to say next.'

Chiara had wanted, as some kind of compensation for the disastrous day, to offer the most precious confidence she had. Even Aunt Mad hadn't yet been told. 'O.K., so you're pregnant,' said Barney sombrely. 'But you needn't worry, Cha, it won't be any trouble for you, you're Italian, or half. Italian women produce them just like rabbits.'

'Oh, of course it won't be any trouble. I only thought I'd like to tell you.'

'Do you want a girl, or a little teapot?'

'Salvatore wants a girl.'

'Who'd have thought it?'

*

187

Warmth met them at the Gentilini flat, the warmth of air used many times and the urgent activities of the growing Gentilini. But where there had always been confusion there was now a strange calm. The Signora, proud to have conjured up this foreign friend, held her head high. The little girls, with two or three friends who had been allowed in on sufferance to look at the visitor, crowded onto the sofa to worship. Luca, whose face was now heavily shadowed with dark down, no longer defied the large handsome young woman. He trembled when she said anything to him, and croaked. He was going to get up very early the next day to carry her cases to the bus station. Better, he had decided, not to go to sleep at all that night.

21

At the via Emilio Münz Salvatore wasn't back, but half an hour later he walked in, saying, 'A friend of yours has been staying with the Gentilini.'

'Yes, I know.'

'I mean that very tall large English girl who was having lunch that day with the Harringtons.'

'I know.'

'She was at the wedding, too.'

'Yes, she was.'

'I can't understand how they came to invite her. I've never known them to have anyone to stay. Even Giulia's mother never stays with them. Why should this friend of yours want to come back here at all?'

'She wanted to go to the farm.'

'Did you take her there?'

'Yes.'

'She didn't want to see where we live? She didn't want to see what I was like?'

'No, she wanted to go to the farm.'

22

I have to do something about Barney, Chiara thought. The trouble was, as always, that Barney was not someone who was done something about. She blundered on, not because she couldn't stop herself, but because it was the duty of other people to get out of her way, or stay where she put them.

At first she thought that Cesare might ring up, saying that he had made a mistake. By the end of the week she had heard nothing, and she drove round to the via Limbo. It was still raining – raining in May – and as she got out of the car the cortile's first floor guttering gave way and discharged a quantity of water which fell sharply behind her and rebounded from the stone flags. The whole building might as well have been in competition with the Ricordanza to see which would collapse first beyond repair.

She had made up her mind to ask advice, even if not directly, from her father. He was in, but not alone. The Monsignore was there, Annunziata said. Chiara went into the salone. Her father had his back to her, and Monsignor Gondi was poised, as usual, on the edge of a chair as though to sit down properly would destroy his reputation for overwork.

'My dear child, what a pleasure. I'm on an informal visit, of course.'

'My dearest child,' said Giancarlo.

Chiara, though she was almost without vanity and certainly wasn't thinking of herself at the moment, had a strong impression that the two of them had been talking about her. Presumably they had the world's disasters to discuss, but she did not think they had been discussing them. Probably, she thought, it was the awkwardness of the professor's dinner-party. I'm nothing more than a problem to be solved on a rainy spring afternoon.

But when the slight upset produced by her coming into the room had subsided Gondi said, 'I have been spending the morning at Valsassina.' This was fortunate, perhaps she was going to be fortunate all day.

'I should so much like to know how you thought my cousin was.'

'He was in excellent health.'

'No, I didn't mean his health, I meant how was he altogether?'

Gondi smiled. 'Does he ever change?'

'Surely not,' said Giancarlo. 'That is his speciality.'

'My nephew was born in the large upstairs bedroom,' said the Monsignore, 'as I think you were yourself, Giancarlo, and if we're all spared a third world war I expect him to make a good death in the same bed. A hard-working life, a reproach to the dissatisfaction and restlessness of the times.'

He spoke, not idly, but not very attentively, as near relaxation as he ever got, a professional man on a family visit. Chiara in her anxiety was quite out of key, and she knew it, when she fixed her pale shining gaze on him and asked him, 'Does it strike you that Cesare has something to say that he can't say?'

'Dear girl, in what way?'

'Do you think that perhaps in that half-empty Valsassina, he's becoming not quite himself?'

Chiara had turned to her father, who said, 'You're very much nearer his age, my dear, than I am. Is that how he seems to you?'

'Uncle, when you were talking to him this morning, did he tell you that I came out there with a friend of mine, Lavinia Barnes?'

'Related, I suppose, to the Markham Castle lot,' murmured Gondi automatically.

'I don't know, perhaps. Did Cesare tell you that we came?'

'I think he mentioned it,' said Gondi tolerantly. 'Yes, I think he did. Not at any very great length.'

'What did he say?'

'It was while he was telling me what a wretched season he'd

had. He said you'd spent an hour or so helping to tie up the vines.'

'And Lavinia.'

'He didn't, I think, mention her by name.'

Looking from one to the other of them Chiara felt tired out, and deeply ashamed. She had been a fool to imagine that her father would be able to help her, simply because she could think of no-one else. In consequence she had disturbed him – not much, still, she had disturbed him. And the Monsignore, not allowing himself to become irritated, was obliged to make allowances, exhausting things to make at any time, when he had hoped no doubt for a peaceful few hours. The desire to atone possessed her, the compulsion to make things agreeable, because she had injured them by wanting them to do what they couldn't. She began to talk about the stone quarries in the Boboli Gardens, which had been reopened so that the Ponte S. Trinita could be built exactly as it had been before the war. She heard herself talking away like a child at a tea-party. There was a sale of tickets, you could buy one ticket to replace one stone, or as many as you could manage. The Monsignore was delighted. He took over the subject himself. He knew, not only the exact number of tickets that had been sold but how many were for stones and how many for bricks. The bricks were cheaper, and by that means, no doubt, the authorities hoped to draw in the working classes of the city. His voice rose to a certain recognisable tone, like an engine at cruising speed.

When she left her father kissed her warmly and said quietly, at the door, 'Your uncle won't be staying long. But did I understand you to say that Miss Barnes was here?'

'No, no, papa, she was here, but she's gone.'

Before she left she went to the kitchen to let Annunziata give her further advice on her pregnancy. Some of these hints had been cut out of magazines, some, it seemed, Annunziata had always known. If the expectant mother was sick, the baby was certainly a girl. It was the longer hair which could be felt tickling the end of the mother's gullet. But it could be made to lie down smoothly by drinking a tablespoonful of olive oil.

Even some of the old women at the Asilo, who had told Chiara that they had never been blessed, had warned her about this. Down in the cortile, where the rainwater glittered unevenly, Chiara leant for a moment against the double entrance and felt the extent of her uselessness.

When she got home it was dark, but Salvatore was not back. She knew that he was at a meeting at the hospital, where the neurology and psychiatry departments were to pursue another stage of their more or less open warfare. She rang up 23 Carlisle Gardens.

The telephone was answered by Lady Jones. The line was not a good one and her high-pitched voice sounded like an angel's, giving an intermittent blessing.

'Oh, you dear child, I've been told your good news. You won't mind my saying that there's nothing like your first child. I'm sure that's always so, even in Latin countries.'

23

One thing was certain, and that was that the child mustn't be born at the via Limbo. Otherwise Annunziata would seize the opportunity to introduce onto the premises her favourite niece, who was a Sister in a nursing order and seemed to have no difficulty in getting leave to attend private cases. Giancarlo called her Sister Death. She was obliged to bring with her another member of her community, so that made two of them. The double flutter of black and white and the rattling of pill-bottles, which in itself sounded like a recall to order, meant that these particularly irritating women had arrived and were taking charge. The Monsignore said that it set his mind a little more at rest to think that his relatives in Florence, if there was any question of illness, were in such safe hands.

But Chiara felt, perhaps unreasonably, that Sister Death would never come out as far as via Emilio Münz. She wanted to have her baby there, not in a clinic, but there would be time to suggest this later. Meanwhile the child made its presence felt at the moment only by an uneasy prickling, as though it was a faint-hearted pioneer awash in strange seas.

In the corridors of the S. Agostino, however, Salvatore's approach was dreaded. Anxiously and remorselessly he hunted down the obstetrical and gynaecological staff, usually when they were in transit from one room to another and could hardly avoid him. 'Listen, I'd just like a word of advice. Needless to say I'm not a consultant on my wife's case, she's in good hands, I shan't be professionally connected with the birth in any way, that's why I'm able to take a completely dispassionate view and I thought it might be of interest to you to talk it over.'

'Are there any abnormalities?'

'Of course, at seven weeks it's difficult to get a balanced picture –'

'Let's talk about it in another seven weeks.'

It was suggested by the senior registrar that Rossi should be locked into his office as soon as he arrived. Meanwhile Salvatore waylaid a well-known visiting obstetrician who must, after all, have plenty of time to spare as he had come to Florence for a Professional Convention for Christian Peace.

'There are just one or two points I should like to clear up with you –'

'Are there any abnormal signs?'

'That's what I think you would find particularly interesting. The signs appear to be normal in every way.'

'Let me see, you're Rossi, the neurologist. Where did you qualify?'

'In Bologna.'

'You took your medical qualifications in Bologna, and before specialising you of course conducted your three routine deliveries?'

'Of course.'

'Good, how did they go?'

Salvatore could remember nothing about them.

'They were satisfactory.'

193

The surgeon patted him on the back. 'Like the vast majority.'

But something must have been not quite right, Chiara miscarried and the baby's doubtful experiment came to nothing. There was no assignable reason, no illness, no emotional disturbance, and Salvatore no longer wanted to discuss the point with his colleagues.

'I'm sorry,' said Barney, speaking patiently from London, 'but you've still got five-sixths of your childbearing life in front of you, don't forget that. How do you feel?'

'I don't know, nothing in particular. I'm going to the sea for a bit, to Riomaggiore. The Ricasoli are taking me.'

'Oh, those people.'

'I wouldn't have told them, only it was in their house I started bleeding. I just had to sit tight, picture it, Barney, I couldn't get up until everyone else had left.'

'We're neither of us quite young any more,' said Barney gloomily. 'How long are you going to be away for?'

'I suppose I might be away for a month.'

'Won't your husband think you're leaving him?'

'He wants me to get well, I suppose. No, he doesn't think I'm leaving him. I expect I'll come back sooner than that anyway, I shan't like it without him. When am I going to see you?'

'I'm going to get married,' said Barney. 'I have someone in mind.'

Chiara felt sick with relief. Barney said that she was going to marry Toby Harrington.

'But, Barney, you can't, he's married!'

'Well, he won't be. Of course we shall have to wait quite a while, and fix it. You know, what really broke them up was trying to live at that Scampolo place. They never really recovered from that.'

'Oh, but recovered from what?'

'Of course, it will have to be a registry office. One blessing, my grandmother won't feel that it would be right for her to come.'

It turned out that when Barney had arrived back, as she put it, 'last time' she had gone up to Scotland and had found her father and Toby Harrington by themselves, drinking whisky. She said that this had given her a new slant on things.

'But you still haven't told me, when am I going to see you?'

'Well, we shan't be coming to Italy.' Barney's voice changed to one which the nuns at Holy Innocents would have recognised – calmly dismissive, the voice of authority. 'You must let us know, though, if ever you're in Chipping Camden.'

Chiara had never heard of this place, it was entirely new to her. But during the later stages of her life, at times when things were not going well for her, the bewildering phrase used to come back to her without warning: You must let us know, though, if ever you're in Chipping Camden.

24

Salvatore had had it in mind that while Chiara was away he would get rid of the flat on via Emilio Münz and devote all his energies, outside his work, to bringing the S. Agostino to their senses on the subject of his 100% mortgage. Meanwhile he would stay with the Gentilini (since they appeared to have become so hospitable) as a pensionante. Gentilini, however, told him that he was going back to Borgoforte.

He had never mentioned (and didn't do so now) that he too, after several years of waiting, had been disappointed in his hopes of a mortgage from the S. Agostino. His request had been much more modest than Salvatore's, but perhaps even more necessary. One of the marks against him had been his friendship with Dr Rossi, which had made him mildly, but distinctly, unpopular with the administration. The reason he gave for moving, which was also a perfectly genuine one, was that Luca had become very unsettled. It was almost impossible to manage him either at school or at home. 'In Borgoforte we can share a decent-sized house with my brother-in-law,' he said. 'After all, everyone returns in the end to his first love.'

Gentilini was fond of these proverbs, or popular sayings. Salvatore looked at him in dismay. He decided, after all, to stay on at via Emilio Münz. Without fail he rang up Chiara every evening. The weather in Florence was getting hotter, gusts of warm air blew round the street corners from the bed of the river. She was better off at the sea. Chiara said that she wasn't, that she was soon going to come back, and that after this she never intended to go near a cliff or look at a fishing boat again.

25

One morning about this time Aunt Mad, waking in her flat on the second floor of the via Limbo, felt a pain, as though an unwelcome hand was wringing her dry. It wasn't by any means the first time, and after a little the pain went away, but she had the impression that something decisive had happened. She said aloud, 'It's imagination.' Her mind answered silently, 'Why should you imagine it? It's nothing.' Her body replied, 'No, it's not nothing.'

This was confirmed by old doctor Manzoni, who looked after her whenever she was in Florence. 'But she doesn't take my advice,' he told the Count, coming downstairs and into the library.

'What have you advised?'

'The question is, what is wrong? What did your father die of?'

'He lost interest in life.'

'Well, hypertension is often hereditary,' said Manzoni. 'By hypertension I mean high blood pressure. My patients imagine that's caused by the blood trying to force itself through their arteries, which thicken of course as time goes on.'

'And are they right?'

'Nowadays we think not. We incline to the view that the hypertension causes the arteriosclerosis. It's a natural change, in any case, in later life.'

'Then there's hardly likely to be a remedy.'

'To most patients I would say "lose weight", but the Contessa has none to lose.'

The Count noticed that, as usual, Manzoni said 'we' when giving unwelcome advice and 'I' when it was acceptable.

'There's a possible operation, we can sever most of the sympathetic nerve fibres which lead to the abdominal organs.'

'Did you suggest that to my sister?'

'She gave me to understand that she was against it.'

'And are you in favour of it?'

'No. What I've done is to leave a bottle of 500 microgram tablets of trinitrin, and told her not to exert herself. If she can't make herself rest, she should enter a clinic.'

'Could they help her there?'

'No, but it's better to be beyond help in the right place for it,' said Manzoni, 'I mean, among professionals.'

Indestructible Dr Manzoni had lived without incident under the German occupation, but compromised himself during the forty-five days when Mussolini fled and Badoglio took over, and had to spend almost a year in hiding in a warehouse in the Abruzzi. He often ended his stories – or rather, his one story – by saying that if he closed his eyes he could still smell the tallow and olive oil in which the rats, who had become half crazy, often drowned themselves. If Maddalena were to die, the Count would never have to listen to this story again. The Manzoni era would be over.

'Yes, a clinic,' the old doctor repeated.

'You speak as though I had some kind of influence over my sister. No-one has. Where does she want to go?'

'She spoke of staying here for some time.'

'If she wants to do that she must be in a bad way. She never wants to stay for long anywhere.'

Manzoni accepted a vermouth, and recalled how he had first seen the Contessa Maddalena as a bride, that would have been, wouldn't it, about 1920, after the Socialist Front collapsed, yes, well, as a young bride on the terrace of the Ricordanza, a radiant sight. He's becoming idiotic, the Count reflected.

After the doctor had taken his leave he got slowly to his feet. He went up the stairs, pausing where they changed, above the piano nobile, from marble to stone to look out at the glimpse of the Arno. The river, beginning to sink low in spite of the earlier rains, reflected the yellowish light in its yellowish water and threw over the nearby buildings a curious transparency, like a painting on glass. Giancarlo had seen this so often that he no longer noticed it, just as he no longer pretended to himself that he wasn't pausing for breath.

His sister was already up, and getting ready to go out. He tried to adjust himself to what he had just heard, and was no more successful than anyone else has ever been. Without so much as putting it into words they agreed not to talk about the matter to Annunziata, otherwise there might be no way of warding off Sister Death. No need either, as yet, to say anything to Chiara. They both suffered at the idea of practising a deception on her, but deception, to a quite unexpected extent, gets easier with practice.

Maddalena dragged the pain about with her like a tiresome guest, bearing with it when it showed signs of getting out of hand, but counting on its going away. There was no chance that it would do so permanently. At the moment it made itself known as a violent headache in the early morning and again in the evening. She saw that she must accommodate it into whatever remained of her life.

26

For some reason she felt a little better at the Ricordanza. The opening of the villa to the public had been a success, the Turismo had congratulated the Count, who had not been congratulated on anything (except for his daughter's beauty on her wedding day) for many years. Visitors were now allowed to stay rather longer and could buy a glass of Valsassina or a gasosa at a bar in the salone. This was the perquisite of the gardener, and so was the sale of lemons. Almost overnight he had transformed himself into a character, inviting the company (in a mixture of broken English and German) to tap the vast old thermometers and iron stoves in the limonaia, and telling them that there were more than forty different kinds of lemon and that the juice was unrivalled as a stomach remedy. 'Cannibals, signori, use lemon juice, without it they could not digest human flesh.' Unlike Bernardino at Valsassina he had grown not odder but increasingly shrewd. His instinct to restore some of the horrors which the Turismo had tried to get rid of was a sound one. He had copies of the brochure but had never troubled to read it. 'Picture yourself, signori, cut off just here, at the knees.' His truce with Annunziata had become strained. But the Ricordanza was not her proper territory and she could enter it only by invitation.

As part of the process of getting above himself, as defined by Annunziata, the gardener had been allowed to attend the meetings of the local association of Custodians of Public Monuments. There he had learned, among other things, that Englishwomen, and possibly Englishmen, above a certain age were liable on a short visit to steal plant cuttings. So he was careful to explain, on a more sober note, that lemons, if they were to stand a cold winter, must be grafted on to a sour orange stock, anything else would mean certain failure. As to the famous thickets of roses, they looked more likely to take cuttings from the tourists than the other way about. Apart from that there was nothing else to steal. Any disappointment on that account would disappear when they looked northwards from the terrace at the view of the opposing hills. They were requested, for their own safety, not to lean on the balustrade.

Maddalena had an idea that at the Ricordanza her pain seemed less, or she was successful in thinking about it less. She had a working arrangement with the gardener that as long as she was there he must talk sensibly. Towards the end of an afternoon she was idling down a path between two neglected box hedges, at a distance from the paying customers. An elderly man, whom she had noticed earlier on, straying away from the others, came up to her and said:

'Are you the mother of the dottoressa Rossi?'

He sounded like an old-fashioned schoolmaster, setting for the hundred thousandth time an example of correct pronunciation.

'I'm nobody's mother,' Aunt Mad replied. 'Look at me closely and you'll see that I couldn't be.'

She saw that he was sober, but trembling slightly.

'I'm the Contessina's aunt,' she said. 'This is our family home. Did you come out here with the others?'

'No, I took the bus from Piazza Ferucci and walked the last part.'

He must have come in unnoticed, she thought, at the end of the coach-load. Like a man under a spell, he must have assumed that he could walk in, and had walked in.

'I came from Mazzata yesterday,' he said. 'They gave me three addresses, and one of them was the address of the hospital. I was unsuccessful there and that was what caused the delay. Now under the terms of my return ticket I must take the long distance bus again this evening.'

'Did you want to speak to Dr Rossi?'

'I spoke to him once before, but it was useless, to be honest, worse than useless.'

'Have you telephoned him?' She added with more attention, 'Are you ill?'

'I don't want to speak to him on the telephone. I was his

father's friend. It's a matter that has to be discussed face to face.'

What can Salvatore's father have been like? she thought. Surely not like this. The old man glanced at her from time to time, as politeness required, but it could be seen that he was totally pre-occupied. Meanwhile the last of the tourists had left the Ricor-danza, and the dark green gardens, which had been grossly overcrowded for the last hour or so, stood ready to sink into their own recollections. The gardener, before locking up, was search-ing the limonaia and even the rose-bushes, in case of lingerers.

'What's your name?' Maddalena asked.

'Pericle Sannazzaro.'

'Well, I shall be driving back to Florence as soon as they've shut up here. Come with me, and I'll find Dr Rossi for you in one place or another. By the way, did you get something to drink with the others?'

'No, I took nothing.'

'You should have said you were a friend of the house.' But, pressed on by his overwhelming anxieties he burst out, 'Excuse me, Eccellenza, but I haven't the time now to look for my friend's son. If you are driving, I must ask to be put down at the long distance bus stop in via Caterina di Siena. I should like to have spoken at length, nothing less would have satisfied me. As it is, I shall have to ask you to take a message.'

'At least we might sit down for a few minutes.'

'I am not tired.'

'But I am.'

He apologised, and they took their place side by side on a stone bench whose arms, carved with grotesques, were any-thing but comfortable. Now, disconcertingly, he looked directly at her. In his very much worn black suit he looked pale and battered, almost on the farther edge of respectability. 'Try to understand me,' he said. 'Follow me carefully.'

Although he was quite sane, he was evidently past the point of estimating the importance of what he was saying to anyone other than himself. In this way Maddalena heard for the first time, and in rather more detail than she could take in, about Salvatore's piece of land at Mazzata.

'There's a chance of recovering the land. That is what I have come here to say. The brothers and the sister-in-law would sell at once if the money was available. Quite possibly they would take what they gave for it. All they want is to lay their hands on capital. They don't see themselves as farmers any longer, they've been induced to invest in the building of a hotel. A second category hotel, in Mazzata!'

Maddalena saw that she was supposed to smile.

'A hotel in Mazzata! Treasure that up, Signora Contessa, to laugh at on winter evenings, or in the bad times which, politically and economically, are in store for all of us.'

'Good, but surely Dr Rossi must know all this already? You say you don't want to telephone him, but I shouldn't have thought his brothers would have had any objection.'

'If they did, Salvatore would not be interested.'

'In that case, I don't see . . .'

'He ought never to have sold the sixty hectares in the first place.'

'Then why did he?'

'To afford to marry, Signora Contessa. He thinks quite differently from the rest of the world. You can't judge him by other people.'

His empty jaws moved with a slight chewing motion. Maddalena, meanwhile, was not judging, but, as she usually did, allowing certain pictures to form and dissolve in her memory. In 1911 the great liberal, Gaetano Salvemini, had sold his little bit of land in Molfetta to finance a new weekly paper. As a young woman, a young radical, she had helped to pack and distribute the paper from a cellar in Lungo Il Mugnone. After Salvemini, she saw in her imagination the white cloths of the wedding tables and Salvatore on his feet, saying that he would give his life for Chiara.

'He did quite right,' she said.

'Of course. Nino Gramsci told us that all that Italian men look for in marriage is a hen, a hen with something substantial in the Post Office Savings. It's not a fault in my friend's son that he is determined to be the opposite of everyone and everything.'

Mad half-shut her eyes.

'I can't follow you. What has Gramsci got to do with it? Does Dr Rossi want this property or doesn't he?'

'He believes that he doesn't. He needs it, rather than wants it. He has a duty towards the community of Mazzata.'

'Well, he can't go back and practise there. He's a specialist.'

'He is an intellectual.'

'I suppose so. One would hope so.'

'Therefore he has the duties of an intellectual.'

'I don't know what those are. I suppose they're the same in Florence as anywhere else.'

Sannazzaro, watching her minutely, said, 'He has to make his career in Florence, that's not in dispute. But there's a sickness and craziness about him because he has cut himself off from the place where he was born. In reality, although he's not able to admit it, he can't be happy without his piece of land in Mazzata. You don't think that's possible?'

'Of course it's possible. It happens every day. But I still think he must know what he wants.'

'Don't you think that on some occasions we have to judge for others, I mean as to what is really best for them?'

'Yes,' she said. 'If we're competent to do so.'

'Perhaps, Signora Contessa, I don't look quite competent.'

'No, frankly, I don't think you do.'

Not disconcerted, he repeated: 'Whether he admits it or not, Salvatore will not be happy without his piece of earth.'

'Is this what you want me to tell my niece?' Maddalena asked.

'I believe that would be the best course. You see, I have tried to persuade Salvatore – I'm speaking of the time shortly before his marriage – and I was not successful. He must have known that what I was saying was true, but he couldn't listen.'

'Why couldn't he listen?'

'Because he is unable to diagnose himself.'

Because she was struggling with her own queasiness and at the same time with her impatience with Doctor Manzoni, Maddalena was struck by this remark. This Sannazzaro can't have come more than six hundred kilometres and then spent a day and a half looking for Salvatore, she thought. What he's been doing is to spend a day and a half avoiding him and finding someone else to talk to him. That makes one think better of his intelligence.

'Tell me, what is your profession?'

'I like to think of myself as the follower of a great man,' replied Sannazzaro.

The gardener watched them, uncertain as to what to do and whether to start the evening watering or stand by to lock up. He would not have gone so far at this point as to jangle his keys, but they were in his hand.

'When I spoke to you just now of the bad times coming,' Sannazzaro went on, 'I didn't mean that they won't be succeeded by good, only that you and I can hardly expect to live until then. And by "good" I'm not referring, you understand, to the improvements brought about by science. Science has to take its proper place, it mustn't try to take over from witchcraft. "Good sense is dead, its child, Science, killed it one day to find out how it was made." Who wrote that, Signora Contessa?'

'I don't know,' said Maddalena.

'Nor do I, but Nino quoted it often. But what is damaged, and what even may seem dead, can be brought to life again. There is infinite good sense in the working people of Italy. All that is needed is patience.'

'There I can't agree with you. I don't put much value on patience. I find it's best to act on impulse.'

Sannazzaro looked at her in surprise. Then he asked for the lavatory. She called to the gardener, who had to reopen one of the side doors of the house. Levering himself off the comfortless seat, Sannazzaro followed, walking in a distinctive manner, as though it required some thought to synchronise the different parts of his body. Maddalena saw that he might be even older than she had imagined. Well, we all are, she thought.

Those who refuse to give way to disappointment are able to accept almost any improbability. From this point of view, there was not much to choose between Maddalena and Sannazzaro. When he came back from the house he took a notebook out of his inner pocket, and out of the notebook a piece of paper.

'It's time for me to go back now. You understand the message with which I have charged you. I hope it won't be too much for you. Here is my address, it is on this letter from my former employers. You will let me know what you have done.'

'I'll let you know,' she said.

There was no parking near the long distance bus station in via S. Caterina. She put him off at the corner. If she had been liable to doubt, this would have been the moment for it. Sannazzaro looked, under the street lamps which had just come on, dishevelled by life. But he said goodbye, gallantly mentioning that he had seven minutes to wait and would perhaps take a cup of coffee.

Then as though it had just occurred to him, he put his head in again through the open car window.

'I can't wait here,' said Maddalena.

'One more word, Contessa, one more question. Tell me this. Is Salvatore happy with his present home? Does it seem to you that, wherever he's living at the moment, he is satisfied with it?'

He disappeared into the lighted jaws of the bus company's câfé-ristorante.

27

While Aunt Mad was discussing him at the Ricordanza with a stranger, Salvatore was discussing Aunt Mad. Only, however, because there seemed no way to get out of it.

It was some time since he had come across the lawyer Andrea Nieve. Nieve had never quite given up hope of enlisting Rossi as a party member, but was now inclined to admire him for having married a Ridolfi. True, the via Limbo place was mortgaged and the villa was in total decadenza. If he himself had been dealing in Ridolfi property on behalf of a client he would have recommended forcibly against it. But the fact that Salvatore, apparently without calculation, had got an interest in it appeared to him as the lucky stroke of a lucky man. How had it happened? It was Nieve's theory that all women were obsessively interested in their own bodies, that was why they found doctors attractive and why doctors were so much more fortunate than lawyers.

Salvatore agreed to meet him provided that the situation in Hungary was not discussed, or the disagreements within the Italian Popular Front.

'No, no, it is an entirely private matter.'

'There's nothing private between us, nothing that we couldn't shout aloud in the street.'

'It will be easier to explain when you come.'

The place, it turned out, for all this privacy was Nieve's place of work, no longer just an office, for he'd gone up in the world, but a Legal, Technical and Commercial Studio above a marble-fronted bank on via Lamarmora, not far from the law courts. No desks here, but large inconveniently low arm chairs for client and consultant alike. One might have been in Milan. The technical and commercial colleagues, whoever they were, seemed to have been got rid of for the morning, but there was another man whom Salvatore didn't know, and who was introduced as a junior colleague, Gattai. Gattai was young, and his slight frown gave him a look of not quite being able to catch up. Why he was needed at this delicate and private conference Salvatore couldn't see, unless, as was quite likely, Nieve wanted a witness of what was said.

Nieve began by asking after his wife, hadn't he heard that she was away?

'She hasn't been well, she is spending a few weeks by the sea,' said Salvatore, 'she was quite all right when I rang up yesterday evening.' At once he was seized with a violent compulsion to call up again and to hear Chiara's voice and to ask her whether she felt the same as she had done yesterday. He checked the impulse. Nieve meanwhile was saying that he was occasionally asked to advise the child welfare service, the Opera Nazionale Maternità ed Infanzia.

'Perhaps you knew that I did some work for them?'

'Frankly, I've no idea who you work for,' said Salvatore. Nieve and Gattai both smiled, as though at a compliment. Nieve's remarks, precise but apparently reluctant and almost wistful, came round to the subject of hospices and asili, and then, gradually, to Maddalena di Ridolfi. By the shadow of a hint of a gesture he suggested that the Contessa might be considered not quite like the rest of us.

'You mean my wife's aunt is mad. Is that what you wanted to tell me?'

'Don't excite yourself. You're the doctor, it's for you to tell us. Of course we're not discussing her personally. It's a matter of trying to protect her, as I shall hope to show you.'

'Very well,' said Salvatore with unexpected calm. 'Most of the Contessa's actions are very shrewd, and, I imagine, well-directed towards their objects. She is not a patient of mine, of course, and I'm not an alienist. What are you talking about?'

'About her asilo for old women and babies in via Sansepol-cro. May I ask whether you know anything about it?'

'Not much.'

'Would you say that it's well run?'

'I'm sure it isn't, but I don't see what concern that is of yours or even of mine.'

Nieve explained that he'd been approached by the Prefettura and the Inspectorate of Health, as well as the O.N.M.I., to see how the affair could be handled in the most tactful way.

'She's sane,' Salvatore said, 'and what's more, if there's any criticism of her, she has a lawyer.'

'Guardone, via Strozzi,' said Gattai, who looked relieved at having made some contribution. Salvatore was a little taken aback. He had been thinking of the Ridolfi family lawyers. He hadn't known that Aunt Mad retained someone on her own account.

'Yes, Guardone,' said Nieve. 'Naturally we have to collaborate with him, but I'm speaking to you first because this may be considered a family matter and you are now one of the family.'

'Then why haven't you spoken to my father-in-law? He's in Rome at the moment.'

'Precisely, we thought it best to make the first moves while the Count was away, so as to cause less distress.'

'I don't think he feels the least distress about these old women and orphans.'

'But he prefers to be spared trouble.'

'We all do.'

'You're with me, then, in thinking that the best thing to do is to arrange affairs a little so that when your wife and the Count return to the city everything will go forward without disturbance?'

'What's been happening, out with it.'

The troubles, Nieve explained, were of long standing. The orphans (in so far as the asilo had any legal recognition at all) were only allowed to stay until they were two years old, but Mad had always believed that the ancient women wouldn't mind this since, at their time of life, one baby would be as acceptable as another. One would go, another come. But, quite recently, a kind of turbulence, a hankering for the good life, seemed to have overtaken the senile inhabitants. Determined not to part with their present lot of infants, they had hidden them and kept them hidden.

In Florence, anyone who doesn't like the look of things can get a denunciation form from the tobacconist's, fill it up and send it to the Questura. Recently these forms, asking what was happening to the little angels at the asilo, had been arriving in great quantities. 'But we don't, above all, want it to become a matter for the police.'

Why doesn't he? – thought Salvatore. – However, what Nieve expected in return for his discreet negotiations would certainly be made clear in good time. What effect would it have on Chiara? He knew that she was fond of her aunt, but then she was fond of everyone and everything, although he had demonstrated to her that this attitude was wasteful and illogical. Best, surely, to find out what was what and then, the next time he rang up, or perhaps the time after that, to break it to her as something that had happened but was not to be worried about. He would begin in a level, reassuring tone: Oh, by the way, about your aunt –

'What had happened to the children?' he asked.

'They were quite well, but the inspectorate found them

stowed away in cupboards and washbaskets. That is why they're investigating the legal position.'

'What do you want me to do?'

'I want you, as a connection of the family, to come down with me now to via Sansepolcro and to meet Guardone there, with the object of seeing what preliminary steps we can take.'

Nieve put on a pair of dark glasses and hung his light summer jacket over his shoulders. As they went out Gattai, who had been hovering about, came close to Salvatore and said with a release of repressed excitement, like a jet of steam: 'Dottore, I have been told that you knew Antonio Gramsci.'

'Gramsci died in 1937,' said Salvatore. 'My God, how old do you think I am?'

'Don't misunderstand me, but as a child you might have met him, or you might have been taken to his funeral.'

'Nobody went to Gramsci's funeral.'

'Dottore, what line do you think he would have taken in the present political and economic situation?'

Nieve turned sharply and told him to find a taxi. Gattai went off, frowning pitiably.

'I'm sorry, he's an idealist. There'll be no need for him to come to the asilo.'

'No.'

28

The asilo wasn't directly on via Sansepolcro, but in a turning off it, one of Florence's darkly greyish blind turnings. After Nieve had paid off the taxi he went into a bar to get some telephone discs, as though without them he might be cut off, like a castaway, from his base in via Lamarmora.

The building was awkwardly crowded into an unwelcoming three-cornered site, so that the entrance gate was at an angle. Oddly enough, it was open. In the courtyard the caretaker's dingy lodge was empty. The place was in silence. All the old and all the young must be asleep or have gone out together.

'Ah, Guardone.'

A man in gold-rimmed spectacles, with an air of being beyond surprise, came out of the main building, such as it was, at the back of the courtyard. He was introduced, and shook hands. 'Forgive me, Nieve, dottore, but I'm afraid you're wasting your time.'

'We're only here to ask you to show us round. I know your position is delicate. We haven't any specific authorisation to act, none at all, and I imagine you haven't either.'

'I follow my client's instructions,' said Guardone.

'You're on the committee of management here?'

'There is no committee of management.'

The balance of power was doubtful. Nieve was a very much more important person than Guardone, but Guardone appeared to be in possession and what was more to know what he was talking about. He turned now to Salvatore.

'Your wife will have told you that this building is mortgaged to the Order of S. Vincente di Paoli, the interest being kept low as a form of charity. The only property which the Contessa is free to dispose of is, as again you must know, the wash-house.'

The caretaker had at last appeared through the street entrance, carrying a loaf of bread and a tin of paraffin. 'The asilo is shown only by special permission,' he said immediately. 'The wash-house is never shown.'

It was explained to him that this was Dr Rossi, the husband of the Contessa's niece. Nieve also offered him an English cigarette. He repeated: 'The wash-house is never shown.'

Guardone indicated a point where the wall was interrupted by an outbuilding. The windows were boarded up, but the door was open. The three of them stood looking in. Salvatore got the impression of a stable. There were solid stone troughs, and the floor was hollowed and ribbed with drains. But beyond that there was nothing. Where the taps should have been, the tap-seatings, the drain-pipes, the plugs and their chains, nothing.

Nieve rounded on the caretaker. 'How could the residents ever have done their washing here? There's no equipment.'

'No, it has disappeared.'

'When did that happen?'

'It disappeared little by little.'

'Did you make a report?'

'The taps were made of brass.'

As time went by the old women had sold off the wash-house fittings in order to buy one thing or another, cigarettes sometimes, but much more often presents for the infants.

'What did the Contessa say about this?'

'She wasn't surprised,' said the caretaker. 'Of course, the price of brass varies from time to time.'

'Guardone,' said Salvatore, in the voice he used for consultations, 'I know something about the Contessa's troubles, but not what she had in mind. What is she intending to do next?'

'Nothing. She sold the wash-house yesterday. My instructions were to go ahead as quickly as possible, even if it meant accepting a lower price.'

Struggling not to show astonishment, Nieve asked: 'Who were your clients, if it's not confidential?'

'Bimbi Auto-Wash,' replied Guardone in a gloomy tone. 'There's no secret about that.'

Nieve tried to recall his position of authority. 'We'll see the main block next.'

'It's empty.'

'Where are the women and children?'

'They have been taken away.' The caretaker supported this. 'Yes, they went early this morning.' He put down the tin of paraffin and pointed towards the street.

'You mean they were removed by the Inspectorate?'

'No, by the Contessa,' Guardone said. 'There were only eight of them left, and six infants. All this is like the taking of the Bastille, Nieve, so much exaggeration, so much effort for so little result.'

'Where have they been taken to?'

'I'm not empowered to say that.'

Guardone took off his gold-rimmed spectacles and wiped them.

'They must of course be traced,' said Nieve.

'Of course.'

'And enquiries must continue in respect of the use of the premises.'

'There you will have to deal with the Order of S. Vincent, also with the Bimbi AutoWash.'

He seemed to be quietly dissociating himself from whatever might happen next.

Salvatore had been right in thinking that Nieve had hoped, in return for his tactful interference, to make a reasonably good thing out of the shut-down of the orphanage. The truth was that he had thought in future he might handle part at least of the Ridolfi legal business. After this afternoon, however, he no longer had any ambitions of the kind.

'Does it ever seem to you,' he asked Salvatore as they left the via Sansepolcro, 'that everything conspires to frustrate you? So often I have that impression.'

Salvatore stopped dead in the middle of the blank white pavement.

'You have that impression too?'

'I suppose most people do at some time or another.'

'You'd call it commonplace?'

'A commonplace, yes,' said Nieve soothingly. Salvatore looked as though he had been struck a blow in the face.

You can't tell what will upset him next, Nieve thought. Certainly it must be a doubtful advantage to be connected with the Ridolfi.

29

At Valsassina the first crop of hay had been cut and they were harrowing the fields to let the sun dry out the weeds. Cesare bought another sheet of paper and another envelope and, this time without hesitation, wrote a letter which he posted to his aunt. In it he told her that he was sorry to seem disobliging, and certainly hadn't forgotten her many kindnesses towards him. Still, the case was as follows: when he had come in from the fields he had found eight old women and ten infants in the upstairs bedrooms and a further three old women in the kitchen, asking what they were to prepare for themselves to eat. These people could not remain at Valsassina. They had brought with them large quantities of dirty washing. Bernardino had locked himself up in the pigeon house. The dog, to prevent its going crazy, had had to be locked up in the office. The business of the estate was the production of wine. He had thought it best to put all this clearly in writing.

Maddalena drove herself out to see him. In her elegant old linen dress she looked as pale as wax. She seemed unmoved by the cackling and wailing from the back quarters of the house and what sounded like the clashing of metal against metal.

'Lately I've been distressed at the thought of your loneliness out here,' she said. 'I don't like to think of your being all by yourself at Valsassina. I don't believe in Providence, but I do believe that there's such a thing as a moment of inspiration when one can judge what's best for others. Under this arrangement you'll have both the very young and the very old about you, as in the natural order of things.'

'Not after tomorrow.'

'What are you going to do with them?'

'The Welfare are fetching them.'

'You'd have become used to them, Cesare. Your life would have expanded. You're very hard to help.'

'I'm sorry.'

'Now I shall have to think what I can do for Chiara and Salvatore.'

'Don't do anything.'

'What?'

'Do nothing.'

30

Giancarlo had never taken his sister quite seriously, even now, when she had embarked on the process of dying. In fact, she didn't take herself quite seriously either, in the sense that she did not believe she had the capacity to do harm. Perhaps this in itself might be considered a little crazy, but sometimes those who are considered crazy or even malicious are only those who choose the wrong moment.

Maddalena wrote an aunt's letter to Chiara at Riomaggiore, hoping that her periods had established themselves again satisfactorily, and sending her a list of the autumn concerts which had just been published. She sent her respects to the Ricasoli, and said nothing about Sannazzaro. Then she sent for Guardone and gave him twenty-four hours to check that Mazzata existed, that the Rossi land existed and was purchasable under the regulations of the Cassa del Mezzogiorno, and that Sannazzaro existed and was in good standing in the neighbourhood. 'On the first two points I have confirmation,' he told her. 'As to the third, Pericle Sannazzaro is considered simple, but entirely honest.'

'In what way is he simple?' Mad asked, and was told that he was thought to have only one idea in his head, not just one idea at a time, but the same idea for many years. Maddalena then instructed him not to pass the Bimbiwash money through the bank (this he had taken for granted) and to undertake the purchase as soon as possible in his own name. Guardone had no intention of doing this, but began the negotiations through a property agent, Domiciliolux, in which he had a small interest. He didn't know whether the Contessa expected him to go down and make a personal inspection, but he had no intention of doing that either. Soon she would be going away for the summer, indeed from the look of her she ought to have gone already.

'The purchase won't be the work of a moment, Signora Contessa,' he said.

'You probably don't want it to be,' she said, undisturbed.

'Certainly I advise against it. It didn't take me long to ascertain that no enterprise in Mazzata has ever shown a profit.'

'I'm not buying for myself. The title will be assigned at once to Dr Rossi.'

'I can't think that the dottore is indifferent to profit either. In any case we shall need his signature at an early stage as proof of acceptance, that is if you really think it wise not to consult him in advance.'

'Guardone, haven't you ever given anyone a present? Not something that they expect, but a present del cuore, like grace itself, unasked for, to put matters right with one stroke?'

'I have arranged for such things occasionally on behalf of clients,' said Guardone. 'They can put a considerable strain on a relationship.'

'But, my God, it's better than quarrelling.'

'Not in my experience, Contessa.'

'You're as dry as a toad, Guardone.'

'May I repeat that all I'm likely to be able to show you in the near future, if all goes well, that is, is a draft for a preliminary contract. You want an extra copy of this for Dr Rossi?'

'Well, you understand me.'

The copy was ready before Maddalena – having refused absolutely to try the water cure at San Pellegrino Spa with Mimi Limentani – set out for the Dolomites. He had time, but only just, to notify her, at five o'clock in the afternoon, that it was on his desk.

'Send the copy round, then, to Dr Rossi at the S. Agostino.'

'Tomorrow.'

'At once.'

Guardone had no clerk to spare for the job, but hanging around his office was the caretaker from the asilo, now unemployed and unable, it seemed, to claim his social security payments. To begin with, his wife and children were with his wife's parents and family allowances were not paid to those living in the country. Guardone cut all this short, as he did practically every afternoon.

'Today I've got something for you to do. Take this envelope to Dr Salvatore Rossi at the S. Agostino hospital. If he's gone to his private clinic you must find out the address and take it to him there. Get a receipt for it and come back here tomorrow and when you hand it to me I'll give you two thousand lire.'

Salvatore was still at the hospital. He had put back his private appointments, and was waiting in the hope of another few words with the Director of Administration. He had heard that there was a possibility not of building, or even of rebuilding, but of repairing a house in Bellosguardo village, with nothing like the same view, of course, as the Villa Hodgkiss, indeed with not much of a view at all, still, at Bellosguardo, not in the via Emilio Münz. He had at least the illusion of making progress.

'From the office of Avoccato Guardone.'

More rubbish about the wash-house, thought Salvatore.

'You will sign the receipt for it, signor dottore.'

He recognised the caretaker from the asilo and gave him a reassuring smile. 'You've found another job, I hope. If not, come and see me.' He signed the piece of paper which was put in front of him, and, having missed the Director of Administration, left for the clinic. It was eight o'clock before he reached via Emilio Münz. The lift wasn't working, hot weather affected it badly, and he walked sweating up the stairs. The two rooms were now as tidy as his office at the S. Agostino, and had lost entirely the air of just-controlled wildness which Chiara had created there. Her clothes were hung up, her few things were put away in the wretched little cupboard with its frail plastic handle. The flat, in fact, was ready to show to whoever wanted to rent it next.

He had taken to eating in the bar on the opposite side of the road. It meant, of course, walking down and up the stairs again and it was a singularly dull place, surely there must be better ones, but he couldn't be bothered to look for them. Before he went out he opened Guardone's envelope.

31

He had made no objection to her going to stay with these friends of hers, even when she had changed her mind and declared in tears that it wasn't possible for her to get well without seeing him every day, quite the contrary, he remembered that he had shouted, 'I'll pack for you, I'll show you how to pack,' and had begun to heap everything he could lay hands on, her photographs, her missal out of which bits of dried palm-leaves and holy pictures showered onto the floor, a heap of sandals with straps as thin as bits of string, all of them into her protesting suitcase. This had made her laugh, which was not what he had intended. He saw now that she had laughed because she had wanted him to believe that she was better already.

When he had read through Guardone's draft document twice he understood with absolute certainty what was being done against him. He was also able to grasp correctly everything that had happened since his marriage. It was even clearer if it was taken in order. He had been supposed to believe that Chiara, when she ordered those miserable dresses, had truly not known who Marta was, and that she hadn't been taking pity on his little weaknesses, now safely over and done with. He had been supposed to believe that when that monstrous English girl came to stay with the Gentilini it was not a device to spread the news from one end of Florence to the other that he himself hadn't provided a place fit for his wife's friends. Now he was supposed to believe that the mad aunt, out of her own invention, was proposing to enter into some kind of contract to buy back the wretched twenty and a half hectares. Why should the mad aunt's lawyer allow her to do any such thing? It was Chiara, who, having no money herself, had appealed to the Contessa, pedlar of the orphans' wash-house.

Chiara had been seized with the idea of surprising him with a toy, just the thing to keep him quiet, the unpredictable husband who disgraced himself at the Professor's dinner-table, so hard-working, so clever, but too stupid after all to guess what was wrong with him and too crass to know that he was homesick, which accounted for his tiresome fantasies, homesick like a sucking infant but grossly satisfied when his handful of earth was given back to him. But he would hardly have thought it possible that at nineteen – even though she loved him, which of course gave her an unfair advantage – she would have known how to cut down a grown man.

He had stood with his father in front of the Quisisana Clinic, waiting for permission to visit, and outside the Ricordanza, pressing his forehead against the iron gates. The mistake, in both cases, had been to go inside. Of course, as a boy he had had no choice. There was only one thing to be thankful for, and that was that no-one had been there to see him on the day when he had so grotesquely hung about the Ricordanza.

32

Cesare was sitting at one end of the dinner-table at Valsassina, the same end as usual, doing nothing for the moment, and apparently thinking of nothing. The plates had been taken away. The radio was playing Monteverdi, which stopped and was replaced by a translation of *Mrs Dale's Diary*. In summer the doors and windows were never shut until Cesare locked up for the night. Anybody might walk in, and Salvatore did walk in.

'You weren't expecting me.'

'No, but come in and sit down,' said Cesare. 'I heard the Vespa.' He switched off the radio. Salvatore took a chair at the opposite end of the table. The presence of the other chairs oppressed him.

'Do you always sit here in the evening?' he asked. 'I don't think I could stand it here without company.'

'Did you come here for company?' asked Cesare.

Salvatore looked at the violet night sky and back at the immovable table.

'What I want to talk about can't be settled without a second opinion. But, on the other hand, it can be discussed only within the family. I came here because it seems to me that you're the only member of the Ridolfi family who can take a detached view of my case, and in fact I would say the only rational member at all.'

'I should have thought that, whatever it is, you would do better to discuss it with my cousin.'

'Chiara is very dear to me, but she's not rational.'

'I've known her since she was born. She's quite rational enough for ordinary purposes.'

'Is that how you think of her?'

'I don't want to talk about her.'

'Nor do I. I appealed to you as a detached intelligence for quite other reasons. Don't smile, I know that anyone who comes forty kilometres out into the country at night to see someone he knows only slightly is certain to want to talk about himself.' Cesare did not smile, however. Salvatore went on, 'You know my story, I started off without advantages, my father was a bicycle mechanic but not a good one, I studied medicine at Bologna, I did what I could, here I am. Would you consider me an unnecessary person?'

'Doctors are necessary,' said Cesare. 'How many doctors, I don't know.'

'I should have added that we had some land, not much, and I myself had twenty hectares and a half, which I sold, I sold it when I thought the time had come to do so. You'll understand that, I imagine.'

'Well.'

'Now I find that behind my back and without a single word to me Chiara's aunt proposes to buy back the terreno and hand it over to me. I've only just been allowed to find out about it. Guardone sent the papers round to me at the hospital.'

'You're upset because my aunt, who has a good heart but isn't altogether accountable, wants to make you a present of 20.5 hectares.'

'I agree that your aunt isn't accountable. Really, though, that has nothing to do with it. It's Chiara who has arranged it.'

'What makes you think she knew anything about it?'

'How else could the Contessa know anything about Mazzata? No-one knows anything about Mazzata, still less about my 20.5 hectares. To Chiara I did talk about it. I told her almost everything about myself. Marriage is like the second stage of drunkenness in that respect. Tell me, can you see any other way that the aunt could have known about Mazzata?'

Cesare gave the question his usual serious consideration.

'No, I don't.'

'Chiara has no need of me whatever as I am. It would be absurd to blame her, I should have forseen it, but I'm not ashamed of taking it seriously, if I didn't do that I should deserve what has happened to me. There are dilettantes in human relationships just as there are, let's say, in politics. To people like that a crisis of faith or trust is only a passing annoyance, or even a diversion. It's no more important than finding you can't afford to pay one of your bills for a month or two. I wanted to explain that I'm not like that. But unfortunately I'm a consultant, and I don't know how to consult. I had a friend, who's leaving Florence now. I used to talk to him. I realise now that I didn't consult him either, I just told him where he was wrong.'

He looked past Cesare at the open doors each side of the great fireplace.

'Does anyone else sleep in the house?'

'Yes, Bernardino and the old woman.'

'His wife?'

'Yes, if she is his wife.'

'Where are they now?'

'At a guess, she's saying the rosary in the kitchen. I don't know where Bernardino is, probably shutting up the pigeons.'

'It's been dark for some time.'

'It takes him some time.'

'Have you got a gun?'

'Of course,' said Cesare. For the first time he took his two hands off the table.

'I used to go out with my father when I was a boy, of course. We used to get up before it was light when the air was still fresh but quite often we couldn't find anything to shoot, we'd walk for two hours and get nothing but a couple of thrushes or a lizard.' He added, 'I need a shot-gun now, the kind I had then, not an automatic.'

'I don't keep anything in the house,' said Cesare. 'You'd have to come across to the office.'

'Yes, but perhaps I ought to explain a little further what it is I'm doing. The main consideration is that Chiara and I are not able to accept each other, and I believe that on balance she would be better off without me.'

'Don't despair,' said Cesare. 'By my calculations, in twenty years there should be legal divorce in Italy.'

'By what calculations?'

'When the European Community gets going, we shall have to join to sell our wine, even though Germany is against it. Join them in one thing, join them in all.'

'Do you think that your cousin ought to wait for twenty years to be happy?' Salvatore cried ferociously. 'To take a broader view, if I were eliminated the whole world situation would be shifted to a tiny degree, no more than that, no more than a grain of sand, for the better. That's not only because there's an incompatibility between love and the ways of showing it that are open to us. It's also because I've come to think that it's not impossible that at an early point in my life I took a wrong direction. That direction was a reaction against another one which was indicated to me by feeble and irritating people, sick people, failures, prisoners. However, as I've just said, it's possible that as far as this country is concerned, and I've never lived in any other, I've become what might be considered from one angle a strongly growing organism and from another a deformity which can only be removed by surgical intervention. To turn to practical matters, I have an adequate life insurance with Previdenza, the beneficiaries of course are my mother and Chiara, but in the event of my suicide the company pays out nothing.'

'That's not in my policy,' said Cesare.

'Probably not, it's occupational, Previdenza includes it only for journalists, doctors, artists, speculators and degenerates. It follows, however, that if I were to put an end to myself this evening your evidence would be necessary as to its being an accident. What do you feel about this?'

'On the whole I feel sorry for you.'

'You wouldn't try to prevent me?'

'I don't know.'

They went out together through the front door, acknowledging that this was a formal occasion of sorts. The night was pitch dark and starless, breathing relief after the disagreeable heat of the day, and like all country nights it was unquiet, with rustlings and creakings. The fragrance of the viburnum, which this year had flowered exceptionally well, followed them relentlessly round to the back of the house.

'I'll go ahead,' said Cesare. 'There's usually something to fall over.'

The office was lit with a 40-watt bulb, which gave it exactly the same bleakness as it had by day. It looked just as it had done when Giancarlo came to discuss the arrangements for the wedding, except that the catalogues of agricultural machinery had disappeared under a new set of regulations from the Consorzio. The card announcing Chiara's engagement was still on top of the desk.

Cesare opened the door of the cupboard, which was built into the thickness of the inner wall. The old dog, who had been napping in her corner, and was very well aware that the shooting season wasn't due to open for another long stretch of existence, looked up at the cupboard with a flicker of hope. The end of her tail moved itself.

'Well, you can see what I've got. Those on the top rack are my father's Holland and Hollands. They were here for the whole of the war, no-one ever found them. They were made for him. I don't use them. He shot from the left shoulder, so they were adjusted for that, and I don't. That one below them is the one I use. It's Italian. It belonged to my father too, but it wasn't made for him. I'm taller than he was, so I had the stock lengthened. They had a job to get the right bit of walnut. You can hardly see the join.'

'Certainly I can't make it out,' said Salvatore. 'What about the shot-gun?'

'That's just for the vermin, rats and snakes and so on.'

Cesare took out the little .22, broke it open, loaded it, and handed it to Salvatore. The dog lifted her head and turned it slowly from one to the other of them.

Salvatore thanked him, and Cesare left him there and walked back again round to the front of the house. A very slight breeze was now getting up, as it often did at this time of night. He went into the entrance hall, leaving the doors open behind him, and as he passed the painted cassone, running his hand along the top, he heard the telephone begin to ring.

'Cesare, it's Chiara.'

'Well, I know your voice,' he said. 'Where are you?'

'I'm speaking from the Riomaggiore, from the Ricasoli house where I'm staying, it's so good of them to look after me, but Cesare, Salvatore rings me up every evening and this evening he hasn't, and I can't get him at the flat, or the hospital, or at the Gentilini.'

'Why should you think he's here?'

'I don't, I'm just asking you what to do, come sempre.'

'Well, he is here.'

'He's come to talk to you, he's lonely, I knew it.'

'I don't know whether he's lonely or not. He wanted a gun.'

'But he never has a gun.'

'I know, he wanted to borrow one of mine.'

'But what for?'

Cesare considered a little, and said,

'He said he was thinking of shooting himself.'

Chiara, so often misguided, so rarely knowing the right thing to do, now, by a miracle, did know. She said nothing at all. The unexpected silence had its effect on Cesare. After waiting a moment and finding that she did not ring off, he went out once again. He had meant to spend the evening in peace, sitting in his dining-room.

This time the corner of the back yard seemed to have sprung to life. There were disputing voices. The office door was still open, the weak light poured out, the dog, who never barked, who had not barked when Cesare's father was killed or when the orphans arrived, was barking now. The disturbance was irritating.

'Signor, dottore, that gun does not belong to you.'

Salvatore said something in a low voice, like a sufferer, and Bernardino cried, 'It's not his to give. If it was daylight, you would have to acknowledge that everything up to the north wall of the second olive grove is mine.'

Cesare stepped into the light, took the shot-gun, broke it once again and unloaded it.

'Salvatore, you're wanted on the telephone. It's your wife. She's speaking from Riomaggiore.'

Salvatore threw up his hands.

'What's to become of us? We can't go on like this.'

'Yes, we can go on like this,' said Cesare. 'We can go on exactly like this for the rest of our lives.'

Leaving Salvatore to go back by himself, he put the little gun into its correct rack. As soon as the cupboard door was shut the old dog settled off to sleep again. Bernardino disappeared, either into the large spaces of the country night or more probably to the kitchen entrance. Cesare put out the light and locked up. He didn't mind tedium, he was trained to it, but it struck him that he didn't want to walk in and out of his house any more on this particular night.

As he turned the corner Salvatore was coming into the courtyard to find his Vespa. He called out that he was going back to Florence and would be starting first thing in the morning for Riomaggiore.